ABOUT THE AUTHOR

Gwyneth Steddy is originally from Omagh, Co Tyrone and now lives in South Wales.

Her crime novels are set in West Tyrone, a place she says will be forever be home.

The series backdrop is a beautiful, and much overlooked part of the world. The stories are peopled with funny, tough and extraordinary characters – although Gwyneth freely admits she has taken some liberties with geography and no characters are based on real people.

She has worked as an occupational therapist for more years than she is willing to admit. In the free time she has between working and writing, she runs (slowly) and mountain bikes (even slower).

Published in Great Britain in 2022
By Diamond Crime

ISBN 978–1–7397448–3–0

Diamond Crime is an imprint of Diamond Books Ltd.

Thanks, first and foremost, to the people of my home town of Omagh who inspired me to write about that wonderful part of the world. Thanks also to Katherine Standfield, author, teacher, and mentor. She has guided me through such a steep learning curve while writing this book. It's an absolute joy to work with Kath and long may it continue. Finally, thanks to the gang at Diamond Books who have got me over the publishing line with humour, fun and honesty.

Book design: jacksonbone.co.uk
Cover photograph: Jason Mac

Coming soon to Diamond Books:

Better The Body You Know
Volume Two of the Tyrone Mysteries

For information about Diamond Crime authors
and their books, visit:
www.diamondbooks.co.uk

For my husband, Paul, and my sons Matthew and Alex. You are my world.

DO SLEEPING DOGS LIE?

THE TYRONE MYSTERIES
VOLUME ONE

GWYNETH STEDDY

CHAPTER ONE

Friday 12th April 1989

"You're taking the piss..."

Duncan Gallagher glanced across at his old friend in the passenger seat, then returned his eyes to the road. You couldn't be too careful in these back lanes.

Trevor Mulholland snorted with laughter. "Serious, the man couldn't do a deal to save his life. All I did was wait for him to give in. And sure enough the oul fool dropped the price. I could sell the same machinery tomorrow and double my money."

"So the drinks are on you," said Duncan, smiling.

Although he appreciated the profit Trevor was going to make, Duncan wasn't sure he could have taken advantage of Mr Tobin in the same way. The man's machinery-hire business was in dire straits. Poor business sense could only be to blame, but Duncan felt sorry for the wife and children. A son still at home and a daughter over in England. But you had to live with your conscience. Trevor had never been troubled in that way. Maybe that was what made him such a good laugh when they were out on the town. Christ, the times they'd had over the last fifteen years. Mates at first sight. Bonded by disagreeing with the referee despite playing for opposing rugby teams, and sent off for their trouble. Duncan had asked the ref when his optician's appointment was and Trevor had questioned if his parents were married.

"How far out is this place?" asked Duncan.

"Not far now. Here – turn right just after this petrol station. Another mile at the most."

Duncan loosened his collar with his free hand and pulled down his tie. He had heard of Kealey's, of course, but had taken care not to visit, even when it was suggested as a meeting place by a prospective customer. The green, white and gold painted kerbstones didn't help. He'd been straight with Trevor when he had asked for a lift. "Not comfortable" was the phrase he'd used. And he didn't tell Pat where he was going. She would've played hell. Four miles from town in a staunchly republican area? Brilliant. Still, they should be safe enough this time in the afternoon. He hoped.

He pulled up in the deserted car park Trevor looked at his watch and reached down awkwardly for a bulging envelope at his feet. That bit of weight he had put on since their rugby days was clearly getting in the way. When Duncan dislocated his shoulder and Trevor twisted his ankle in the same match, they both realised that at the age of thirty-six, it was time to hang up their boots. Duncan knew that his effortless ability to keep his weight down irked Trevor. But maybe he should lay off the stout – that would be a start.

"Stay for a quick one before my meeting?" asked Trevor. "But no need for you to wait for me. Probably best you don't."

"OK. I'll come in for one." Duncan felt relieved that he wouldn't be around for long. Trevor hadn't said who the meeting was with, and Duncan had absolutely no intention of asking. In this country, what you didn't know kept you safe. And Trevor had kept more and more from Duncan over the last two years.

"Bout yeh, Tony," Trevor greeted the barman.

"Usual?" replied Tony. He rose slowly from a stool positioned beside the cash register, carefully folded his newspaper and stretched out his back. He ran a hand through his steel grey hair.

Duncan looked at Trevor in surprise. A regular in this place? He knew Trevor liked his drink, but this couldn't be a regular watering hole. Surely he had higher standards and more regard for his safety?

With a practised movement, Tony dragged a wooden box towards him with his foot to reach the pint glasses on the shelf over the bar. The dimensions of the bar hadn't taken into account his short frame. He stepped up onto the stool with an agility that belied his advanced years.

"Aye, a pint for me and a wee chaser." Trevor turned to Duncan. "Usual?" Duncan nodded. "And a half of the black stuff for my friend here."

Trevor sat on one of the bar stools.

Duncan looked around him. The pub was typical of the type. No refurb here for many a year. Chipped formica tables stained with years of spillages and basic wooden chairs with little thought given to comfort. The floor was scrubbable lino. A pool table placed close to the toilets. Maybe you'd be distracted from your game by the bleach-and-urine scent coming from the gents. The ladies' toilet would be rarely used. Duncan walked over to the pool table and started to rack up the balls in the triangle. A quick game would do no harm. It was a while since he'd beaten Trevor.

"Game?" Duncan asked.

"Naw."

"Fiver in it?"

Trevor looked at his watch. "Sure, if yeh want to get beat again I can meet yeh in McAteers this evening. "Bout seven? Should be well done by then."

"There you are." Tony placed the drinks on the counter in front of Trevor. "As I'm not rushed off my feet here, I'll be out the back. I'm due a delivery."

Duncan watched Tony push the swing door that led to the rear of the pub. He moved back to the bar and took a sip of his drink.

Trevor was leaning over the bar, fingering the envelope he had placed in front of him.

"Trevor, I'm sure you know what you're doing, and I'm happy enough not knowing what you're up to. But…"

"Thanks for your concern." Trevor smiled. "In my line of work, you have to make sure you keep everyone happy." He tapped the envelope with his index finger. "As they say, it's not pleasant but yeh have to do it. A fact of life if you want to quarry in this province."

He took a sip of his whiskey and a gulp of his stout.

"I know Trevor, but…"

The door to the pub slammed open. A man in dark clothes and a balaclava, a hand gun held out, was walking towards them. Duncan felt his drink slip through his hand. It fell to the floor. The glass shattered. Trevor pushed past him. Moved towards the gunman.

"What the fuck is this? We had a deal! Look." Trevor held the envelope out in front of him. "It's all in there. Go talk to the top man."

The gunman shook his head, his weapon still pointed towards the two men.

4

"Fuck sake, it's all there," insisted Trevor, his voice weaker.

Duncan reached out to Trevor, finding his left arm. "Trevor, calm..."

A flash. A deafening noise that echoed from the walls. Duncan's ears popped, then started to ring. Trevor slammed into him as if he was jumping backwards. Duncan fell to the floor, Trevor on top of him. Duncan's face was wet. His eyes stung. Through blurred vision he could see that the gunman was now closer, his eyes narrowing. Duncan cleared his face with his left hand. The gunman lowered his weapon, turned and walked out of the room.

Duncan pulled himself to a sitting position, and leant against the foot of the bar, his legs spread wide. He pulled Trevor's body towards him. Wrapped his arms around his dead friend and held him like a child, Trevor's back resting against his abdomen. Duncan's bladder and bowels opened.

"Help. Help me. For Christ's sake, please..." Duncan tried to shout but it came out a whisper. Tears began to roll down his face. He held his friend close and rocked. "Jesus, Trevor..."

CHAPTER TWO

Constable Edward Daniels pushed open the door to Kealey's bar and scanned the room. He detected the pungent smell of body waste and blood. In his first year as a constable, he had witnessed the after-effects of both deadly bombs and shootings. It hadn't got any easier to stomach. He started the, by now practised, technique of concentrating on breathing in through his mouth and out of his nose, which helped stop the heaving in his stomach. Sometimes it worked.

When the call came in to the station, Edward had recognised the names straight away as the two men at the touchline when he played for the Omagh Academicals rugby team, shifts allowing.

At this moment, in front of him, Trevor Mulholland was lying in a pool of his own blood. Duncan Gallagher was at a bar table sipping a whiskey, his hand shaking as he raised the glass to his lips. He appeared to be concentrating on a spot on the far wall, away from the body of his friend. Duncan's suit jacket and trousers were soaked in blood, but as far as Edward could see, he was uninjured. Physically, that was. From his ashen colour and blank stare, Edward guessed there might be some hidden injury.

DI Robinson walked in the room

"Daniels, get this place sealed off. No one comes in unless I say so."

Edward straightened up. At the bar, Duncan tensed up and put down his drink.

Robinson moved to Edward's shoulder. "Fecking mess to clear up again…" he muttered. Then looked up. "You!" he shouted over to the man at the bar. "Your name?"

"Tony Muldoon." Tony was holding an opened bottle of whiskey, about to give Duncan a top up.

"Houl your horses. I need this man sober." Robinson moved to the bar and put his hand on the bottle to stay the process of pouring.

Tony twisted the cap. Placed the bottle on the bar with a bang.

"Have ye keys to this place?" asked Robinson.

"Aye, they're…"

"I don't care where they are. Give them to this lad." DI Robinson nodded to Edward. "I need the place shut."

"I'm not sure if big Frank would appreciate that. It's Friday night."

"You can tell your boss I'm shutting the place. And ye never know, it could be a while before I'm done. Could be a good few days, maybe a week. Depends on the help I get. Now, go get the keys."

Tony sneered at the DI and reached under the counter and drew out a large bunch of keys. He pushed them towards Edward and headed for the storeroom.

"Stay in there until we're sorted," Robinson yelled after him. He sat down next to Duncan.

Edward returned from securing the door.

"So… Tony was out the back when the gunman arrived," DI Robinson said. "Handy. He only came back in when he heard the shots. Best to see if Duncan here can help." He reached over and touched Duncan's arm gently. "Right, Duncan?"

Duncan looked at Robinson as if seeing him for the first time. He glanced up at Edward and then back at the DI.

"Are ye not getting an ambulance?"

"It's too late for Trevor. We'll get someone for you, though."

Duncan took another sip of whiskey. Edward's stomach was starting to settle, but he felt it would settle a good sight better if he could share that drink.

"Go easy on that." DI Robinson put his hand over the top of the glass. "I need you to tell me what happened. A nice wee cup of tea, that's what you need. Edward, get that clown out the back to make Duncan a cup of tea. Plenty of sugar in it."

Shelving lined the walls of the large storeroom, ready for the crates of beer. The door at the rear of the pub was open. Tony was deep in conversation with a tall man who looked as though he could do with a good meal or ten. This man's reddened complexion and sunken eyes suggested that he received most of his nutrition from alcohol.

Edward spoke up. "We need a hot sweet cup of tea for Duncan."

"I'll come now. Just sorting out the drayman here." Tony nodded towards the skinny man and turned back into the room.

"Hang on a minute." Edward put his hand on Tony's chest to stop him. "How long has he been here?"

"Him? He got here just before the shooting. But he was in here the whole time. Weren't yeh?" Tony turned to the man.

"Yeh. Saw nothing. Heard nothing. Was in here the whole time."

"Name?" asked Edward. Might as well to get it, even though he knew the man wouldn't be any use as a witness, regardless of what he did or didn't see or hear.

"Paul McGonigle."

"Don't leave. DI Robinson will want a word."

As Edward returned to the bar with the sweetened tea, he heard the familiar noise of a helicopter landing – the brutal growl of a Chinook, by the sound of it. An army patrol from the town's barracks to seal off the area, just in case it was one of those traps the terrorists were fond of. Something inside Edward unclenched a little. DI Robinson rose to his feet.

"Constable, get that tea into Duncan and then take him home. We'll catch up with him when he feels up to it. He's had a wile shock." The DI patted Duncan on the shoulder. "He needs to get home and change out of those clothes."

Edward placed the mug on the table in front of Duncan. Robinson gestured for Edward to follow him towards the door.

"Can't get a word of sense outta him. And he's honking of shit and piss. Use his car – he's in no fit state to drive. I'll send a Tangi out to fetch you back."

Edward knew Duncan lived just outside Seskinore.

Not the best place to hail a taxi from, even if they would go that far from town. "Right Sir... Oh and the drayman Sir. Name's McGonigle. He was here the whole time, but says he saw and heard nothing."

"I'll deal with him. And Edward...

"Yes Sir?"

"Best take the cap and tie off. I don't think Duncan's Sierra has much armour plating. You just don't know who's waiting to take pot-shots in this neck of the woods."

Edward shook his head. Some disguise his DI was suggesting. He took a final look at Trevor Mulholland's body. Regardless of any potential risks, he was pleased to get away.

* * *

The DI was right about the need for a nose peg. Edward found a blanket in the boot of the car. It was covered in dog hairs, but it was better than Duncan sitting directly on the passenger seat.

As Edward drove away from Kealey's Inn and towards the town, Duncan started to sob quietly. Edward looked across at him, unsure of what to say. Or if he should say anything to this man who he had only previously seen laughing and shouting instructions to rugby players from the side line.

"He didn't shoot me."

Well, obviously, thought Edward.

"He was going to but he didn't." Duncan spoke through his sobs. "He didn't want the money."

"What money?" Edward asked. He hadn't noticed any money. Not on the floor, or on the table where Duncan had been sitting, or on the bar.

"He shook his head," Duncan continued. "He didn't want it. Trevor was sure it was enough. Maybe it wasn't enough."

"Duncan, what money?"

But Duncan's body was now racked with sobs, and he was unable to speak at all.

CHAPTER THREE

29th March 2022

"For feck's sake, would you leave the lead alone!" Malcolm Bell shouted at the dog.

He had just been enjoying a wee sit down on the bench, taking in the view of the East Strand in Portrush. The sea and weather were calm, the beach now filling up with the parkrunners ready to head out along the sand to the White Rocks for their usual Saturday 9.30am, or thereabouts, five-kilometre run. His wife had told him it was good to take a wee walk and sit awhile, letting the world go by. But when ex-DI Bell was honest with himself, he bitterly missed the pressure, the always-present tension of working as a policeman in the West Tyrone town of Omagh that had been his home and working patch for thirty years. He had been looking forward to retirement, had told himself it would make all the difference to the nightmares, to the memories he wanted to leave behind. But when retirement and the accompanying move to this seaside town on the north coast arrived – what did they say? Be careful what you wish for.

But Billy, the two-year-old Cairn terrier from the rescue shelter, was having none of the wee sit down. The dog had twisted around to get the lead still attached to his collar between his teeth, determined to drag Malcolm on to finish the walk, pulling the lead this way and that. Malcolm couldn't understand why this thing had been able to take over their lives. The bloody animal had been timid for the first few weeks, and his wife had done nothing but nurse it. Malcolm had left her to it. For God's sake, it's a dog, not some sort of substitute wean. But the die had been cast, with the dog as meek as you liked with his wife, she forgiving it every transgression. But when the good Mrs Bell was out of sight, Billy had taken every opportunity to growl and, on the odd occasion, nip at Malcom. This bloody animal would not get the better of him.

"We will go when I'm good and ready."

The dog let the lead drop from his mouth and turned his attention to something behind Malcolm, staring intently. His tail started to wag his ears up and alert. Maybe there had been a breakthrough in this war of attrition. Maybe the damn dog realised at last who was boss. Billy made a yipping sort of sound, and then Malcolm heard an answering bark. He twisted around and saw another man with a dog similar in size and shape to Billy. He walked towards Malcolm with a slow gait suggestive of someone of advanced years. He was wrapped up well against the sharp wind of the sea, his lined eyes and grey eyebrows just visible over the scarf covering his mouth. The dog was pulling on its lead.

Another man, dressed for the cold winter wind in an overcoat and a beany hat pulled down low, strode past Malcolm towards the man with the dog. A quicker, younger walk. Yes, with that ease of movement, definitely someone who was at least twenty or thirty years younger than Malcolm. The younger man grabbed the older one's arm. He stopped and looked at his assailant with surprise and then – what was it? Not exactly fear, more like apprehension or confusion. The younger man was saying something. He dropped the older man's arm and then, shaking his head slowly, opened out both arms in a gesture of exasperation. The older man kept his head down and continued walking slowly towards Malcolm's bench. The younger man turned and stared, then turned once more to walk away quickly, shaking his head, his hands in his overcoat pockets, shoulders slumped.

"'Bout yeh," greeted Malcolm, when it was clear that the two dogs were determined to get acquainted, both pulling at their leads and wagging their tails. "Sharp enough wind today."

"Your dog is friendly enough," replied the man who loosened his scarf from his mouth.

Malcolm saw that he had been right in his guess of the man's age and recognised the slow drawl of a Tyrone accent.

"I may as well stop while they carry on."

Malcolm slid up the bench to ensure that no personal boundaries were broached. "Sit yourself down. If yeh don't mind me asking, everything all right? I mean, I couldn't help noticing..."

"I like this view," said the man, sitting down and unbuttoning his coat. "Especially when you see thon eejits running like lemmings." The man pointed towards the runners on the beach.

Malcolm got the message. No enquires were welcome.

But as the man spoke, Malcolm was convinced more than ever that this was definitely a Tyrone man. No doubt about that. He glanced sideways. The lines around the man's eyes confirmed he was older than Malcolm. His hair was white with a tinge of grey, cut in a style that suggested his heyday was the seventies or eighties. Under his thick coat he was slightly built.

"Malcolm Bell," said Malcolm, extending his hand for a handshake.

"Duncan Gallagher," Duncan smiled as they shook hands.

"Are you visiting these parts?" asked Malcolm.

"Yes, I'm a visitor. From Tyrone," replied Duncan.

"I used to work there, in the police."

"You'd be busy enough then!"

Silence fell. Malcolm had hoped the mention of his previous job might have triggered something more from Duncan. He tried again. "The man yeh were chatting to, he's from Tyrone too, is..."

"Duncan... Jesus, I've found you!"

Malcolm looked towards a petite woman of, he guessed, around seventy years of age walking quickly up the path towards them. She was holding a pair of man's shoes.

"Please, Duncan, when I say to wait, just wait."

"Sorry, love. I thought you said to go on."

The woman turned to Malcolm. "I'm his wife. I only left him for a minute to go to the toilet. I thought he wouldn't go out without changing into his shoes. I thought it was safe enough."

Mrs Gallagher knelt in front of her husband. Malcolm now saw that the man was wearing leather slippers. They were soaking wet and covered in dirt. Mrs Gallagher pulled some fresh socks out of her coat pocket and, shaking her head, started to change his soiled footwear.

"Can I help? I mean shall I hold the dog?" asked Malcolm.

"Yes. Thanks." She concentrated on her task.

Gently, Malcolm took the lead from Duncan's hand.

Duncan looked towards Malcolm with a puzzled expression. "I always take the dog for a walk. Don't I, Buddy?" He leant down to pat his dog.

"Yes, but with me, love. Don't want you getting lost again, do we?"

Duncan's wife leant on the bench to rise to a standing position. She patted her husband on the shoulder, sighed and sat down next to him.

"I think we come from the same part of the world. The name's Malcolm Bell. I'm a... I mean," Malcolm cleared his throat. "I used to be a DI in Tyrone."

Mrs Gallagher turned to study Malcolm. "No, sorry. I don't recognise yeh. Did you ever use our post office in Seskinore? It was that busy it was hard to keep track of people."

Malcolm smiled. "No, but if yeh were never in trouble, our paths wouldn't have crossed."

Mrs Gallagher smiled back, but it was a tired smile.

"Just now," Malcolm said, "just before you arrived, there was a man here. I'm not sure, but I think he was bothering your husband."

Mrs Gallagher's smile turned to a worried frown.

"Not again." She turned to Duncan and stroked his arm. "Did he hurt you?"

"No, it's OK." Malcolm held his hand up as if to stop her train of thought. "He didn't do anything. Nothing really happened. He just spoke to Duncan for a bit and then left."

Abruptly, Mrs Gallagher got up. "Time to go, Duncan, love. Thanks for your help, Malcolm. Duncan will have the dog back. Come on, love. Nice cup of tea waiting for us at home."

"The police, do yeh say?" Duncan asked, turning first to Malcolm and then to his wife. "Is it about Trevor?"

"Let's go. Nice cup of tea. Remember?" Mrs Gallagher turned to Malcolm. "He gets confused. He needs his medication. Thanks again."

As the pair walked off, Billy strained at the lead in their direction, ears up, posture alert. Then his tail slowly wagged to a stop. Malcolm pulled on the lead.

"Not sure what happened there. I think we were both dumped."

He reached to pat Billy in commiseration. Billy turned his head towards Malcolm and growled.

* * *

Back at the bungalow Malcolm and Harriet had bought six months ago, he took off his coat and released the dog from its lead.

His wife had left his cup ready on the kitchen counter next to a plate with two slices of Fifteens, his favourite wee bit to go with his tea – it would be too wet a cup without them. It mightn't do much for his waistline, or lower his chances of being told he had diabetes at his next medical check-up. But sure, that was some walk all the way over to the East Strand. So probably there was already a calorific deficit.

"Are you there?" Malcolm called, already knowing the answer due to the way Billy had careered off.

"Yes. Be there now. The tea's just made," Harriet replied from the conservatory at the back of their bungalow. Good weather isn't guaranteed on the north coast of Ireland, so it had been Harriet's idea to have one built. Then they could at least pretend they were outside when the weather wasn't the best. Malcolm could hear her making a fuss of Billy, as if she hadn't seen him for a week rather than the half hour they'd been out.

He poured the tea into his cup from the metal teapot he knew would have been on the hob for at least five minutes. His wife knew how to prepare the best cup of tea. A good strong brew.

"Do you remember a Duncan Gallagher from back home?" Malcolm asked when they had settled themselves in the comfort of the conservatory for their elevenses, which they tended to take at 10.30 each morning.

"Duncan the finance man?" Harriet asked.

Malcolm put down his cup with a bang. "Of course. Jesus, my mind's going to mush. Of course. And his wife?"

"Do yeh mean Pat?"

"I never met her," Malcolm replied. "What she look like?"

"It's a good few years since I've seen her. Not since she sold the post office. That was a great post office. Nothing too much trouble. Heart of the village. She knew just about everything that was going on." Harriet took a sip of her tea, looking into the distance, remembering.

"Is she wee?" Malcolm said. "I mean, like a neat-looking wee woman?"

"That'd be her. Never a hair out of place. Always bought clothes well. A lady, but in a good way. No airs and graces. All common sense and kindness. Why do you ask?"

"I think I met them over the East Strand this morning."

"Yes, I heard they had moved up this way."

"But Duncan said they were visiting."

"Ah... Poor Duncan. I heard he was living in the past. Not much of a retirement for Pat Gallagher. She worked hard all her life. And now she has more hard work ahead of her looking after Duncan."

"Have they any family?"

"Two lads, but they're away across the water. Pat was all for them going to university in England. And then of course they stayed there."

Malcolm watched his wife smoothing Billy's coat, the dog stretched out over her lap looking like he might purr with pleasure.

"When I mentioned about me being in the police, Duncan mentioned a name. Trevor. Then his wife practically dragged him away."

"They're very decent folk, so I suppose not people you would recall. Not the types you would have come across in your work." Harriet tilted her head to one side. "Trevor… Trevor… I wonder, would that have been Trevor Mulholland?"

"Christ, yes!" Malcolm said. "The murder just before I came to the town as a probationer. It was all put on the shelf by the time I started. Usual thing. Terrorist attack with no one caught for it."

"Wasn't there a bit of a scandal around it? That lad getting sacked?" asked Harriet.

Malcolm shifted in his seat. Police officers who didn't stick to the right side of law and order were the worst of all. "Aye. Something to do with money going missing. After the enquiry and he was shown the door, they offered the position to me."

His wife reached over and squeezed his knee. Billy growled. "Well, his loss was definitely my gain," she said. "Otherwise, you might never have come to Omagh and we wouldn't have met." She returned to smoothing Billy's fur and the growling stopped. "It was a terrible time when Mulholland got murdered. I remember the funeral well. Sure, the whole countryside was at it. And that young Eileen Mulholland walking behind the coffin with the two youngsters, them not even started school. Just awful." Harriet shook her head as if trying to rid herself of the memory.

He nibbled at the slice of Fifteen and sipped his tea. And pondered… No one had been brought to book for the murder of the very prominent and successful quarry owner Mulholland. Not that it was unusual in the 1980s for death to go unrewarded with a prison sentence. Sure, there would be no harm in checking it out. After all, he had plenty of time.

"Malcolm?"

"What?" He was brought back to the present by his wife's sharp tone.

"I know you like I know the back of my hand. You've left the job behind, and after all these years I want you to have peace of mind. Do not start thinking about that or any case. Peace and quiet. That's what you promised me. Right?"

"Yes, dear." But the cogs of Malcolm's mind were turning, and he wasn't sure if he wanted them to stop.

CHAPTER FOUR

Tommy Smith took a sip of his tea and looked around the church hall. The women had done a good job. His mother would have approved of this funeral spread. Maybe even the wake too. The house had been fit to busting in the two days since she'd died. But the one person Tommy needed hadn't been there. He checked his phone for any missed calls. A text maybe. Nothing.

All the old paramilitary paraphernalia had long since disappeared from the family home in East Belfast. His mother had made sure of that after his da had died three years ago. But there was no mistaking the backgrounds of some of the mourners at his mother's funeral. A large number of the congregation were around seventy years of age, still sporting UVF tattoos on the knuckles. His mother had insisted that he displayed no such artwork. He had started to raise the subject when he was in his teens, wanting to emulate his da. But she had chased him round the house with a sewing needle.

"Do yeh want a needle in yeh? I'll do it now!"

He had run from the house with the sound of his da's laughter ringing in his ears.

Tommy smiled as he thought of the complicated relationship between his ma and da. She was a weekly churchgoer who would clip Tommy around the ear if she thought he was even thinking of swearing. He knew from playground gossip that his da was a respected member of the local 'volunteers of East Belfast'. Da had worked in the shipyard all his life. But it was the other times that caused the problems between Tommy's parents. When his da was collected by men Tommy only ever saw at night, he was sent to bed, but could never sleep until he heard the door bang shut behind his father when he returned. He would creep out of bed and sneak down the stairs and peer around the door of the sitting room. Da would be pacing up and down, sweating. Tommy would be chased back to bed and his da would be greeted in silence by his wife, who would bang a glass of whiskey in front of him, muttering under her breath.

That had all stopped in 1998. Life had settled. But his ma still couldn't get his da to church. No such option for Tommy. He had been told the stories time and time again by his mother. How she had him christened when he was barely three months old, his father sweating by the baptismal font having celebrated a bit too much the night before. His ma had made sure he was confirmed in the Church of Ireland when he was eleven, and was frog-marched to church every Sunday until he grew tall enough to say no. Became the hard man, just like his da. His ma had cried then. But his da had told him, "Good on yeh, son. Yeah don't want to be listening to oul superstitious crap."

Tommy looked round the hall at the groups of people huddled together in twos and threes. The minister was working the room, targeting parishioners he hadn't seen for a while, avoiding the tattooed men – the lost causes. Tommy knew the minister wouldn't come near him either, not after what had happened when the minister came to say prayers over his mother's body. The minister knew better than that.

The church jungle drums had worked as usual, and the minister had been at her bedside not more than an hour after she had breathed her last. Donal had been there too. Tommy's ma had slipped into unconsciousness the night before, so Tommy had felt it had been safe enough to bring Donal into the family home. And he so needed him to be there.

Donal, who he had met at a Van Morrison concert in Dublin.

His ma had begged him not to go, saying it was too dangerous for a Protestant from East Belfast to go to the south. Especially with their connections. But Tommy had the best night of his life. The music – oh heavens, the music. Van the Man was a god. To think he came from Tommy's neck of the woods. And then the chance look across the room and the returned gaze of the dark-haired, dark-eyed, tall, taut man. Tommy had known at once that this was different. This was meant to be. So different to the perfectly pleasant girls his mother had tried to introduce him to at church events when he was barely into his teens. And then, a few years later, the secret fumbles he had in the alley behind that bar in the city centre, where he would go alone.

But with Donal, Tommy knew from the start that this was real and it was deep. There had been five glorious months of travelling to Dublin each weekend, where what he and Donal had was accepted, where it was OK for Tommy to be.

Donal had held him as he cried beside his mother's still body on her last day. Cried that he could now never explain to his mother this love, this passion he had discovered. She would have understood, wouldn't she?

Tommy hadn't heard his mother's bedroom door open. They had pulled apart at the sound of the deliberate cough.

"Tommy, a word please." The minister spoke softly, as if he was scared of waking Tommy's ma. "Alone."

Tommy looked between the minister and Donal. "No. He stays."

"OK, but Tommy, I don't think – I mean, your aunt will be arriving soon... I'm not sure she would want ..." The minister nodded towards Donal. "The likes of him..."

"The likes of..." Tommy looked again between the minister and Donal.

"Tommy." The minister's tone became more determined. "What you get up to in the south is one thing, but not here, OK?" He shook his head. "Your mother would be ashamed of you; God rest her soul."

Shock ran through Tommy, despite the fact that he had lived with such views all his life. "Fuck away out!" He pushed the minister from the room. His breathing heavy and fast. Anger building in the pit of his stomach. He turned to see Donal picking up his jacket from the bedside chair.

"It's as well I go," Donal sighed. He pointed at Tommy's mother. "For Christ's sake, you have to do this

25

properly or you'll never forgive yourself. Look, I'll be in touch. It's been grand." He glanced at Tommy's mother and made the shape of the cross.

Tommy leaned against the wall and closed his eyes. Every aspect of his life was starting to crumble. The front door slammed, signalling Donal's departure. Tommy sank onto the bedside chair and reached for his mother's ice-cold hand.

* * *

A gentle slap on his shoulder brought Tommy's thoughts back to the funeral tea and announced the arrival in the church hall of Jeff Henry, his da's oldest friend. "Bout ye, Tommy."

"Jeff," replied Tommy stretching out his right hand.

Jeff grasped Tommy's hand in both of his and shook it. "Sorry for your loss. She was a great woman."

"Yes." Tommy had run out of words with which to respond. The funeral service had been long, the queue of mourners to shake his hand had been longer. The committal as cold as the north-westerly wind blowing in from the Lough. He needed Donal here, but there had still been no answer to his calls.

"Her and your da, sure they were a great couple. They..."

"Tommy, a word!"

Tommy turned at another familiar voice, sharp and piercing as ever. "Alberta... More tea?" Tommy asked his stout, grey-haired aunt, who was dressed in a close-fitting black suit, the skirt of which strained across her generous stomach.

"No, just a word." Alberta stared intently at Jeff.

Jeff dropped the forced smile he had directed at Alberta. "Right, I'll just get meself a wee cup of tea. Some lovely-looking sandwiches. And is that your cake, Alberta?"

Alberta frowned. Jeff made his way towards the funeral tea laid out on the church trestle table disguised with a spotless white tablecloth.

"What's the like of him doing here? Have ye no sense? I always knew your head was full of sweetie mice!"

"You know he was a friend of me da's. He's just being respectful…"

"Respectful?" Alberta spat the word out. "That buck eejit wouldn't know the meaning of the word. Him and your da, nearly breaking my sister's heart working for the cause. Much bloody good it did. Your da died with blood on his hands."

"For God's sake, Alberta, will ye give it a rest. People are looking." Tommy glanced towards the nearest mourners.

"Just get rid of him. Now. The man and his cronies are no better than dirt under my feet."

Alberta straightened her jacket and returned to her two seated companions – a dark suited, thin small woman with crow sharp features on one side, and a steel-haired matron on the other wearing a tent like black dress with a white collar and bow that seemed to be a failed nod to Princess Diana circa 1990. They puffed themselves up in support of Tommy's aunt.

Tommy followed Jeff over to the table of sandwiches and cakes. Jeff held a paper plate in one hand, with two sandwiches and a slice of wheaten bread and was contemplating which cakes he should add.

"Jeff?" called Tommy.

Jeff grabbed two iced buns and followed him to the door of the hall.

"What's the story?" he asked between the bites of a sandwich.

"Jeff, I'm wile sorry. I'm going to ask ye and the boys to leave. Alberta there..." Tommy gestured to his aunt now sitting with between her two friends, all three staring at them. "She's not happy ye are here. So thanks for coming, but maybe it's best you all left."

"Jesus, that woman will never let up or let go. Christ Almighty." Jeff put the remains of the half-eaten sandwich on the plate and thrust it at Tommy. "Your da was a great man and it's because of him I'm here to pay my respects to your ma. And a wee bit of advice. Man up yourself." He nodded towards Alberta. "Not for you, not for your ma, but for your da. Don't forget the boys."

Jeff pointed at the four men moving towards them. "The boys look after their own. Don't you forget that." He patted Tommy on the arm and turned to the group of elderly men dressed in suits brought out of wardrobes only for funerals and Court appearances, hair with number one cuts and tattoos over their knuckles and creeping up their necks. "Come on lads. Let's start a proper wake – at the pub!"

Tommy watched them leave. A group of ageing men. But he knew they had the blood of a good few innocents on their hands. He turned. Alberta was standing behind him now, arms folded. His breathing quickened at the sight of her. Sweat ran down his neck. He reached for the band on his wrist and pulled at it. It helped. A bit.

"Glad to see you've a bit of sense and got rid of them."

"I just didn't want a fuss." Tommy tried to keep his voice even. This was his ma's funeral, for God's sake. He couldn't lose it here. Not now.

"He was right about one thing. Not much backbone in you. Never was. All that anger covering up weakness." Alberta face curled into a snarl.

"For feck's sake, they've gone. Isn't that what you wanted?"

"They should never have gotten through the door in the first place. But then I was against you coming into the house too. But your ma, God rest her soul, she was the soft one."

Tommy's voice rose. "Jesus, Alberta, what are you on about?" He looked around to see if he had drawn attention. "I have just about had enough today. Why don't you go back to the rest of the old hags over there?" He pulled at the elastic band around his wrist and let it snap back against his skin. He counted his breaths – his therapist had told him he should aim to get to ten.

"Don't you ever speak to me like that." Alberta poked her finger into Tommy's chest. "You're nothing but a foundling, and my sister took you in. She never should have. She should have had her own. That da of yours brought you home. Probably the result of some dirty secret. My sister was never your mother. You never deserved her. She was too good for the both of you."

Tommy stared at this suddenly unfamiliar woman. What was she talking about? A cold feeling crept over him. What was she saying? It didn't make sense.

"Here." Alberta was reaching into her black handbag. Her hand reappeared from its depths holding an envelope. She thrust it towards Tommy. "That'll show yeh. You're no blood relative of mine. Your mother gave this to me to get rid of, but I knew I'd need it someday."

Tommy stared down at the envelope in Alberta's hand. He looked up. Alberta's eyes were blazing with anger. His arm reached out as if of its own accord. He took the envelope with a shaking hand. All that he knew to be true had ended.

CHAPTER FIVE

"Why do they organise retirement training?" asked Malcolm. "Bloody waste of money."

"Have yeh found your shoes yet?" responded his wife.

"I don't know where ye have put them."

His wife sighed, reached to lift the brown brogues from under the breakfast bar, and thrust them at him.

"Right. Thanks." Malcolm sat and put on the new shoes his wife had bought for him. He had been looking for his police standard black ones. Of course, they were now at the back of the wardrobe.

Harriet had been all for him attending this course when the invitation had arrived last week. He suspected another motive. As she opened the front door and handed him his coat, she muttered something about him getting under her feet.

Malcolm paused and kissed her on the cheek. "Thanks, love. See you later." Yes, retirement meant adjustments all round.

* * *

Philomena Begley belted out Malcolm's favourite songs on the car CD player, entertaining him as always. She had been there through thick and thin. Pity Harriet didn't see it that way, refusing to have her on when she was in the car. The two women in his life just didn't seem to be compatible.

So he was off to be trained how to retire. Such nonsense. What was there to learn? Retired from the job that was in his blood, that had defined him for the last thirty years. But you couldn't just stop, that was for sure, and that was what he would tell them. Watching that man with Duncan yesterday morning, and chatting with Duncan and Pat afterwards. How could you not start thinking about what happened all those years ago? Well, not that many years ago. Malcolm's whole working life had passed in a flash, but youngsters would think it an age. Those like William Fyffe, for example.

Good lad, he was. When William joined the Police Service of Northern Ireland, Malcolm could tell he was sound straight away. He had been delighted to take the boy under his wing. And there was still plenty of potential in the lad even if he had had a rough time last year. God, had a whole year gone by since William's uncle had tried to kill him and his father had ended up in psychiatric hospital?

Yes, William would be the type to have another look at the Mulholland case. And it would be very interesting to find out the whole story of how there came to be a vacancy in the town for Malcolm to start his own career. There was never much chat about it at the time, and, well, Malcolm had just been very grateful for the opportunity. It had taken years for a close-knit community to open its doors to an outsider from Antrim.

But he'd settled well in the town and in the community. And he had met Harriet, the love of his life, at the Young Farmers dance.

The closer Malcolm got to Omagh this morning, the more his desire grew to know more. To find out why Trevor Mulholland had been killed. Sure, it could be a wee hobby. No harm to anyone, and it would keep him busy. You could only walk the damn dog so much.

As Malcolm approached the turn-off for the hotel which had been hired for the retirement training event, he could see further down the road to the outline of the upper offices of the police station. He pulled into the hotel car park, then reached into the glove pocket and flipped open his Nokia 6263. He'd had some stick for this phone over the years, but it did what it said on the tin – it was a phone, not some fancy mini-computer. He dialled the number he had somehow found easy to remember.

"William, "bout yeh?" Malcolm greeted the man he now thought of as a son. Not that he would ever say it. After all, the lad had a father.

"Jesus, sir, everything all right?"

Malcolm smiled. "I've told yeh a hundred times, no need for the "sir" now." But it felt nice all the same. "I'm about to go to one of them retirement training days, but I don't think I'll stick it much past the lunch."

"Don't miss the free lunch! But what can I do for yeh?" asked William.

"I was wondering, are yeh about at all, for a cup of tea? The training is in the Birches hotel, so I'm only round the corner."

"So happens I'm off this afternoon. So is Hannah." There was a slight pause. "We have an appointment at four."

Malcolm knew William was still seeing a counsellor in his continued recovery from his head injury. His wife, Hannah, had mentioned it when they last visited Malcolm and Harriet in Portrush. Hannah seemed to think it a great help, but Malcolm had never been sure about those "talking therapies". Better just to get on with things. His wife had suggested counselling for him, saying he needed to "man up" and get help after all these years, and that she was sick of waking up next to him shouting, thrashing and sweating. After all, it was twenty years since the day the bomb had ripped out the heart of the town. The day when he had been one of the first to arrive on the scene. But he wasn't ready. Not yet.

"Your place isn't far from the hotel," Malcolm said. "I can be with you by two. That OK? It will be great to have a catch up."

* * *

Hannah answered the door. She threw open her arms and reached up to kiss Malcolm on the cheek. He had nearly gotten used to this Englishwoman's free and easy approach to hugging and kissing. He stood still and surrendered. Over Hannah's shoulder, he saw William smiling at his discomfort.

"You're looking well, Sir," he said, shaking Malcolm's hand.

"I'm damn grateful I've escaped that nonsense."

Malcolm nodded in the general direction of the hotel. "Do yeh know they had us doing some sort of slow-motion karate? Whatever next!"

He followed Hannah into the sitting room. William went to the kitchen to re-boil the kettle. Malcolm sat in his now favourite chair and looked around. It was good to be here.

"How is he?" he asked Hannah.

"Getting there. It was the best decision to pause his career until we get this all sorted. It was a hell of a year last year."

"It was that!" agreed Malcolm. "What about yourself? Did yeh get that promotion? What was it? Social worker team leader?"

Hannah looked towards the open door of the kitchen. "Yes, well, I suppose there was no one else. It's just a shame we didn't both get the step up at the same time."

"His will come when the time is right."

Back from the kitchen, William placed the mug of tea on the side table beside Malcolm.

"So what have ye been up to, with all that leisure time?" he asked. "I bet ye have the legs walked off that dog."

"I can't say me and the dog see eye to eye." Malcolm took a gulp of his tea. "I was thinking of taking up a hobby."

William and Hannah looked at each other with bemused expressions

"Like stamp collecting?" asked William.

"No. I was thinking of using the skills I've got."

"Right," replied William, bemusement now turning into confusion.

Malcolm put down his mug and leant forward in his chair. "I met someone, not far from here, who has a link to an unsolved murder in Tyrone from thirty years ago. Got me interested."

Hannah chimed in. "Shouldn't you be leaving all that to the Historical Enquiries Team?"

"Aye, well, I'm sure they have enough on their hands. Ye see, my interest is a little more personal. I got my first job here in the town because a probationer they had before me went rogue."

"Go on," urged William.

"So… It was your usual terrorist murder – from memory, this man Mulholland didn't pay enough protection money."

"Protection money?" Hannah said. "Dear God, how much more is there to learn about this place? Does that still go on?"

William rubbed Hannah's arm. "No, no more bombs to protect your business from. More drugs, though. Change of income for hoods of both colours," he explained. He turned back to Malcolm. "So what's the connection between the probationer and this murder?"

"Well," Malcolm said, "it was all brushed under the carpet before I arrived. And after that there was enough to deal with. The terrorists upped the ante during the 1990s. From the rumours at the time, this probationer, he was the first officer on the scene. Duncan Gallagher, the guy Mulholland was with, swore there was an envelope of money. That would make sense. Mulholland was on his way to make a payment. Something went wrong and he was killed. And the money disappeared. The probationer got the blame. His DI was a bit of a bastard. He was mine, too. Not the easy-going guy I was." He grinned and shook his head.

"And this probationer got the sack…" Hannah said.

"It was suggested to him that he resign. There was no court case or the like. So it must have been that way."

"And you want to find out… what, exactly?" asked William.

Malcolm reached for his cooling mug of tea and nursed it in his hands. "Ach, I suppose it sounds daft. Daft notions of an old man."

"No," replied William. "It's not stupid, looking back. I just wondered what exactly you were looking for."

Malcolm sat back. "I'm not sure. Maybe to go full circle? Where I started from? Why I was here in the town." He shook his head. "Would you just listen to me. I'm an oul fool already. I just know I have to keep my brain ticking over."

Pat Gallagher's worried and tired face came to mind and the care she had now to provide for her husband. Malcolm didn't want that for his wife. Maybe that was it? Was it just an effort to keep his mind sharp and clear? Williams cleared his throat. "Right, Sir, I mean Malcolm. How can I help?"

Malcolm looked at this great lad who had gone through so much. He didn't want to make life any more difficult for him. "Naw, you're all right. It was a silly notion. I'll be on my way." He got to his feet.

"Sir, you wouldn't have asked me if it wasn't important to you. And if its important to you, it's important to me. Just let me know what you need."

* * *

Malcolm felt a good thirty years younger as he drove back to his bungalow. William had promised to pull what he could from the "bunker", where the records of unsolved murders were kept. Then together, he and William could review them. See where they led. There might be something that would shed some light on the missing money – if there had been any money in the first place. And if there was an unsolved murder attached, well that would make it more interesting. Happy days.

Harriet had left the porch light on. Oh, and the door was open. Malcolm had a feeling he was in trouble.

"Enjoy the course?" she asked with a stony face.

"Yes, love, there was a very interesting karate lesson." Malcolm smiled what he hoped was a winning smile.

"Is that so?"

His smile sagged and collapsed. "Ah now, love, I did me best. Honest to God, it was crap."

"Where did you go?"

Jesus, had she put some sort of tracking device on him? He played for time. He needed to think of a believable answer.

"What do you mean?" he said.

"They rang. Asked if you had got home all right after your bout of sickness. And as it was after the lunch they had given you, they've put in a complaint to the hotel."

Malcolm's heart sank as he realised the string of problems he had caused. "Sorry. I went to see William and Hannah. But the course really was crap. I mean, that slow-motion karate –" He stopped, as he saw tears welling up in Harriet's eyes. "Aw, love. I didn't mean to worry yeh." He wrapped her in his arms and guided her to the conservatory.

Over a cup of tea, he explained as best he could. He would just have a look at the records, see if he could make sense of what had happened, what had led to him having the opportunity to start his career. But mostly to keep the old cogs going round.

"OK," Harriet said. "As long as it goes no further. Look, love, I know you're bored, but you have to make an effort to fill your day with something else." She put her cup down on the side table and placed her hand on Malcolm's arm. "You have given enough to the police, and to the people. I need you to be well. Put the nightmares behind us."

Malcolm picked up Harriet's cold cup of tea from the table and took it to the sink in the kitchen. He washed out the cup and placed it carefully on the draining board. It was her favourite one, a china mug with a picture of a Cairn Terrier and the caption Don't Panic and Carry On Walking the Dog – bought for her by Hannah last Christmas.

He shouted through to her, "Look, if you don't mind me just having a wee look at what William comes up with, then I promise to go to any club, or whatever you come up with, to keep me occupied. Deal?"

CHAPTER SIX

Malcolm closed the front door behind him. The weather had brightened up, but his overcoat, cap and scarf were still necessary to keep out the cold wind that blew in from the coast. It was only a ten-minute walk to the library. At least he didn't have to take the dog with him. That was a bonus. The damn animal had been unusually quiet last night, seemingly happy to stay in its basket. But when Malcolm had looked closer, he saw that Billy had only been chewing his good leather gloves. His wife had excused the beast, saying, "He must be teething."

Malcolm could not believe the efficiency and speed of Harriet in her task of finding a class for him. It was only a matter of days and she had come up with this Information Technology course at the local library. He had counted on having at least a few weeks of peace and quiet. To be fair, he did need some help in that direction. Using the police IT systems was one thing he certainly didn't miss in his retirement. He had been forever getting into trouble with IT Support. He had refused to have a computer in the house. But Harriet's wee machine seemed to be never far from her hand, so there must be still some use for the things. Strange name for it though – a tablet?

Malcolm had counted on young William getting some paperwork to him to have a read and think about.

William had suggested he post hard copies, as that way there would be no email trail. Malcolm could see the sense in that. He wouldn't want William to get into trouble just because he was bored, but it had come to something when posting a letter was less risky than using email.

Malcolm had checked the letterbox each morning. Nothing yet. Maybe the stuff had got lost in the post. He reached into his pocket and took out his phone. He flipped it open. His right forefinger hovered over the numbers. He snapped the phone shut again and shoved it into his pocket. No, he wasn't going to put pressure on the lad. Access to a computer at the library would just have to keep him going for the moment.

* * *

"Can I help you?" asked the young man behind the reception desk. His slight frame was stooped and all his attention was on his phone that was clearly a much more recent purchase than Malcolm's. The lads' eyes flicked from his mobile phone to Malcolm and then back again to his phone.

Malcolm knew just where he would like to put that phone. "I'm here for the Information Technology course."

"The Information... Oh, you mean the IT course." The young man frowned at Malcolm. "Of course you are. Third door on the right." He looked back at his phone. "I think you're late. She won't like it."

Malcolm nearly turned on his heel to walk out of the library. But no, he had made a deal, and it was only fair to stick to it. He knocked on the third door to his right and pushed it open.

"Yes?" The woman asking the question didn't turn round. Her attention was on the screen in front of her. She was sitting next to a grey-haired woman also staring at the screen. Malcolm looked around the room. There were two other women and two men, all sitting at desks with computers and all leaning forward as if they were being sucked in.

"I'm here for the course. Malcolm Bell."

"Right, just a moment. Mrs McCartney, make sure you spell "photography" correctly and you won't be bothered by those images again."

The woman stood up. She was tall, her hair flecked with grey but still mostly brown, an untidy bob cut. This woman was definitely a librarian, with her sensible flat shoes, tweed skirt and blouse buttoned up to the top. But as she turned round, Malcolm could see that her clothes belied her age. He had never considered that makeup improved a woman's look, and clearly this woman felt the same. She was fifty at most, but her clothes aged her more than they should.

"Mr Bell?" she asked, running a pen down a list on an A4 paper attached to a clip board. "You were the only one missing. I was about to call your wife."

"Aw, Jesus, no need to do that. Sure, I'm here now."

"Mr Bell, I do not hold with swearing in my classes. It's my third rule."

"Sorry." There was no way he was going to ask this stern woman what rules one and two were. No doubt he'd find out. He was bound to break them sooner or later.

"My name is Emily Baxter." She pointed to an empty desk with a keyboard and monitor. "You can sit over there." You know how to turn a computer on?"

"Yes, we used them in my old job." Malcolm didn't bother to explain that he mostly delegated any online tasks to subordinates. What else were junior officers for?

"Great. So, today's lesson is research. And the topic is ourselves. It's always enlightening what is on the net about ourselves. So, if you just type..." Emily leant over Malcolm and reached for the keyboard.

"Do yeh think I could research someone else?" Malcolm knew that a search on his name would bring up a multitude of stories relating to his police work, enough to fill a good many screens. He had never been one to enjoy attention. For goodness sake, he was paid to do the job. No need for any glory. "A cousin of mine. I haven't heard from him in a good while. Do yeh think I could look him up?"

"Well, it's not our topic for today, but OK. What's his name?"

"Mulholland. Trevor Mulholland."

"OK, so if you just click on this box."

"Yes, I'll do that. I think your man over there is having a bit of trouble." Malcolm pointed to an elderly man sitting at a terminal on the other side of the room, who was pushing the mouse around vigorously.

"Mr Samuels, I'm just coming. Please, take your hand off the mouse."

"Don't you worry. I'll be grand," Malcolm reassured her.

"Just shout if you need help. Coming now, Mr Samuels."

Malcolm typed Trevor Mulholland's name and pressed return. The first search came up with two Facebook accounts and five LinkedIn and a couple of eejits that felt the world needed to know their day to day ramblings in the form of Tweets. Nothing so far that would suggest a link to the Trevor Mulholland that Malcolm was interested in. Two recent by far. Best narrow it down. Even adding Northern Ireland didn't help much. Seems it was still a very popular name. Malcolm added "Tyrone" and "1989". Now this was better. He clicked on an article from the Tyrone Chronicle. Well, wouldn't you know it. Written by Alfie Hamill.

That reporter had been the bane of Malcolm's life following the bomb in the town, the one that came after they'd said peace was agreed. But, thanks to his wife, Malcolm had made some amends with Hamill in the last year, the year of his retirement – and he was now just about on cordial relations with his old acquaintance. Just. But it had been hard for Malcolm to put what Hamill had done behind him. He was nearly coming round to accept that they had both been at fault all those years ago. Him for embellishing a little evidence – they knew who had planted the bomb, but the physical evidence wasn't strong enough – and Hamill for doing the exposé on Malcolm, trying to get a leg up in the journalist world. It hadn't worked out well for either of them. Malcolm had nearly lost his job, and his promotion to Detective Inspector was a very long time coming. Hamill's story was used by the province's national paper, but promises of a job for him never came through.

Malcolm sat forward in his chair. He found the button to increase the size of the document. He must get his eyes tested again.

ANOTHER MURDER IN OUR COMMUNITY

Trevor Mulholland, a 36-year-old respected businessman from South Tyrone, was killed on Friday night in a shooting incident. Mulholland had been having a relaxing end-of-week and well-deserved refreshment in Kealey's pub. He was set upon by a single gunman who made his escape with no witnesses able to shine a light on the incident.

No witnesses? But wouldn't there have been a barman? And what about Duncan?

The Police arrived within thirty minutes of the shooting. Mulholland was pronounced dead at the scene. The RUC is appealing for anyone with information to contact them on the confidential helpline, 0800 666 999. No claims for responsibility have been made.

No claims for responsibility? Unusual. One side or the other always claimed responsibility. That was the whole point of terrorism. Frighten the general population.

Mr Mulholland is survived by his wife, Eileen, and their two children, Philippa, four, and Henry, two. The funeral, held in Seskinore Parish Church, was attended by businessmen from all over Northern Ireland. In a statement to the newspaper Mrs Mulholland said she was heartbroken, but would ensure that the family quarrying business continued its financial support for the police-run Blue Light Discos. She said, "My husband was particularly supportive of the excellent work done by the police in their efforts to develop links between young people of both communities. He would have wanted that work to continue."

The photograph showed a young woman in her mid-twenties holding the hands of two small children, walking behind the funeral cortege. Her head was held high.

Malcolm felt a presence behind him. He turned to see Emily standing with her arms folded, wearing a frown.

"So, this cousin of yours?"

"I was just – what do they call it – surfing?"

"When your wife booked you in to my course, she mentioned she was trying to get you interested in things other than..." Emily coughed and looked around to see who was listening. "Interests relating to your previous occupation."

Malcolm sighed. Even now, although peace had reigned in the province for the last twenty-two years, the instant reaction was still to hide any potential links to the police. Just in case.

"OK, sorry. You don't need to mention this. I'll look up something else."

"You do that. I wouldn't want to have you stop attending."

Jesus, expelled from his first course? Harriet would go spacers.

Emily turned back to Mr Samuels, who was clearly still struggling.

Malcolm moved the mouse over the "Print" button and clicked. He hadn't seen any printers in the room, but there had been one behind the reception. And as the computer didn't come up with any sort of error message, Malcolm guessed his document would pop up out there.

"Emily?" Malcolm called over to her.

"Yes?" Emily sighed.

"All right if I pop out to the gents? Weak bladder."

"Of course. Past reception and first on your left."

Malcolm knocked on the reception desk to get the attention of the young man now seemingly lost in his phone, his shoulders hunched and the screen not more than a foot from his face.

"Emily asked me to collect a document she had printed."

The young man quickly put his phone down on the reception desk. He walked to the rear of the reception and picked up a sheet of paper. "Here it is." He frowned as he glanced at the document in his hands. "Unusual. She has a thing against looking at historical information. Always saying we should be looking forward, not back."

"Aye, well." Malcolm took the document from the young man's hands. "Maybe she's has had a change of heart." As he headed back to the computer room, he folded the paper and slid it into his back pocket.

CHAPTER SEVEN

"Would you just look who's here!" Harriet said. "Malcolm, get the kettle on! William, com'on ahead in. Don't mind the dog – he's wile friendly. Och, would you look at that. Billy likes you. Can yeh see his wee tail wagging?"

Malcolm had thought the information would come by post. William must have something good for him if he had decided to drive all the way here to deliver it.

"Wasn't expecting yeh. But it's great to see yeh." He guided William to the conservatory. It might be teeming with rain just now, but this was still Malcolm's favourite room. Outside but still inside.

Harriet retired to the kitchen to make the tea and, Malcolm would guess, to pull together a plateful just to keep William going. A round of salad sandwiches and a wee bun would be Malcolm's best guess. Thankfully, Billy went with her.

"Sit yourself down," Malcolm said, gesturing to a chair. He shut the door between the conservatory and the kitchen gently so as not to alert his wife. "Well?..." He sat down and looked hopefully at William.

William shifted awkwardly in his chair. He reached into the inside pocket of his jacket and pulled out a thin A5 envelope.

Malcolm looked at it in surprise. "I thought there would be a bit more than that."

"It's the best I could do. It's harder than ever to get stuff out of the murder archive, with all the retrospective enquires going on. I had to spin some yarn about Mulholland's name coming up in a current enquiry. Even then I had a message back from the Chief Detective Inspector's office asking difficult questions."

Malcolm dropped his shoulders. The last thing he wanted was to put William's career at risk. He had been through enough in the last year, and he had the makings of a great police officer. He just needed time.

"No, lad, you've done great," Malcolm reassured him, working hard to keep the disappointment out of his voice.

"It's just a timeline they pulled together of the events leading up to the shooting and the immediate aftermath," explained William.

"Thanks. I appreciate it." Malcolm took the envelope and slid it between the seat cushion and the side of the chair.

The door opened and Harriet came in carrying a tray of tea and a well-laid plate. "Help yourself, William," she instructed. "Malcolm, remember the waistline." Malcolm withdrew his outstretched hand. "I'll leave yeh to it. Billy needs his wee walk." The dog was behind her, with his lead in his mouth, head cocked to one side, looking like butter wouldn't melt.

Malcolm waited until he heard the front door close. "I do appreciate it, lad, but don't be getting yourself into trouble. I'd never forgive myself."

He handed William one of the mugs of tea and offered him a traybake. The rain had stopped. The sun was breaking through the clouds and streaming into the room, giving a taste of spring warmth.

"It's no bother. But it's not all I got. I spoke to the desk sergeant, Charlie. He started just after Edward Daniels, the probationer who was first on the scene. The one you replaced."

"Yes, Charlie always was reminding me he was there before me. How is the oul bastard? Have they not retired him yet?"

"They're trying." William smiled. "Enticing him with a backroom job."

"So what did Charlie say? 'Bout Daniels. Why was he sacked?"

William shook his head. "Daniels wasn't sacked. Encouraged to resign. You were right. Charlie reckoned it was all brushed under the carpet too. The force didn't want the negative publicity, not with the Troubles still in full swing. Things were bad enough."

"Aye, I remember," Malcolm said quietly. "Daniels having to leave his job, it was about the missing money."

"The day of the shooting, Mulholland was meeting someone. Duncan Gallagher, the guy that gave him a lift, was very clear about that. But he didn't know who Mulholland was meeting. He didn't want to know."

"I can understand that. What yeh didn't know couldn't hurt yeh in those days."

William gestured to his mug. "Where can I put this down?"

"Stick it on there." Malcolm gestured to a side table

that had a neat stack of Harriet's well-thumbed cooking magazines on it.

William put the mug down and moved on. "Duncan was clear that Mulholland had a shedload of money with him. In an envelope."

"He saw the money?" Malcolm said.

"No. But according to Duncan the envelope was busting at the seams. Couldn't be anything else. What Charlie heard was that Daniels was first through the door of the pub, and by the time the DI came in, there was no sign of any money."

"And Daniels got the blame?"

"Looks like it," William said. "He was from a rough part of Trillick, family as poor as church mice. The story went round the station that he'd taken a chance and paid the price."

"After Daniels left, did Charlie know what happened to him?"

"He did this and that, apparently. Took to drink in a big way. Charlie said Daniels had little choice but to stay around Trillick. If he did take the money, God knows what he did with it."

"Does Charlie know if he's still around?"

"He heard that Daniels died about twenty years ago. Nothing much improved in his life. Sad, really."

"Any family?"

"I have no idea."

"I remember that DI," Malcolm said. "Robinson was his name. He was there for my first couple of years. Right difficult bastard."

Williams laughed. "God save us from cantankerous

senior officers!" He stood up and took the two empty mugs. "I'll make another brew."

* * *

The rain returned and hammered down. The sound in the conservatory was almost deafening. Malcolm hoped William's drive home hadn't been too bad.

He spread the unfolded A4 sheets on the coffee table: the one he had printed out at the library and the two sheets from William. He leant forward, resting his forearms on his knees, and studied them.

He began with the Case Timeline, dated Friday April 12th 1989, signed as collated by DI Robinson.

The sources of information were listed as Duncan Gallagher, Jane Mulholland Tony Muldoon, Paul McGonigle, PC Edward Daniels and Di Robinson. Times recorded were based on the recollection of witnesses, and confirmed in some instances by other sources.

The Timeline covered the chain of events from the moment Trevor Mulholland had been picked up at his home at 1.45 on the Friday afternoon, until he was pronounced dead on the pub floor at 3.45. Two hours, detailed with all the care and attention Malcolm would have expected from a police crime report.

He sat back in his chair. The rain had started to ease off, the clatter on the conservatory roof now reduced to a murmur. He began to wonder about the events after the shooting…

2.26pm: Record of 999 call from pub requesting ambulance and police.

3.11pm: Police arrive at scene. PC Daniels enters pub lounge. DI Robinson remains in squad car to request army backup.

3.14pm: DI Robinson enters the public lounge.

3.24pm: Army backup arrives to secure the area.

3.25pm: DI Robinson instructs PC Daniels to take Mr D Gallagher home.

3.30pm: Paramedics arrive.

3.45pm: Mr T Mulholland is pronounced dead following examination at the scene of the crime.

It was clear to Malcom that the crucial time period was between 2.26 pm and 3.11 pm. Forty-five minutes to give Muldoon or Gallagher time to pocket the money before the police arrived. But Duncan was a good friend of Mulholland. Would he have had the mindset in that moment to take the envelope? It seemed, from what Malcolm knew of the Gallaghers, and from his own wife's opinion – rarely wrong – such an action would be totally out of character for the man. A better shout would be the barman. But then both PC Daniels and DI Robinson would have had time as well. It would have been easy enough for either of them, given the chaos. Malcolm had experienced enough of that at crimes scenes in his time.

Other questions kept coming at him. One shooter and no claims of responsibility. And why leave the one witness alive? Muldoon was out at the back of the pub. By accident or design? The drayman made a regular delivery every Friday. Apart from Muldoon, who was aware of that? Yes, getting to the bottom of the missing money, if there had been any in the first place, that was one thing.

Maybe there was more to know.

Just in these two documents there was enough

information to get his teeth into. Most important were the gaps in the story – they said more.

Malcolm looked at the timeline again and sighed. Sixty minutes to destroy a family. How did the widow Mulholland cope with bringing up two small children? She may have carried on with the quarrying business. Or did she sell up?

He felt his wife's hand on his shoulder.

"Find what you're looking for?" she asked.

"Still looking, love. No answers yet."

CHAPTER EIGHT

Tommy spread the documents on the table. A letter confirming that his parents were fit to adopt. Advice on getting support. A court order confirming the adoption. They did it by the book, which meant there must be a way, an official way, of finding his birth parents, of finding out who he really was. Had he been rejected or was he a by-product of some fling his da had? Alberta seemed sure enough of the latter. But then she had never liked his da.

Tommy glanced at his phone screen. Still no call back from Donal. One last try. He pulled out the other phone he had bought that morning from the supermarket. A burner. Donal wouldn't recognise the number. A small chance he would answer, but still a chance. Tommy dialled the number.

"Hello?"

"Don't hang up, please." Tommy hated himself for the pleading he heard in his own voice.

"It's you. I don't think..."

"Please, Donal. Just listen. Look, my aunt, she's not my aunt. And my parents – I don't know who the fuck I am."

"Tommy, you haven't been honest with me. I did a little digging. Your da, Christ, he was in the UVF, for fuck's sake.

You are too, for all I know. There is no way I am getting involved with you. I'm keeping my kneecaps."

"No, you don't understand. I'm not in the UVF. My da was, but not me. Anyway, there is no UVF now. At least, they're not active. I thought you and I—"

"You must think I'm stupid. Or you're bloody naive if you think those connections just go away when it's convenient. Sorry. It was good fun, but it's over."

"But I need you!" shouted Tommy. The phone was dead. Donal had gone.

Tommy threw the phone at the wall. It dropped to the floor. The screen splintered. Tommy put his head in his hands. How had something so right gone so quickly wrong? Tears stung at the back of his eyes, but just as quickly a surge of anger started growing in his stomach. He reached for the band on his wrist and pulled it so far back it could have snapped.

* * *

Jeff's terraced house stood in a time-forgotten street in East Belfast. Tommy stopped outside and peered through the window, past the greasy curtain.

Jeff was slumped in his armchair, staring at the electric fire, a glass of something in his hand. His grey hair was slicked down into place. His feet were in tartan slippers. A small side table was piled high with Jeff's essentials: brown plastic medication bottles, a packet of fags with a lighter on top, a plate with the remains of a sandwich. A half-drunk mug of tea and a tumbler with a few fingers of amber liquid. Tommy hadn't considered Jeff old, until now.

He knocked a few times on the window, smiled and waved as Jeff turned around. Then he moved to the front door to wait.

The door opened. ""Bout yeh, Tommy lad!" Jeff smiled. "I wasn't expecting anyone. Come on ahead in. Don't mind the mess. Sure, I was just about to get the hoover out."

Tommy doubted the hoover had seen the light of day for some considerable time, maybe not since Jeff's wife Maureen had died five years ago.

He followed Jeff into the sitting room. His host moved a pile of newspapers from the second armchair facing the fire. "Sit yourself down, lad."

"I just thought I'd pop by as I was passing."

Jeff rubbed his chin and his eyebrows squished together. "Passing to go where? Are ye not back at work?"

"Naw, they've given me a bit more time off. I'm... I'm just not there yet. Ye know?"

Jeff sat heavily in his chair. "Your da had to pull a few strings to get yeh started in Bombardier's. Don't go throwing it all away. Death is as certain as life. Just need to crack on."

"It's about me da I'm here."

"Oh aye?"

"Alberta—"

"That bitch. She been slagging your da off again? Take no notice. Your da is a hero round these parts. I remember the time—"

"She's told me... about me being adopted."

"Has she now?" Jeff said. "Well, let me tell you, it makes no odds. You had good decent parents. Alberta's nothing but a meddling cow."

"She said – well, I think she said – that me da had a fling and I was the result."

"That woman is talking through her arse. Always has done. Your da was devoted to your ma. Talk about opposites attracting. When they got together there was nobody else for either of them."

"Jeff, I need to know. Christ's sake, I've lost me ma and da, and now I don't know who I am."

"Look, Tommy, if you must know, Alberta was right about one thing. It wasn't straightforward. Your ma and da, they'd tried for weans for years. And your ma was heartbroken. Your da was doing a few jobs, yeh know, for the cause, in Tyrone. It so happened someone wanted a favour, someone who was important to us. It was a win-win situation. Your ma got you, and a major favour had been granted."

"I saw the court order."

"Like I said, it wasn't wile straightforward. Your da had to call in a few favours of his own to get the paperwork in place. Your ma insisted on it. She wasn't going to risk losing you. You can be assured there was never a more wanted youngster than you."

Tommy stared at the single red bar of the electric fire. Bit by bit, the foundations that had underpinned his life of his life were being eroded. Just when he had thought, some few weeks ago, that it was all making sense, that he had – despite the loss of his mother – a future in Donal.

Jeff reached for his glass and sipped. "Do ye want one?"

Tommy shook his head. "Where?"

"Where what, lad?"

"Where in Tyrone? Where about was this favour done?"

Jeff put his glass down and sighed. "There's still harm that could be done to our people. Peace process be damned. Some things have to be kept quiet, even now. Can ye not just forget about it? What good will it do to rake everything up?"

Tommy leant forward in his chair. He picked up Jeff's lighter from the side table and flicked it. The flame popped up.

"You know, an oul man living alone could be in danger of falling asleep with the drink, and setting fire to the place. They say it happens a lot. That would be a very sad way to end your days. A lonely, drunk old man burnt to a crisp."

He grabbed the glass from Jeff's hand and threw the contents over his face. Jeff tried to stand up. Tommy reached over and clamped his hands on Jeff's wrists, pinning him to the arms of the chair. It didn't take much effort to keep him down.

"What the fuck?" Jeff shook his head, trying to get the liquid from his eyes.

"I'll ask you again, old man," Tommy said. "Where in Tyrone?" His face was now a foot from Jeff's. He could smell the alcohol combined with staleness from the old man's breath. Jeff's lips and chin trembled. It was good to be in control.

"For fuck's sake! Near Ballygawley. We always met him in a lay-by near the Ballygawley roundabout. He kept guns for us. He'd somewhere he could hide them."

"A name, Jeff. Since you're doing so well, give me a name."

"I was never given one."

Tommy put all his weight into his arms. His pectoral muscles tensed with the effort.

Fuck sake!" Jeff shouted. "I wasn't given a name, Tommy. Your da was the only one who knew his real name. He only ever called him Tractor Man."

Tommy released his grip and stood up. He tapped Jeff on the face with the flat of his hand, which might have looked friendly to an observer but had force behind it.

"Much obliged."

He made for the front door.

Jeff called after him. "What the hell has gotten into yeh? I suppose your wee friend from down south put yeh up to this. That'll end in tears, one way or the other. The likes of him aren't welcome around here. Not with his preferences. Your da would be ashamed of yeh!"

Tommy paused. He turned to look at this man he had admired for so many years. Now an old, crumpled figure clinging on to bigotries that gave meaning to his life. Tommy slammed the front door behind him.

* * *

Tommy pulled at the edge of the lino that covered the floor of the bathroom. He remembered the fuss his mother had made to get the lino changed. He must have been around fifteen. She had argued that it had gotten tatty and she was ashamed when visitors asked to use the toilet. His da had changed it one Saturday, when his ma was shopping in Belfast. He told her there was no sense using a tradesman when he could do it himself.

Tommy remembered how doubtful his ma had looked. His da tried to avoid all DIY – a man had to rest when he came home from a day's work, he would say. Tommy was roped in to do the heavy lifting. He was already starting to grow tall and his gym workouts meant he was filling out in a good way. His da was always complaining of the aches and pains in his back.

It was where Tommy remembered it. Where he and his father had cut the floorboards before they put down the new lino. Next to the toilet. Back then, they had hollowed out the floor underneath to create a space that was just big enough. The wood was starting to rot – years of decay from his father and him sometimes missing the toilet bowl.

Tommy pulled at the cut floorboards. They came away. He reached into the hole underneath, pulled out the oilskin parcel and placed it on the kitchen table. He cut the cord keeping the parcel together with his Stanley knife. The 9mm pistol fell out, together with a box of bullets.

CHAPTER NINE

It didn't seem so hard for Malcolm to leave the bungalow today. There was a potential purpose in his visit to the IT course. Christ, would you believe it, he was even starting to get the lingo. He pulled his hat down firmly and buttoned his overcoat. That wind would go through you. He dug his hands into his pockets. He still had not got round to replacing his gloves that the bloody dog had destroyed.

The boy behind the reception at the library – he couldn't have been more than a teenager – was still staring at his phone, his thumbs battering away at the screen.

"You're back, then," the boy greeted him, not looking up.

"You're still here, then," returned Malcolm.

Malcolm walked on towards the meeting room.

"Toilets on the left there," shouted the boy after him. "You old blokes and your prostate, got to be careful."

Malcolm turned and drew a breath to respond to the wee skitter, but stopped when he heard the meeting room door open.

"You're early!" exclaimed Emily.

It sounded like a reproach.

"Do ye want me to..." Malcolm gestured towards the reception and the way out.

"No, no, come on ahead in. I suppose you can wait for the others."

Malcolm followed her and sat at the terminal he had used before: already it was his. He was never one for the old "hot desking" approach. Didn't see the point in it.

The room was warm. Malcolm took off his coat shoving his hat into his coat pocket for safety. Emily moved efficiently about the room in her sensible shoes, tweed skirt and button-up cardigan. Her hair was shorter, tidier than last week, glasses perched on top of her head, pushing back her hair so that the grey around her hairline was showing. Her expression was intense as she placed a printed handout beside each terminal, including Malcolm's. It was entitled Project.

"Emi... I mean, Miss Baxter?" Malcolm didn't feel that he had permission yet to use her forename.

"Yes?" Emily's glasses dropped onto the bridge of her nose as she peered at him.

"I have an idea – for a project."

"That's wonderful. I thought, well, after last week – I mean, I wasn't sure if you would come back."

"Oh yes." Malcolm remembered the excuse he had given when she started the whole "let's get to know you" nonsense at the end of the session. Tell us an interesting fact about yourself. He had no time for all that touchy-feely stuff. "I had a bad stomach."

Malcolm knew that look she was giving him. It was the one his wife used when she could see straight through him – which was practically all the time.

"Glad to see you have recovered," Emily said. "So, your project?"

"You know what I used to do, what I was?"

"Yes, and don't worry. With GDPR we are very tight on confidentiality, so you have no worries."

"No, it's not that. I mean, I'm sure my privacy is safe with you. I saw from the start that you are a very competent professional librarian." Malcolm could see the beginnings of a smile twitching at the sides of Emily's mouth. "It's just, well, there's this case. What they call a cold case."

Emily's potential smile turned into a scowl.

Malcolm pressed on. "It's an interesting one, from years back. A murder in which some assumptions were, I believe, made. Of no consequence now. Just professional interest. That's all. You understand, I mean, as one professional to another…"

The vanished smile was now replaced with a frown. "My rule number two. No looking back."

"I thought that's what research involves?"

"Mr Bell…"

Malcolm drew breath, ready to correct her, but then stopped. Of course it was Mr, not DI anymore.

"Given the nature of our wee country," Emily said, "it is my policy, or rather it is my rule…" Clearly her rules were far more important that any library policies "… that we do not go poking about in the past. Especially our recent past."

"And by recent past you mean…"

"Anything that is going to upset anyone. The last hundred years. That should do it. It's no good for anyone." Emily made to walk away.

"But…"

"Yes?"

"You asked us to research ourselves. Isn't that looking back? "

"It's always enlightening to see ourselves as others see us. Well, usually, anyway." Emily fiddled with the top button of her cardigan. There was a catch in her voice. She cleared her throat. "But I will not allow digging around in the past when it involves..." She shuddered. "Well, to be clear, anything to do with the Troubles. We have had enough of that. You'll just have to think of something else." She pushed her glasses back onto the top of her head. "Something positive. Now, I have to get the room sorted."

Malcolm pushed the mouse back and forth on the mousepad aimlessly. What could he research that would keep Emily happy, and at the same time advance his knowledge? Emily counted out more of her handouts, placing them on each of the workstations and tapping them into neat individual piles.

His fellow students started to arrive. Emily greeted each of them with a curt "hello". Malcolm felt her attention lingered on him a little longer than the rest as she reminded her class of the "house rules". She moved from workstation to workstation to turn on the computers – clearly her students were not considered collectively competent enough to do so themselves just yet – and the little blue lights started to flash one by one.

Blue lights flashing.

Malcolm sat up.

Mulholland's widow had mentioned the Blue Light Discos in the newspaper article. Something about continuing to support them, continuing her husband's good charitable work. And surely Emily would be happy enough with that. Yes, going back in time, but to a good thing, something positive, that would help bring the divided communities together. Or so the police hierarchy said when they were trying to find volunteers in Malcolm's ranks police to run the damn things. He'd managed to get out of it all but once. And that once was bloody memorable. Teenagers being sick out the back of the scout hall, and all over his boots as he held them up. He had been delighted when his DI got word that there would be no more calls for volunteers because the plug had been pulled.

He clicked onto the search bar and typed "Blue Light Discos" and "Tyrone".

Tyrone Chronicle, 19th April 1990

Demise of the Blue Light Discos

The RUC has announced that, due to budgetary constraints, the popular Blue Light Discos will no longer be run by the community engagement department of the RUC in Tyrone.

So the widow Mulholland's financial assistance had either not been enough or it hadn't lasted.

These very popular events have been an asset to the community, giving our young people an opportunity to socialise, and enabling them to make new friendships. DI Robinson, from West Tyrone PSNI, stated, "It's a sad day when opportunities like this are taken from our wonderful young people, who I know have benefited from these social events to integrate with others."

Malcolm snorted. The lying bastard. DI Robinson had prefaced his persuasion to 'volunteer' to help at the discos with the words 'bloody waste of time' and 'wee terrorists in the making'. In fact, Malcolm recollected that the DI had campaigned long and hard to take these events off his list of responsibilities, and boasted about doing just that at his retirement do the following year.

The article also said that the Blue Light Discos in Tyrone had been supported by both the community and local businesses for the last twenty years, and have done much to promote community cohesiveness, despite negative publicity in the last few years linked to a poster campaign.

Negative publicity? Yes, there had been something. Weren't a couple of posters put up on lampposts in the Ballygawley area saying that any attendance at the Blue Light discos was tantamount to collusion with the security forces and not something that the nationalist community would endorse? But it was something and nothing.

Malcolm checked out the reporter's byline. Yep, wouldn't yeh know it – Alfie Hamill trying to rake up the dirt. Yes, the discos were a pain in the arse, but there were that many illegal bloody posters about instructing the populace to vote this way or that, reminding them where their loyalties had to lie.

Malcolm sensed a presence behind him.

"I'm looking at the wonderful history of the Blue Light Discos," he said. "Weren't they a great thing?"

"Hmmm. Well, I suppose..." Emily pulled her glasses from the top of her head, pushed them into position and bent down to peer at what Malcolm had brought up on the screen.

"Yeh can't say it's looking back, at, yeh know, other stuff."

"OK. I suppose. I'll let it pass."

"Miss Baxter?" The request for help came from across the room.

"Coming now, Mrs McCausland," Emily called back, standing up straight. "But Mr Bell…" Emily placed her hand on his shoulder.

"Yes?"

"I'll be watching you."

CHAPTER TEN

Malcolm leant on the window sill in the front room. He recognised the two figures walking on the public footpath that bordered the front garden of the bungalow. If he hurried, he could catch up with them.

"I think I'll take the dog out for a walk."

"You'll what?" Harriet looked out of the window at the grey sky, then back to her husband.

The rain had just stopped, but there was a dampness in the air, a cold that seeped into your bones.

"Com'on, Billy." Malcolm shook the dog's lead.

Billy growled quietly from his basket.

"I'm not sure he wants to go."

"Course he does." Malcolm knelt in front of Billy, got a strong grip of the dog's collar and attached the lead. "Look, he's dead keen."

Billy continued to growl but accompanied Malcolm to the front door.

"Back in a bit!"

"Are yeh sure..."

Malcolm pulled the door shut and hurried to the footpath, Billy trotting alongside him. The two figures were about fifty metres in front, but Malcolm and Billy walked at pace and closed in fast. Billy's ears pricked up and he strained forward on his lead.

"Yes, it's that wee dog you're fond of. Aren't I giving you a treat?"

Malcolm knew where Pat and Duncan Gallagher would be heading. The East Strand. Had to be. He was starting to puff with the effort, but he could see the bench he hoped they would rest on. Pat and Duncan reached it. Yes, they were sitting! Thank God. Malcolm slowed his pace, but Billy still pulled at his lead.

"For Christ's sake, don't appear too keen! We're meant to be undercover."

Malcolm waited until he was within speaking distance of Pat and Duncan. "Wile chilly, isn't it? But it's great the rain's stopped."

"Move up, Duncan, let the man sit down." Pat nudged Duncan with her elbow. Then, to Malcolm, "You're looking out of breath."

Malcolm hit his chest with his fist and forced a cough. "Just recovering from the cold. Och, would yeh just look at the pair of them." Billy was circling their dog, nose firmly towards the other's behind. "Making friends. Mine's called Billy."

"Ours is Bella. Have you had him neutered?" asked Pat.

"Oh aye. That was all done before he arrived with us," Malcolm reassured her, hoping he was right. "Are yeh enjoying the view, Duncan?"

Duncan turned to look at Malcolm, his expression politely puzzled. "Yes, lovely view. And you are…?"

"Do yeh remember we met the other day. Just here. Watching them eejit runners. Name's Malcolm."

"Yes, of course." Duncan looked towards Pat, tilting his head and blinking.

"Duncan, it's Malcolm the policeman. From back home." Pat sighed and took Duncan's hand. "He isn't having a great day. Didn't sleep too well. It makes it hard for him to remember."

Pat's complexion and the dark rings around her eyes suggested she hadn't had a great night's sleep either.

She gathered up her bag and stood. "Come on, Duncan, we need to get some milk and the paper."

"But we have some."

"No, love. We don't." Pat adjusted Duncan's scarf, which had come loose. "He tried to make me a cup of tea this morning, but he knocked the whole bottle of milk over. Coordination isn't that great. Not when he's tired. He does his best. Don't yeh, love?"

"Look, why don't I just sit here with Duncan?" Malcolm asked. "You'll be half the time on your own. And the dogs are getting on great."

Pat frowned. "If you're sure? Duncan, you'll be OK?"

"He'll be fine," reassured Malcolm

Malcolm watched Pat's petite figure move in the direction of the Spar shop. She stopped and looked back. Malcolm gave what he hoped was a reassuring wave. Pat carried on walking.

"Grand view." Malcolm pointed to the sea front.

"Aye."

"So yeh used to live in Seskinore?"

"Yes…" Duncan strained to look in the direction of Pat's receding figure.

"She'll be back in a minute." Malcolm searched for topics that would get a response longer than one word. Omagh Academicals rugby team. That may do the trick.

And it would be a good way to get Duncan onto the topic of Trevor Mullholland. "The rugby team is doing well."

"I play rugby... I mean, I used to."

"So I hear. I was a forward meself. Had the figure for it." Malcolm patted his stomach.

"I was a... the ones at the side."

"Ah yes, you would've definitely been a winger. Sharp and light on your feet would be my guess."

"That's it – a winger." Duncan smiled with relief. He reached down to stroke his dog.

Malcolm considered his next question. Surely it would do no harm? "Duncan, if ye don't mind me asking, you had a friend who played with you. Name of Trevor Mulholland."

Duncan's smile faded. "Trevor was great craic. A great friend."

"I heard what happened. It must have been an awful shock."

"Yes... a shock." Duncan tucked his scarf tighter into the neck of his coat and frowned.

"You were there I understand, you know, when he was shot."

Duncan didn't reply.

"I was just wondering, I mean, can you remember what happened?"

Still no response.

"Maybe it's too long ago."

"Long time ago." Duncan bent again to stroke Bella.

"Aye, I know." Was he was getting through? He wasn't sure. "Somebody said there was money that went missing."

No response.

"Duncan, did yeh hear where—"

Duncan turned quickly towards Malcolm, his eyes wide and bulging.

"There was money. I told them. I told you all!" He spat out the words. Bubbles of spit gathered at the side of his mouth. Bella jumped up and put her front paws on Duncan's knees, her head cocked to one side.

Malcolm put his hand on Duncan's forearm. "I was only asking..."

Duncan shook the hand away. "I said the money was there!"

Malcolm looked around to check if Duncan's raised voice had attracted attention. "OK, mate, OK. Course you did. I remember," he said in a soothing tone.

"I told them, over and over..." Duncan's voice was now quieter, pleading. "They just wouldn't listen!"

Maybe a distraction would calm Duncan. Malcolm had to do something before Pat returned.

Malcolm pointed down to Billy, who was stretched out in the weak sun that had now made an appearance. "Look, the dogs are getting wile fed up." Duncan followed his gaze. "Why don't we take a wee dander to the shore?"

Malcolm helped Duncan to his feet. Billy growled.

They walked to the beach with their dogs, in silence. Progress was slow on the soft white sand. The wind had eased and the sea rippled onto the shore. They stood a while, looking out at the rocky outcrop of the Skerries. To Malcolm's relief, Duncan's face relaxed, the tension disappearing. They turned to walk back to the bench. Malcolm could see Pat approaching in the distance, struggling with a plastic shopping bag. A man was moving towards her. He looked familiar.

They climbed the steps from the beach. The man was now talking to Pat. The same one Malcolm had seen the first day he had met them on the East Strand? The man had grabbed Pat's arm. She was trying to shake him off.

Malcolm wanted to go to Pat, but knew he couldn't leave Duncan.

He waved, and shouted. "We're over here!"

The man looked towards Malcolm, raised his hands in a gesture of frustration and walked away, picking up speed.

People and dogs met at the bench. Pat was sitting, arms clasped tight to her abdomen, looking down at the ground.

"Thought we'd have a wee walk to keep the dogs amused, didn't we, Duncan?" Malcolm gently elbowed Duncan. "Everything all right?" he asked. "I mean, that man... was he bothering yeh? Some sort of nutter?"

Pat looked up sharply. "No. He was just asking the way."

"Oh. It just looked to me..."

"It was nothing. He was... lost."

Pat reached to take Duncan's hand. "Com'on, love. You're looking tired. Time to take Bella home." She smiled at Malcolm. "Thanks for keeping him company. It's a help."

Pat and Duncan got to their feet.

"Pat, before yeh go..."

"Yes?" Pat's voice was weak.

"I'm sorry. I might've upset Duncan. I didn't mean to."

"How?" Pat looked at Duncan, her brow furrowed. He smiled back at her. "He seems fine."

"I asked him about Trevor Mulholland."

Pat looked at the ground and then looked up at Malcolm. Her eyes were brimming with tears, and her voice was rising.

"Will no one leave us alone? Have I not enough to cope with? Trevor Mulholland was no good. I wish Duncan had never met him." She wiped her tears away with the back of her hand. Managed to pull on a smile again for her husband, her voice now controlled, with a false brightness. "Let's get back for a cup of tea."

Malcolm watched as Pat and Duncan walked away, her arm tucked in to Duncan's. She seemed smaller than before.

Malcolm felt guilty. Had there been any point to his questions? Had he needed to ask them? What had he achieved?

"Do yeh know, Billy, sometimes I'm a selfish arse."

CHAPTER ELEVEN

Tommy dialled the number. He hadn't needed to for nearly three years. Not since his da died. That was when he had finally got it under control. The anger. Mostly. But not without help, he knew that. He wasn't stupid.

It had always been with him, but when the police had wanted to charge him with GBH his doctor had intervened. Said he had a "disorder that could be treated". And it had worked, the counselling. Mostly. What did they call it? Talking Therapy. His da wasn't keen, of course. Said it was for women. Until now. It had started again.

"Tommy? It's been a while," said the woman. "All OK? Sorry. Stupid question. I guess not if you're contacting me."

"It's been… difficult. I mean, it was getting better. The strategies – they were working." Tommy pulled the band on his wrist.

"That's good." There was a pause. "But not now? What's changed?"

"Things."

A light chuckle. "You'll have to give me a little more than that."

Tommy smiled. She could always make him smile. No matter how much the anger was churning inside him.

"I met someone."

"That's good. Is he right for you?"

"Yes… he was." She was the first he had been able to tell, before he had even accepted it fully himself. That was when he had started to understand what he wanted. The beginning of the process of taking down the barriers that he had put in place, the barriers that had contained his rage for so long. "But he's gone."

"I'm sorry."

Silence. Tommy knew she was waiting for him to continue. This was how it worked. "And me ma, she's gone too."

"Sorry for your…"

Fuck's sake. "Please – please don't say that."

"OK. Tommy, you're grieving."

The voice was irritatingly soft.

"I know that. But there's more. Me ma and da, they… lied to me. They fucking lied." Tommy's voice started to rise. "They all did!"

His head began to pulse, to thump through his skull. He rubbed his eyes, pressing the phone to his ear. Any sensation to stop what he knew was coming. But he also knew it wouldn't stop.

"Tommy, breathe deeply. I want you to count to ten before you speak. Find the band on your wrist. Pull the band."

Tommy counted his breaths. The churning, the throbbing calmed. The band snapped onto his wrist. He focused on the pain. The pain was a friend. Made the anger go away.

"Tommy…?"

With effort Tommy suppressed his voice to a quieter tone. "Yes?"

"That's good. You're getting control. They lied? What did they lie about?"

"I wasn't theirs. I'm some fucking cuckoo. Some piece of shit no one wanted." The anger was growing again. The band snapped onto his wrist. Once. Twice. Three times. "I wasn't theirs. Alberta told me. The bitch loved telling me." He took a deep breath. He was trying. Really trying. "I thought… I was beginning to… I was getting… me." He trailed off. How could he explain this storm of thoughts in his head?

"Tommy, there are ways of sorting this."

"Oh, are there?" Tommy heard the sarcasm in his own voice. "Have yeh a magic fucking wand?"

"Proper ways." She paused. "You have made so much progress. Your friend – that was a start. That was good. And there will be other good times."

"I know. I've checked."

"Checked? Checked what?"

"There's a form I can fill in. To find them."

"Sorry – find who?"

"Find the fuckers who threw me away! My darling real mother and father! To ask them why."

"Tommy. Take a deep breath. I know you can do this. Control it. You can do it. Look, I know your ma and da loved you. You have talked about them so much. I know you loved them too."

Tommy tried to take a deep breath but his chest was tight. "Loved who? The ones who lied to me? Everyone knew but me. Laughing stock. That's me."

Tommy held the phone tightly, pushed the handset even closer to his head so it hurt. His breath was shallow and quick. He started to hit his fist in a rhythm on the door frame of the kitchen door. Physical pain, that's what he needed. To block out the pain and hurt that was deep within him.

"Tommy, listen to me. I want you to take a breath in and count to five, then breathe..."

Tommy took his phone from his ear and held it close to his mouth. "Fuck off!" he shouted. He slammed the phone down on the sideboard. He paced back and forth, back and forth, back and forth. His chest was tighter, the throbbing beating an ever-increasing rhythm in his head.

He looked at the form on the kitchen table – CR part 1. An official impersonal name for a form that could mean so much. He had downloaded it off the internet and printed it at the library. The librarian had raised her eyebrow when she'd seen it. Nosey cow. He had wanted to tear the eyebrows from her fucking face. But he needed the form and didn't need the aggro. Not now.

He had studied the form over and over. He had made sure he had kept it clean. No creases. No folds. No careless grease stains.

There were questions on it he could answer. Some he couldn't. Birth name. How the fuck did you find that out? Wasn't that the point of the form? Birth mother? Birth father? They were taking the piss. And the icing on the cake: the requirement of a cheque for fifteen pounds. You had to pay to find out who you were.

But he started to fill in whatever he could. Did the

best he could. Because this was the only way. Because this would give him the answer. It had to. To tell him who he was. Why he was thrown away. And when he found his answers?... Tommy didn't know what he would do then.

CHAPTER TWELVE

Malcolm hadn't slept well. The nightmares were back. Running, running, running towards where he knew that people, so many people, would need him. The familiar street now unfamiliar, debris everywhere, mixed up with bloody body parts and the sound of silence. Then moaning, then screams. Piercing screams. Screams that got into his soul. That never would leave him. Never had. But this time Duncan was there, asking "Where's the money?"

Malcolm had woken in a sweat. As usual. No change in twenty years.

Harriet had insisted on a two-bedroomed bungalow, and he knew she was right. Sometimes his turning and shouting and thrashing destroyed a good night's sleep for her. Malcolm was worried that someday it would be dangerous for her, too. She said she didn't fear so, but then she would, wouldn't she?

He put the kettle on. A cup of tea ready for when she woke would make amends, to some degree. She deserved it. He knew that. Maybe the cup of tea would tell her how much he appreciated her. Needed her. Loved her. He left the china mug on her bedside table. Her deep breaths told him she was catching up on what she had lost during the night. He returned to sit in the conservatory. Watched Billy stretched out on the rug, his head resting on the floor between his front paws, watching him back.

Malcolm resolved to stop. Stop the digging and hoken around. What good did it do? Look what he had done to Duncan. And to Pat. They hadn't deserved the upset. They both had enough on their plate.

The phone rang and he heard Harriet answer. So she was up. Maybe she needed a fresh cup. As he padded towards the hallway, he stopped dead.

"Pat, how are you?" Harriet asked. "No, not too early at all. I've been up a while."

Malcolm looked at his watch. Nine thirty. Harriet would be mortified if anyone thought she would still be in bed past eight thirty. Was this Pat calling to complain about him?

"Really?" Harriet said. "Are you sure?"

Oh Jesus, he was surely in trouble now.

"If it's not too much bother for you."

What?

"This evening would be grand. About six thirty?"

Shite… He had just nine hours to work out how to get out of this. Clearly Pat was keeping her powder dry. No doubt she'd tear a strip of him face to face. What would Harriet think of him?

"That was Pat Gallagher," Harriet said, catching sight of him. "She's inviting us over for a meal. Isn't she kind? I told you she was a real lady."

"I think I have an IT class this evening."

"Malcolm. We're new to Portrush. And I don't have that many friends here, not like home…"

"I know, love, it's just…" His wife's quizzical look stopped him. "That'll be lovely."

* * *

He stood behind Harriet as they waited for the doorbell to be answered. He ran a finger around his collar to loosen it a fraction. He was getting increasingly annoyed with himself. For God's sake, was he not a grown man? OK, he might have stepped over a line yesterday, but to feel this wretched? The only thing he could put it down to was that in his career he hadn't been used to dealing with decent people. Scoundrels, liars and occasionally, murderers had been more his line.

The door was opened by Pat. Malcolm smiled what he hoped was a friendly, guilt-free smile over his wife's shoulder. It was returned by a nod. Maybe, just maybe, he wasn't going to get a dressing down.

"Thank you so much for the invite. It'll be great to catch up." Harriet extended her hand to Pat, whose eyes had lost their deep shadows since Malcolm had last seem her. Perhaps she'd enjoyed a better night's sleep. Malcolm resolved once again not to do anything to upset the situation.

"Come on ahead in," Pat said.

They followed her into a neat and tidy sitting room. A three-piece suite with cushions covered in the same material as the sky-blue curtains and perfectly positioned and angled. Precision and tidiness clearly meant a lot to Pat. Maybe it was her way of keeping order in her life. Duncan was sitting in one of the armchairs, stroking Bella on his lap with a contented rhythm. He was wearing the slippers he had worn when Malcolm had first met him. But now they were spotlessly clean.

"Sit yourself down. Duncan?" Pat called, to move her husband's attention from Bella to the visitors. "Malcolm and his wife are here."

Duncan looked up. "Have we met?"

Pat sighed. "Duncan, you had a walk with Malcolm yesterday. With the dogs. I'll go and get the food ready." She sighed again and left.

Malcolm was glad that Duncan did not remember their last conversation, but was at a loss as to how to start one now.

Harriet rescued him. "I remember you from way back. You haven't changed a bit. You were in the post office. Helping out Pat. I'd come in around once a week. You pair were always wile busy."

A smile spread across Duncan's face. Malcolm felt a pride in his clever wife. She had gone to a place and time that was easy for Duncan to access. Malcolm sat back in his chair and listened to the stories swopped by Harriet and Duncan. He wasn't sure which of them was enjoying the reminiscence more.

Soon enough they were ushered to the dining table. The meal was spot on. A lovely piece of beef, slow cooked so that it fell to bits in your mouth. And the vegetables? None of that oul continental al dente stuff. Cooked through and cooked proper. The pudding was an excellent pavlova. Pat and Duncan moved together like parts of a well-oiled machine as they served up the food, each instinctively knowing each other's role and the task in hand.

Malcolm patted his stomach and settled back in his chair. Time enough for calorie controlling tomorrow. He struggled to lean forward to take the offered cup of tea. He added milk and sipped. Duncan had been persuaded to sit too, leaving the last of the tidying up to Pat and Harriet. The silence between the two men was comfortable and had a peacefulness about it.

Harriet returned from the kitchen. "Duncan, I fancy a walk. Do yeh think we can take Bella for a wee dander?"

Malcolm started to rise. A quick walk would help with the calories.

"No, love," she said. "Just me and Duncan. Pat wants a word."

Malcolm sank onto the chair. It had been too good to be true. Pat had probably told Harriet what happened yesterday. But maybe not. He knew his wife well enough. She would have been much sharper with him if she knew how much he had upset these lovely people.

Pat came to the table with a fresh pot of tea. She sat and offered Malcolm a top-up.

"Thanks." He leant his elbows on the table. "Look, I am so sorry about yesterday."

"Yes, well, it was a bad day. It's worse when he doesn't sleep. It's not often. I can cope." Pat smiled weakly. "I have to."

"It didn't help when I put me foot in it, though."

Pat sipped her tea. She placed it carefully on the saucer. "Maybe I overreacted."

Malcolm shook his head slowly. How did this woman have the grace to say that, considering what she had to cope with now, and what he could guess the future held for her?

"Malcolm, Harriet mentioned that you have an interest in what happened. You know, with Trevor Mulholland."

"No!" Malcolm's voice was firmer than he had intended. "I mean, I did. But when I saw what it did to you and Duncan? I haven't the right. So, no. Not anymore."

"But what if I asked you to go on with it?" Pat's voice was almost a whisper.

Malcolm studied this neat-looking woman. "Why would you want me to?"

"I was thinking last night. It might help Duncan."

"How?"

"It's always troubled him, right from the start. He used to bury it, you know, so as not to worry me. But I knew." She smiled. "That's what fifty-two years of marriage does. You know each other inside and out."

"Oh, I know. Harriet can tell what I'm thinking just by looking at me. Hard to get away with anything!"

"But that missing money... what really happened... You know Duncan's as straight as a die, always has been, and it cut him to the bone that he wasn't believed. He told them and told them the money was there, but the official report says no. Duncan felt the police – your lot – had him down as a liar. If you knew my husband..." Pat paused. "You would know how much that hurt him."

Malcolm cleared his throat, uncertain how to go on. "Harriet's not too keen on me... she wants me to leave it all behind."

"I know, she told me." Pat gestured towards the kitchen. "She said you were having a hard job not being a policeman. Said the two of you had a deal – you can have a wee look at what happened back then if you agree to go to some courses."

Malcolm shifted uncomfortable in his chair. "I've started an IT course."

Pat continued. "The thing is, now Duncan's memory is going. In spite of times when he can't remember things that only happened that same morning, it seems stuff about Trevor Mulholland is coming back to him. You've seen how much it upsets him."

"I know. Like I said, I'm sorry."

"No, no." Pat moved her hand as if to sweep away Malcolm's apologies. "Duncan wakes up in the night shouting about it, and sometimes even when he's having a doze in the chair."

So Duncan had the nightmares too.

"There's something else." Pat reached forward and poured herself more tea. "The man you saw..."

"The one that was bothering you? He didn't look much of a lost tourist to me."

"Yes, you're right. And it wasn't the first time. It must be about three times, maybe four now. I suppose you would say he's a sort of stalker."

"Do you know him?"

"No, and I know quite a few people. With the post office."

"What does he want?" Malcolm asked.

Pat smiled weakly. "Same thing you were interested in. The money that went missing. You know yourself that Duncan looks well, but with his memory - you could say that what's wrong with him is invisible."

Malcolm thought back to the first time he'd met Duncan. "Yes. I suppose that's a curse and a blessing."

"Well, that man – that man thinks Duncan can tell him what happened to the money."

Malcolm leant forward. "What age do you think he is? You were closer to him than me. Tell me what he looks like. Anything at all." He was on familiar ground now.

"About forty," Pat said, "maybe late thirties. I think anyway. To be honest I just wanted to get away from him." She shuddered.

"Hair colour? Was he fat, thin? Anything you noticed that was different about him?"

"Quite tall." Pat shrugged. "But most people are to me. He always has a woollen hat on. Hard to see if he was fat or thin. He wears an overcoat. An expensive one. I'm sure he has an American accent, but there's a Tyrone twang to it too."

Malcolm tapped his fingertips on the table. He'd had worse descriptions to start with. But this would take much more digging than the cursory look back he had been doing to date. And he'd have to sort out this bloody man, whoever he was.

They both turned at the sound of the front door opening and laughter from Harriet and Duncan. Pat's shoulders dropped a fraction and she smiled. Perhaps a release of tension?

"Pat, I've promised Harriet not to..."

Pat smiled. "I spoke to her about it earlier. In the kitchen. She says it's OK. Says it may kill two birds with one stone."

"How come?"

"She thinks it'll help us and at the same time get that monkey off your back!"

* * *

More tea and cake were presented by Pat and she wasn't taking no for an answer. Despite the tightening around his waist band, Malcolm did his best to consume a slice of lemon drizzle cake with his tea. Harriet was clearly at home at chatting about the old days, and Duncan was holding court, talking about the past customers they had at the post office. Pat pottered about, smiling at the interactions between Harriet and Duncan. Malcolm hadn't looked forward to this evening but it had been great. Results all round.

Duncan stayed in his chair when Malcolm and Harriet rose to leave. He was close to dozing off; the effort of the evening had taken its toll.

"All sorted between you pair?" asked Harriet as she put on her coat.

"Yes. Thanks, Harriet," replied Pat.

"No bother. He's not bad at what he does, my husband. I mean what he used to do."

So, thought Malcolm, both of us are adjusting.

Pat helped Malcolm on with his coat. "You know, I was just thinking. It was bad then. I mean I know all the Troubles were. But it seemed, for a while, we avoided the worst of it where we were." She laughed. "Sure, nobody had heard of Seskinore." Her voice turned serious again. "But then over two years, first we had that wee girl Liza found dead in the quarry and then Trevor's death."

"Terrible times," agreed Harriet.

On the walk home, Malcolm pushed his hands deep into the pocket of his overcoat, Harriet's arm tucked into his. Damn, it was cold, with that wind picking up. As they walked, Malcolm turned over Pat's comments. A girl's death in the quarry. Would that be Mulholland's quarry?

CHAPTER THIRTEEN

Another sleepless night. But this time Malcolm didn't wake up in a sweat, so it was a good sleepless night – if there was such a thing. The bedside clock said 5:00. There was no chance he would get to sleep now. He padded quietly out to the kitchen and put on the kettle. Billy raised his head and then rolled over in his basket so that his back was to Malcolm. Some morning welcome, but maybe better than growling. There was a brief phutt from the direction of the basket, and within seconds a beef-gone-off aroma wafted around Malcolm.

"Jesus, Billy!"

But there was no response from the sleeping dog.

* * *

Malcolm had expected that the visit to the Gallaghers' home the previous day would have involved him apologising for upsetting Duncan and making Pat's life even more difficult. He had expected to be asked to stop. But they needed his help, and now it was game on.

Malcolm knew what his next step needed to be

Back to the beginning.

* * *

The drive to town gave Malcolm time to think about his tactics for the meeting ahead. DI Robinson must be nearly ninety. The man must have mellowed by now. Malcolm had heard that after Robinson's wife had died – some said he sent her to an early grave with his demanding nature – he had struggled on alone, but had finally been persuaded to go into a nursing home. Robinson's two daughters wouldn't have him in their homes, and from Malcolm's memories of the man, he couldn't say he blamed them.

Malcolm indicated right into the very grand entrance of the nursing-home grounds. He smiled. Yes, Robinson would certainly only have the best. But sure, why not have comfort in your old age?

The reception area was more like the lobby of a five-star hotel. He announced himself to the receptionist, who in turn called for a member of the care staff. The chairs and sideboards were faux antiques and the carpet underfoot had a luxurious feel to it.

"Can I help you?" The lilac-uniformed carer was immaculately turned out, with makeup more suitable for a night on the tiles. Her name badge announced her as Orla.

"I've come to see Mr Robinson," Malcolm said.

"Have you?" It was more of an expression of surprise than a query.

"He's not expecting me. I was passing, so I just thought..."

"No, no, that's grand. It's just he doesn't get many visitors. And now two this week."

"Two?"

"Yes, there was a relative from America. I'll go and ask him. But I'm sure he'll be delighted."

An American. There's plenty of them visit the province investigating their own personal history, Malcolm reasoned to himself, but this was too much of a coincidence.

Orla smiled. "Your name?"

"Malcolm Bell. We worked together."

"Right. Well, I'll go and make sure he's decent. If you could just sign the visitor's book."

Orla strode down the corridor and Malcolm turned his attention to the book. After he had put in his details, he flicked back a few pages to see the names of those who had visited over the last few weeks. He recognised Robinson's daughters' names – one visit from each over the last month. Nothing else.

Orla returned with the good news that Mr Robinson was up for visitors.

"Great," said Malcolm. "Orla, I was just wondering, there doesn't seem to be any signature of any visitors for Mr Robinson other than his daughters."

"Sometimes people just forget. A bit bad, really. What if there's a fire? But they still don't bother."

Perhaps whoever had visited Robinson hadn't wanted to leave any record.

"Third room on the right, at the end of the corridor." Orla pointed the way.

As Malcolm approached the room, he heard a man's raised voice followed by a more conciliatory woman's voice. He knocked on the door. It was opened by another lilac-clad carer. This one was labelled Yvonne.

Her face was flushed. She wiped her forehead and turned to the occupant of the room.

"Your visitor is here." She turned back to Malcolm and sighed. "Good luck. Not one of his better days." She pushed the door wider to let Malcolm in. "Let me know if you need anything."

"Much good that would do," snarled ex-DI Robinson, his thin lanky frame hunched in a wheelchair that looked too small for him. He was dressed in pyjamas that rode up his leg to expose pale, hairless skin, and a striped dressing gown.

"So, who's this visitor?" He squinted at Malcolm and then a look of recognition spread over his face. "Well good God almighty. If it's not Belly boy!"

Malcolm cringed. Memories flooded back. Memories of how this man would find a weak spot and work away at it.

"Lovely to see you." Just in time, Malcolm held himself back from calling him "sir". "You're looking well."

"Huh. Do yeh think so? No thanks to this lot."

Malcolm looked around the room. This belligerent man had landed on his feet. The room was large, with two bay windows overlooking the garden. No urine smell, as was often the case in other nursing homes Malcolm had visited over the years. The single bed had a side table next to it, and the armchairs for visitors were good quality. There was even a coffee table with family photos on display. Two framed commendations hung on the wall.

"Yeh might as well sit down now you're here."

Malcolm knew it was as gracious an invite as he was going to get. "It's been a while. How are the girls?"

"All right, I suppose. Waiting for the inheritance is my guess."

Malcolm had met both of Robinson's daughters in the past and had come to the conclusion they had taken after their good-natured, patient mother.

Robinson focused his rheumy eyes on Malcolm. "This is no social call. Just passing? That's what that Orla said. Bullshit."

His mind was intact, even if he was physically diminished. It would be hard work, this conversation, but it had to serve Malcolm's ends.

He sighed. "You're right. Not a social call. You were never one for socialising."

"What do you want?"

"Information," Malcolm said.

"Do yeh now? What information can a beat-out oul man give yeh?"

Malcolm's best guess was that Robinson could still control those around him, or at the very least have a bloody good try. There was nothing beat-out about him.

"Something that happened before I joined the RUC."

"Not sure my memory would go back that far," Robinson said. Then his eyes narrowed. "Just a guess, but I suppose this isn't exactly an official investigation."

Malcolm smiled wryly. "I've retired too. Consider this a hobby."

"Well, maybe my memory wouldn't be so bad if you're telling me it's not official."

"Do yeh mind the Mulholland case? Terrorist shooting in 1998? I've been chatting to Duncan Gallagher."

Robinson's eyes narrowed. "That is going back some. So?"

"Duncan's a wile decent soul, but he's still upset about not being believed."

"Christ, he's not still going on about the money? Before I retired, he'd taking any opportunity to have a go at me about it. I've managed to avoid him since arriving in this dump."

"It's making him unwell… he's not great."

"My heart bleeds." Robinson closed his eyes in faux sleep. "I'm tired."

Malcolm was going to have to play this man at his own game. Take control away from him. Threaten to leave him to his loneliness.

"Well, if ye can't help, I'll be going. Sorry for disturbing you." Malcolm rose to leave.

Robinson's eyes whipped open. "Hang on. Maybe I can help. No harm after all these years."

Malcolm sank into the chair again. "Duncan is sure Mulholland had a wedge of money with him. But there wasn't any sign of it in the aftermath."

"That would be right."

"Is it, though?"

"It was investigated at the time," Robinson said, "and the conclusion was that if it went anywhere, it would have been that young PC Daniels. No proof, though."

"I understand Daniels left the force soon after."

Robinson snorted. "It was suggested he left. But it worked out all right for you, didn't it?"

"Why did they think it was Daniels?"

"Piss-pot poor and had the opportunity. Never admitted it, though. Wasn't a strong character anyway, as it turns out. Took to drink in a big way. Not the type we needed. Certainly not in those days." Robinson shook his head. "I hear they have all sorts nowadays."

Although Malcolm had often reminisced about the old days, it was uncomfortable to hear this hankering after a way of working that maybe wasn't that good. The pressures on the RUC had been huge back then and Malcolm heard about corners that had been cut in investigations. He had learnt the hard way himself when he had once fallen into that trap. Never again.

"I've looked at the timeline, and everybody bar the drayman had a chance to lift the money. My problem is, Daniels showed no sign of spending any great amount of money after the shooting, and it was Duncan who brought Daniel's attention to the fact that there had been money there in the first place. But that was when Daniels was driving him home."

"Is that right?" Robinson raised his eyebrows. "Timeline? Aren't you the clever one? I won't ask where you got your information from. Who would you put in the frame?"

"The barman, Muldoon, had enough time in the chaos, but he'd be way too scared to lift it. I remember the links his boss had and I wouldn't have recommended taking risks there. And then there was you."

Robinson laughed a humourless laugh. "What the fuck would I need with a wee bundle of cash? Have a look at my accounts. You see nothing there."

"No, I don't think you took it for yourself. But the widow Mulholland might have appreciated it being returned."

Robinson pulled himself up from his stooped posture. "Now look here. That woman had enough on her plate. Mulholland wasn't the shining example of the community everyone would have wanted him to be. Especially after they found that wee girl in his quarry. The last thing his widow needed was for the family to be pulled into a scandal because her husband was stupid enough to give in to the protection rackets on top of everything else."

"You were quite the gentleman."

"Things were complicated back then. You know that as well as I do. And if the whole process showed us that Daniels didn't have the mettle for the job, well, there was another good outcome from a shoddy affair."

The word "affair" raised another question. "So, giving Mulholland's widow the money was nothing more than righting a wrong?"

"Now just you listen." Robinson pointed a bony, arthritic finger at the framed picture of a woman in her sixties that took pride of place on the coffee table. "I would never have done anything to bring shame to Margaret." He shook his head slowly, and his voice lowered a fraction. "I know I wasn't the best to her. But she was a good woman. So no, there was nothing untoward with Eileen Mulholland. I just knew the right thing to do for her."

"The girl yeh mentioned? The one in the quarry?"

Robinson picked at his trousers. "Now that was sad. It was a couple of years before Mulholland was shot. An awful to do. Shook us all. We were used to the noise of the Troubles, but a girl out at a Blue Light Disco? She was just trying to have the life that any youngster deserves."

Malcolm raised his eyebrows. "What happened there?"

"A wee girl from a dodgy background. A mother but no known father. Yeh know the sort. Found in Mulholland's quarry dead and... violated."

Malcolm could see even this hardened, belligerent man didn't have the words.

There was a gentle knock at the door and Orla popped her head in. "Sorry to disturb you, but I need to give you your medication." She pushed a trolley through the doorway.

"They keep me sedated, yeh know," muttered Robinson.

Malcolm looked questioningly at Orla.

She smiled weakly. "Mr Robinson, you know that's not true." She opened the medicine trolley and lifted out a chart. Malcolm guessed she had been accused of this many times by this man. Orla looked from Malcolm and Robinson. "Look, I'll see to Mrs Cook first then. Give you a bit more time to chat." She closed the medicine trolley lid and wheeled it out of the room.

"Thanks for the information," Malcolm said, rising from his seat. "It'll help Duncan." When he reached the door, he turned. "I'm not the only visitor yeh had this week."

Robinson looked up at him, his rheumy eyes now sharp and piercing. "I did. Some Yank who wanted the same information as you. Probably a journalist doing some unwanted investigation. Post-Troubles story, no doubt. The Yanks as a nation don't know when to shut up and go away." He snorted. "Pity all he found was a demented old man who knew nothing."

"Did yeh get a name?"

"As I was playing the old demented bastard, would it have looked right if I'd had enough wit to ask his name?"

"Suppose not."

"Anyway, he would have signed the visitor's book. Call yourself a detective? At this stage you should at least get the basics right."

Malcolm exhaled. Ex-DI Robinson still retained the arrogance and total lack of charm Malcolm remembered. "So why tell me about what happened to the money?"

"I remember what you were like. Painfully straight as a die. You'll do the decent thing." Robinson sighed, bowed his head and rubbed his eyes. The fatigue looked real this time. "You know, I miss Margaret. She was so good. I didn't deserve her. Maybe being left behind was my punishment."

"Look," said Malcolm, "I'll pop by the next time I'm passing."

Robinson looked up. "I really hope you don't have to. Just pray I'll be in my box by then."

* * *

Malcolm drove home on auto-pilot, going over the revelations of the last hour. At least he had an answer for Pat and Duncan about the money. It would be too much of a coincidence for a second Yank to be harassing both

Robinson and the Gallaghers. He had to be one and the same person. And once again the murdered girl had been mentioned. Robinson's view of Mulholland wasn't entirely rosy. Not the great chap Duncan had referred to. Problem was, although he had something to take back to the Gallaghers, many more questions had been raised. The murder of the girl had never been solved. Was she linked to Mulholland somehow? Why was a Yank journalist interested in the case – if he really was a journalist? Pat's interaction with the man hadn't suggested a professional approach, but maybe they did things differently in the new country.

He pulled in at the petrol station just outside the town. After he had filled up, he returned to the car with the best bunch of flowers on offer. A mixture of pinks – Harriet's favourite colour. He placed it carefully on the passenger seat. It would be something to show his appreciation. There was no way he would be like Robinson and leave it too late.

CHAPTER FOURTEEN

Tommy placed the flowers carefully on the fresh earth that just a week ago had been put in place by the gravediggers to cover his mother's coffin. The gravestone had been taken away to add her name to the inscription about his da. Tommy knew it wouldn't be back for six months, to let the fresh earth settle.

He hoped she would understand why he needed to go to Tyrone. Despite his love for his parents, he needed to find out who had rejected him, and why. Looking down at the mound of earth, the floral tributes now blown this way and that, his eyes grew wet, his vision blurred. How much more could he bear? First his da, then his ma, and of course Donal. Maybe that relationship had been too good to be true. Just when life had seemed to be making sense, the bastard had pulled the rug from under him. No one was going to hurt him like that again. And now he needed to find out how his story had started. Maybe that would help him make sense of who he was now.

He walked back to his car. Omagh was only just over an hour's drive from Belfast, but he had packed an overnight bag, just in case. You never knew. Maybe his birth mother was just waiting for her son to reach out. And in case things didn't go well, his da's handgun was wrapped in its oilskin in the bottom of the bag. He couldn't see anything specific he might need it for, but there was no way ever be wrong-footed again. The gun was a little insurance policy – though against what, he had no idea. Da had always said to be prepared, and that was nothing to do with the Boy Scouts. The days of the Troubles might be deemed long gone by the politicians, but how could you trust that lot? Sure, they couldn't draw a straight line between them. Tommy had listened to his da's doubts over the years. Worries about letting your guard down. One advantage about these peaceful times, there was zero chance of being stopped and searched. Made you almost relaxed carrying a piece.

On the passenger seat lay the form that Tommy had printed off the previous night, having filled it in the best he could. The instructions said to post it to the General Register Office. But that seemed a long-winded approach, with the office being in Belfast. Presumably it would be sent on to Omagh, the administrative centre of the district, to be dealt with. The answers he was looking for must surely be in or around Ballygawley itself. That was where Jeff Henry had said the man who had needed favours doing would customarily meet the volunteers when they were on active service. Tommy knew what those country culchies were like – they seemed to stay in their townland come hell or high water.

He turned up Van Morrison loud and headed west.

* * *

Tommy's heart pounded and his hand quivered as he passed the form to the receptionist in the council offices. She shook her head and started to push the form back across the desk. Tommy pulled on the band on his wrist. It snapped back into place.

"Sorry, sir. I think if you read the statement at the bottom of the form here..." She used a sparkly painted fingernail to tap a sentence. "It says you need to post it to the General Register Office in Belfast."

Tommy snatched the form back. The receptionist looked up in shock and withdrew her hand.

"Listen here, wee girl," Tommy hissed. "I can fucking read. I know where the form has to go, but I also know I have to have a meeting with a social worker, so run along and find one while I wait."

"Sir, I don't think..."

"That's right, don't think, just go!"

The receptionist pushed her chair back, rose and disappeared through the door at the rear of the room.

Tommy breathed deeply and pulled at his wrist band. He sat on one of the hard chairs in the waiting area. He wasn't going anywhere. If they thought he'd be going through the bureaucratic nonsense, waiting for letters to be lost, meetings to be postponed, they had another thing coming. He focused on the clock on the opposite side of the room, continuing to pull at the band and taking deep breaths. Slowly, the anger subsided.

The receptionist reappeared. "Someone will be out to see you." Her voice quavered.

"Good... thanks." Shite. He knew it wasn't her fault. Breathe. Get it under control.

"Mr Smith?"

Tommy turned to see a short, slightly chunky woman who looked to be in her late twenties, maybe early thirties. Her hair was spikey and a red that was definitely not natural. She extended her hand and smiled. "I'm Hannah Fyffe, one of the team leaders. Can you come with me? We can have a chat in one of our interview rooms."

He hadn't been expecting the English accent. Looked like the culchies had been invaded. Possibly he would make progress with this unconventional-looking woman. He shook her hand.

"Tommy Smith. Look, I'm sorry about upsetting your receptionist. It's just I've come all the way from Belfast and I was hoping to get some answers."

He followed Hannah to the interview room. She sat in the chair behind the desk. There was a panic button on the side, just visible from where she gestured for Tommy to sit opposite her.

"How can I help?" Hannah asked.

Tommy leant onto the desk and placed his form in front of her. "Look, I know I'm meant to send this form to Belfast to go on the register to find my birth, but—" Tommy paused. He looked down at his hands. "My mother has recently passed away. My da died three years ago. I've only recently discovered that they weren't my real parents. And anyway, I'm supposed to have a meeting with a social worker before anything gets done."

Hannah picked up the form and read through it.

"I think my adoption was carried out…" Tommy searched for the words. "A bit unconventionally. A friend of my father told me it was a favour to someone who lived near Ballygawley."

"A favour?" Hannah rubbed her forehead.

"That's what he said. It was something to do with the organisation me da was in."

"The army? Police?"

Tommy smiled. "An army of sorts. The UVF."

The woman's eyes widened for a second.

"I was wondering if you… I mean, records are always kept, aren't they? Can't you look into it? I have no names or anything, but Ballygawley isn't a big place and people always talk, gossip."

"Mr Smith, it was a very long time ago."

"Thirty-four years ago, that's all. No time in this country."

"And there's other people to consider."

"My parents, I mean my adoptive parents, are dead."

"We have no idea who else may be affected. That's why there are processes in place."

Hannah placed the form gently onto the table and, just as the receptionist had done, pushed it towards Tommy. He looked up at this woman he had placed his hopes in. The slow build of his anger started to return. He reached for his band.

Hannah sat back in her chair. "Look, I appreciate how frustrating this is, but there is a reason for these processes."

"You're one of those pen pushers too, just looking after your job. No intention of actually helping anyone."

"There is nothing I would like more than to give you a quick answer. But Mr Smith, as well as everything else, you have recently been bereaved. You need time to go through the grieving process before taking on anything else. You need time."

Tommy tried to rein in his anger, but it was no use.

"What the fuck do you know?" His voice was rising. Hannah's hand started to edge towards the panic button. "You don't need to bother doing that."

He grabbed the form and started for the door, then stopped and rounded on Hannah. "One way or the other, I will find out who they are. The fuckers who were happy enough to give me to a stranger. I'm not looking for a happy ending, a big family reunion. Just answers, and I'll get them. Thanks for nothing!"

* * *

Tommy broke the sixty-mile-an-hour speed limit as he left Omagh and drove towards the Belfast road. Fucking country culchies. Even an English one. No answers. Not even a hint of possible help. He overtook the Belfast bus on a corner and didn't give a shit. He gave the two-fingered gesture to the pillock who didn't have the sense to slow down when he saw Tommy on the right side of the carriageway. Who cared now anyway if he lived or died?

As he approached the fifty-mile-an-hour sign for some godforsaken terrace, and got stuck yet again behind a slow-moving truck, he saw the sign for Royal Oak Inn. His counsellor had always told him that regardless of what his gut said, the last thing he needed when he felt this way, was alcohol. Well, fuck it. He pulled into the car park. Happy days – they had rooms available too.

Tommy slammed the door of his car and slung his overnight bag over his shoulder. He looked at his watch. 3pm. He was determined to get shit-faced, and as quickly as possible. Disappear into alcoholic oblivion. Drown his demons, if only for a night. He reached for the band on his wrist, tore it off and threw it on the ground.

* * *

The landline phone rang.

"I'll get it!" shouted Harriet from the kitchen. Then, "Hannah, how lovely to hear from you. Everything all right?"

Malcolm looked at his watch. 3pm. An unusual time for Hannah to call. She should be in work. He knew that behind his wife's enquiry was all about concern about William. He had made a steady recovery from his head injury the previous year, and Malcolm and Harriet been relieved that he managed to get back to work.

"I'll get him for you."

Harriet didn't need to. Malcolm was already at her shoulder and took the receiver.

"Hannah, all OK?"

"Yes, I'm fine. William is too."

Malcolm sighed. "Well, there must be something up. You never ring in work hours."

"No, things are all fine. It's probably nothing."

"What's happened?" persisted Malcolm.

"There was a man who came to the office today. He was from Belfast, asking about his birth parents. He was very aggressive."

"Surely you deal with the likes of that all the time."

"This was different. I can usually manage angry people, but this guy was on another level. He left quite quickly, but there was stuff he said I just couldn't get my head around. He said his adoption was something to do with a favour for someone in the UVF. Is that possible? He was adopted thirty-four years ago."

Malcolm did the calculations. Just about the time the UVF was particularly active in Tyrone. "Anything was possible back then. But if he left, what's the problem?"

"Well, I know I shouldn't have, but my curiosity got the better of me. I checked back. We had a case – still have it, actually – that seems to fit. A woman, she's in her seventies now, has had a very troubled life. But from the records I've pulled up, it would seem that she's a likely candidate for the birth mother of this man. This woman's father was a prominent unionist, lived just outside Ballygawley. She's had mental-health issues all through her adult life. When it flares up, she rages about a lost child, a boy. There are no records relating to her having a second child, just one child, a girl. So she's been treated as delusional. She has a period of inpatient treatment and things calm down again. Jesus, what if all these years she was right? What if this man, this Tommy Smith, is her lost child?"

Malcolm could hear the anguish in Hannah's voice. "Look, it sounds to me like you dealt with it very well. As you usually do."

"Malcolm, there's something else."

"What?"

"There may be a link to the case you were asking William about. This woman, her name is Elizabeth Tobin."

There was something about that name, but the memory was just out of reach. "Yes?"

"Her daughter, Liza, the child we knew about, was murdered in 1986. It was her body that was found in Mulholland's quarry."

CHAPTER FIFTEEN

Malcolm could see the smirk starting to form on the young man's face as he pushed open the door of the library. Christ, was that phone never out of his hand?

"Look, lad, if I were you, I wouldn't make any comment today. I'm not in the mood." Malcolm went to walk straight past him and towards the IT room.

"All right, grandad, suit yourself. I was just going to say hello."

Malcolm swivelled on his heel and gave the finger to the cheeky wee git.

"Very mature. Some example you're giving."

Malcolm heard Emily's voice behind him. He shoved his hand into his pocket.

"Emily, the very person I've come to see." He turned and adopted what he hoped was an innocent smile.

"Shouldn't you apologise to Kevin?"

"Apologise?" Did she not understand what a brat this Kevin was?

"It's all right," Kevin shouted over. "I'll let it go."

Once again, Malcolm turned to look at the young man. "You'll..."

"That's very good of you, Kevin. Now Malcolm, how can I help you?"

Malcolm pulled at his ear lobe. He needed her help, for her to be on side. Which meant he needed to swallow this injustice. For the moment, anyway.

"Well?" Emily asked when they were settled in her IT room.

"I was wondering if I could do a bit more research – you know, out of class hours."

"Really?" Emily furrowed her brow. "This is quite a turnaround from the man whose wife made him come here in the first place." She rubbed her chin and studied Malcolm.

He started to take off his coat. He wasn't sure if it was the central heating or Emily's stare that was making him sweat. "Och, I know, but sure I'm really getting the bug. I might even get a computer for the house."

Malcolm didn't think Emily's eyebrows could go higher. This explanation wasn't washing. Last try. "You know the Blue Light Discos meant a lot to me."

Emily laughed. "If you think I'm gullible enough to swallow that nonsense, after your obvious empathy with the youth of today just demonstrated out there…" She pointed towards the reception area. "Try again, Mr Bell."

"Jesus, Miss Baxter, you missed your vocation. We could have done with you in the police."

"Mr Bell, remember my third rule." But there was a smile twitching at the corner of her mouth.

"Sorry. No swearing." Malcolm sighed. "OK. I'll come clean. I'm trying to do a friend a favour. But it's led to other things that don't seem right." He shrugged. "I'm a bit like a dog after a bone. Always have been. Maybe it's a failing – not being able to leave things alone."

Emily put down the clipboard she had been hugging. "It clearly means a lot to you, whatever you're researching."

Malcolm smiled. "They used to call it investigating, whenever I was doing, you know, what I was doing before."

Emily took a pen from the desk and studied it for a moment. She looked up at Malcolm, seeming to weigh him and his intentions. "Go on. Tell me what it's all about."

Malcolm tucked his hands between his knees. "Maybe you've come across Pat and Duncan Gallagher? They're a bit older than me. Moved up here a few years ago from Tyrone."

"I think so. Is she a petite wee lady, immaculately turned out? Her husband is always with her when they come to the library. Sweet really, how close they are. And they have a wee dog! I've always wanted a dog. But with work commitments…"

What was it with people and dogs? Was it only Malcolm who realised there was a downside to having the bloody animals? "Yes, that's them. The reason they're always together is that she can't leave him. He's starting to… forget things." He shifted in his seat, unsure why the idea of giving Duncan's condition a name was so uncomfortable. Like in the days when cancer was referred to in whispers.

"You mean… but he's always so polite and chatty," Emily said. "And he looks so well."

"That's all down to Pat. She looks after him. But once you start digging a bit deeper, he struggles. But still a lovely man."

"This is who you're trying to help?"

"Yes. Years ago, the poor man was involved in a murder. He was completely innocent in the whole thing, but there were a few loose ends that have been distressing him ever since. Really distressing him. I thought it might help if I could get answers for him. Put his mind at ease." He frowned. "But I haven't been the only person asking questions. Pat doesn't know who this bloke is, but he keeps pestering them and doesn't seem keen to give up."

Emily smiled. "I can see you're doing this for all the right reasons. But why don't you just go to the police and ask them to investigate? Shouldn't you be enjoying your retirement?"

Malcolm considered this. Truth was, now he was enjoying his retirement, but only since he'd started looking into this case.

He shook his head. "With all the other stuff the PSNI are having to deal with, they're not going to have time to look into a thirty-year-old case that's not causing anyone else any trouble. Nobody's going to be concerned with the peace of mind of an old-age pensioner."

Emily reached over and pressed the on button of the nearest computer and monitor. "OK. Tell me the whole story, and I'll see where I can help."

Malcolm spent the next thirty minutes outlining the original murder, the missing money, the seemingly unfair dismissal of the PC who Malcolm then replaced, the implicit confession about the money that Robinson had made. Emily listened intently, asking questions:

Malcolm was impressed with her approach to better understand.

"It sounds like you're nearly there, Mr Bell. If you just get confirmation from Mulholland's widow that the money was returned to her, and find out who this man is that's bothering the Gallaghers, it would seem to me that you're home and dry."

Once more, Malcolm shifted uneasily in his seat. Was it an indulgence, him picking at the scab that was this case? Would he be taking Emily into a world that she knew nothing of? There was the angry man that Hannah had encountered and, as yet, Malcolm had no idea what the intentions were of the other man, the one with the American accent. But surely, he had been around the block enough to guard Emily against any potential dangers?

"Miss Baxter, there are a few other things that have come up. The man that was murdered, Trevor Mulholland. It seems he wasn't the good upstanding gentleman that was portrayed in the press. There was a murder in the Ballygawley area two years before Mulholland was killed, and the wee girl's body was found in Mulholland's quarry. She was only fifteen and no one was caught for it. And Mulholland's murder itself – there was no paramilitary claim to it, although it had all the hallmarks." Malcolm patted his stomach. "I have a gut feeling that there's more to be found out."

"OK. You have me interested. It would certainly be a challenge. How exactly do you want me to help?"

"When I was still working, we had this national computer system called Holmes. To be honest, I was sick of the thing. It seemed to rule our lives and proper police work was shoved to the back."

"What – like Sherlock Holmes?"

"Exactly. They probably had a committee to come up with that name. Anyway, the purpose of Holmes was to cross-match and link information so we would never have a situation where information was lost and criminals fell through the net. They put it in place after the murders of those two wee girls by the school caretaker in England. Obviously, the force deleted my passwords and authority as soon as I left work. I was wondering, given your expertise..." Malcolm hesitated. "Is there any chance you could get into Holmes? I mean, with your knowledge, you might find some loophole or something ..." Maybe this wasn't his best idea.

To his dismay, Emily shook her head firmly.

"I'm sorry. Like you, I've only come to computers relatively late in life. I would be able to search on the internet, that's for sure, but I wouldn't get much further than you. Besides, you know very well what you are suggesting is illegal."

Malcolm felt deflated and foolish. This woman, it had seemed to him, had the skills and knowledge he needed. But what on earth was he asking of her? He would have to think again.

Emily frame stiffened. She lowered her voice. "I do not condone anything illegal."

Malcolm shook his head. "Of course not. You're quite right." He moved to stand up. Emily held up her hand to stop him.

"But," she went on, "I am not so naïve as to deny that occasionally a rule needs to be broken." She patted the back of her hair. "I have worked long enough helping the probation services to realise that legal processes don't always get justice for people. Good people like Pat and Duncan Gallagher."

Malcolm studied this woman who he had thought he had worked out. With her rules and that. "Emily, I don't want to you to do anything you're not comfortable with."

He shrank back a fraction as she pointed her pen at him. "Don't worry about that, Mr Bell. I will do what is necessary and nothing more. But I think what you need is more related to the dark side of the internet. And maybe a little bit of hacking."

Malcolm tried to form words but failed. What was Emily suggesting?

"Don't look so shocked." Emily laughed. "I wasn't always a computer teacher for the reluctant and the hopeless. Although I now volunteer helping the probation service through the church, I worked in Lisburn with church youth schemes and safeguarding until a few years ago, so I have dealt with all sorts."

Malcolm scratched his neck. He still wasn't clear where this was leading. "Why did you stop?"

Emily dropped her gaze to the floor. "It was complicated. Let's just say I was... disappointed by someone. Someone who meant a lot to me and I thought he felt the same." She shook her head as if to shake free from the memories. "Anyhow, I decided to have a career change, but kept some of my links. Hence the volunteering. There were some very good people there."

"So how is that linked to hacking and the dark web?"

"The church was developing a rehabilitative approach with the probation service. We worked with local businesses to get placements for young offenders. To try to show those youngsters they were valued, get them some CV worthy experience and hopefully onto a better path."

"I'm still no clearer…"

"Our receptionist, Kevin. He's on placement with us here in the library. And I believe he's your man. He has a conviction for hacking engineering firms and upping the wages for the employees by moving the decimal point one place to the right. I'll go and fetch him."

Emily stood and walked to the door. Her hand rested on the door handle as she turned to Malcolm. "But Kevin will just help you enough and no more. It's a one-time offer."

Emily left the room. Malcolm was left speechless. He surveyed the room as if he had never seen it before. What was happening to his world? He had, only a few weeks before, been, as he saw it, on life's rubbish heap. Then he had found a purpose again and was on familiar territory. And now? This good and decent woman was agreeing to arrange something that no one could consider legal, and suggesting that he could be helped by a convicted criminal. A cheeky skitter of one at that.

Emily returned with Kevin trailing behind her. By the look on his face, he was as unhappy as Malcolm.

"Have a seat, Kevin," instructed Emily.

Kevin perched himself on a desk and folded his arms.

"Right, now we are working as a team, I suggest we call each other by our first names. I'm Emily. Kevin, this is Malcolm. Malcolm, this is Kevin."

Malcolm and Kevin nodded at each other and glowered.

CHAPTER SIXTEEN

Tommy looked at his watch. He could just about make out the time despite his blurred sight. 4.30pm. He looked round the room from his position perched on the stool at the bar. Not a rough dive, that was for sure. A few elderly couples enjoying a coffee after their lunch. Retired, if they were still here at this time. The floor was carpeted, the padded seats carefully placed around small tables decorated with small vases of artificial flowers. No, not his usual taste in pubs, but it had been a useful sanctuary.

"Another one!" He held up his empty pint glass to make sure the barman was in no doubt.

Tommy took his keys out of his pocket and put them on the counter. He pushed them to and fro. Should he head back to Belfast? It was only just over an hour up the road. He hadn't drunk that much and the roads would be fairly quiet. The peelers wouldn't be looking to nab anyone at this time of day.

A hand reached over from the other side of the bar and took his keys.

"What the..." Tommy looked up to see the well-built barman pulling the keys towards him. The broad shoulders and muscular biceps made Tommy hesitate to challenge him.

"I'm happy enough to serve you another, but first, you're in no state to drive, and second, watch your mouth. We have decent people here enjoying their coffee." The barman nodded towards the elderly couple. He handed Tommy a card with the picture of a car and a number. "TJ's taxis. They're reliable. Or you can stay here. We're not busy. The bedrooms are mostly used at the weekends for weddings. And you can collect these," he shook the keys as if they were a bell, then placed them under the counter, "tomorrow."

Tension built in Tommy's muscles. This clown was taking things too far. He stood up.

"I wouldn't try it," a voice said. "Alex there plays second row for the Omagh Academicals."

Tommy turned in the direction of the voice and saw, in a darkened corner to his left, an old man. Painfully thin, with sparse grey hair that looked like he had cut it himself. Tommy guessed the man was in his seventies. He was hunched over his half pint of Guinness, a walking stick propped up against his chair.

"You can houl your whisht, Paul," said Alex. "How long have you been sitting over that drink? I'm minded to throw you out for waiting for it to evaporate."

"I'm waiting for funds to come in." Paul seemed to sink lower in his chair.

The old, sad man reminded Tommy of Jeff Henry. Maybe it was the effect of the drink or the events of the day, that blow-up with the stupid social worker, not getting the information he had been determined to get. Another door shut in his face. He recognised the familiar dark, sinking feelings that always occurred after he'd lost it.

"Look, pal." Alex pushed a pint towards Tommy. "Just looking after my customers."

Tommy carried his pint to the table where the old man sat. "Can I join you?"

"Sure, why not?"

Paul didn't make it sound like Tommy was overly welcome. He sat down regardless. "Could do with some company."

"Whatever," replied Paul. He took a small sip of his stout. When he put his glass down again, Tommy couldn't see that there had been a reduction in the amount of liquid in the glass.

"Can I buy yeh another?" asked Tommy. "Maybe a wee chaser?"

At last, this miserable old man brightened. "Aye, go on then."

Tommy returned with tumblers of whiskey for both of them. The stout had disappeared from Paul's glass. Tommy sighed. "A pint to go with the chaser?"

"Very good of yeh."

At the bar, Alex started to pull the pint for Paul. "Your man there." Alex nodded towards Paul. "He'll take all you're prepared to give. Watch yourself."

"I can look after meself," replied Tommy. "A country culchie won't get the better of me."

"I know that, mate. But you've had a few—"

Tommy slapped a twenty-pound note on the counter. "And I think I'll have a few more. Keep your nose out."

"Fair enough. Happy for profits going up. But your keys stay with me."

Tommy settled in the seat opposite Paul, who had already finished off half his whiskey.

"You're not from around here," said Paul. "Your accent."

"Belfast," Tommy offered.

"What brings you down here? Work?"

Tommy surveyed this man over the rim of his glass. They weren't too far from Ballygawley. Maybe five miles down the road from where Jeff had said the guns had been stored by his da. Where the man who had helped the volunteers and who had needed the favour. And people always knew people.

"What age are you?" asked Tommy.

"Yeh cheeky wee skitter. What is it to you?"

Tommy saw that Paul's whiskey and pint had disappeared. "Another drink?"

With the fresh round on the table, Paul reached forward, licking his lips. But Tommy kept his hand on the glass. "So, what age are you? It's an easy enough question."

"Seventy-four." Paul kept his eyes on the pint as he replied. Tommy released the glass. Paul drank deeply.

"From around here?"

"Yes." Paul was looking at Tommy warily. "What are you after?"

"Information."

"Well aye. I might be oul, but I'm not daft. About what?"

"Something that happened about thirty-five years ago."

Paul's eyes narrowed. "I've a wile bad memory. Can't remember that far back." Paul took another sip of the whiskey and a good swallow of the stout. "But me memory seems to come back when I've had a few of these." He smiled and raised his glass. "It's just I'm waiting on my dividends to pay out." After another sip of the whiskey, he muttered, "But they're getting wile slow about it."

Tommy doubted this man had anything like stocks and shares. But you never knew. Some of these country farmer types probably dressed like paupers and had millions under their beds.

"I'll keep the drinks coming, old man." Tommy opened his wallet and slammed three twenty-pound notes on the table.

Paul's eyebrows went up and he smiled. "All right, son, ask away." His hand on the table started to slide towards the notes. Tommy pulled them back quickly.

"First the information. You've lived around here all your life?"

"Aye. Well, most of it. Was away for a few years – you know, courtesy of Her Majesty."

Somehow, the revelation wasn't a surprise to Tommy.

"So were yeh involved, you know, in the "struggle"?"

Paul's eyes narrowed once again. "That's all long gone... Just who the fuck are you?"

Tommy knew he would have to give some information before he'd make progress. "My name's Tommy Smith. Me da was involved, but mostly up about Belfast." Giving his name was a gamble that he was talking to a man on his side in the Troubles. Then he saw Paul visibly relax.

"Yes, I was involved. Did some good work too." Paul stared sightlessly past Tommy. "Not that it will ever be acknowledged." He re-focused on Tommy. "What do you want to know? You a journalist?"

Tommy tapped the table with his forefinger, his drink forgotten for the moment. There was a chance this old man might know something. "Like I said, it was something that happened thirty-five years ago. A favour was done. An unusual favour. For a man who was a supporter, a friend of the cause."

"There was many a favour done then. What was so unusual about this one?"

Tommy drew a deep breath. "It involved an illegitimate wean. A boy who was adopted. I've been told the mother was the daughter of some man who stored the hardware the boys were using. Hid it close to Ballygawley. My guess is that this man must have had premises big enough and remote enough to avoid any nosey police or army. Ring any bells with you?"

Paul took a good swallow of his whiskey and quickly followed it by finishing the stout. He stared at the empty glasses and money on the table. "Sounds like you have a lot of information already. What do you want from me?"

"A name. The man's name. Or maybe you know the name of the mother? Look…" Tommy put his hand on Paul's arm. "This is a small place. I bet everybody knows everybody. And with your connections back then…"

Paul still stared at the drinks. "What did you say your da's name was?"

What had that got to do with it? Best to keep the man sweet though, keep the conversation going. "Bill Smith."

"Alex?" Paul shouted over to the barman. "Get me a

taxi. I'm going. I'll wait out the front." Paul lifted Tommy's hand from his arm and stood up. "Like I said, too long ago for me to remember."

Tommy stood quickly. Grabbed Paul's arm again. This time the grip was tight. He was satisfied to see the old man wince. "You fucking bastard! You know something!" He heard his own voice rising. Then from behind there was a grip on his shoulder, pushing him back down into his chair.

"I suggest you sit and cool off, mate." Alex had come up behind Tommy. "Like I said before, there are decent folk here."

Tommy knew there was no point trying to move from the chair.

"Paul, off you go and wait outside." Alex bent down and whispered in Tommy's ear. "And you and I will just stay as we are until he goes." He pulled his mobile phone from his back pocket. The pressure on Tommy's shoulder remained firm.

Tommy watched the old man walk quickly to the door, carrying his walking stick. When he turned round for one last look across the pub, Tommy could see from his face that he wasn't frightened. Far from it. He was angry.

"Yes. Alex here from the Royal Oak. Taxi needed for Paul McGonigle. He's waiting outside."

* * *

Tommy got back to Belfast at noon next day, having taken a while to recover from the hangover. After

127

Paul McGonigle had left, there had been nothing else to do but drink himself into oblivion. As his senses had grown duller, he was aware of Alex keeping a check on him, and he hadn't objected when he had been offered assistance to his room. He had woken with his shoes off but still fully dressed, and a headache the like of which he hadn't experienced since his teenage years.

He knocked hard on Jeff Henry's door. A window opened above him.

"What do you want?" Jeff peered over the window sill down at Tommy.

"Let me in." Tommy knocked hard again.

"After last time?" Jeff yelled, and shut the window.

"I need to check something with you." Tommy raised his voice to a shout. "It's about the old days. I'm happy enough to do this in the street if you want."

Jeff pushed the window open again. "All right. Just keep your hands to yerself this time."

When Jeff opened the door, he was holding a walking stick, though he wasn't using it to walk.

"Relax, Jeff," Tommy said. "In here?"

Jeff nodded and motioned for Tommy to go into the sitting room first. There were old photographs spread out on the table next to the well-used chair.

"What's that about?" Tommy picked up one of the photographs. A group of five men in clothes that suggested the late seventies or early eighties.

Jeff grabbed the photo from Tommy's hands. "Our wee chat just got me thinking, that's all." He gathered the photos into an untidy pile. "These will all be thrown

128

out as rubbish when I'm dead and gone. I just wanted to have another look."

Tommy sat on the chair reserved for infrequent visitors. "I've been to Ballygawley."

"Have yeh now," grunted Jeff. "Why can't yeh just leave it alone?"

"I met a man there by the name of Paul McGonigle. Know him?"

Jeff looked up sharply. "McGonigle? What's he look like?"

Tommy pointed at Jeff. "'Bout your age. Skinny. Tall. Doesn't look in great shape."

"There was a volunteer by that surname. Not sure of his first name, though." Jeff shook his head. "The McGonigle I knew was crap. Couldn't keep his mouth shut so couldn't be trusted with most things. If it's the same man, we just used him as a driver. That's all he was good for."

"He said he went to jail for a bit."

"Aye, that might be him. Tall and thin, yeh say?" Jeff started to sift through the photographs. "I don't know how that's going to help you. He had nothing to do with your adoption. He couldn't be trusted with that information." He held up one of the photographs. "You'll have to add a good few years to him, but is that the guy? At the back, right-hand side."

Tommy looked at the picture of ten men posing as if for a school photo, but with the addition of rifles held across their chest. One face had the same narrow weasel-like features of the man he'd met the previous evening.

"That's him."

"Like I said, Tommy. He had nothing to do with your adoption. Nothing."

"But he knew something, that's for sure. Something he didn't want to share. And he was pissed off that I was poking around."

Tommy picked up the walking stick that Jeff had left resting against his chair while he sorted through the photographs.

"But you'll help me, won't you?" He tapped the walking stick on the floor. "The man who wanted this favour. Give me his name."

"It won't do you any good. He's dead." Jeff's eyes were on the walking stick. He licked his lips. There was a sheen of sweat on his upper lip.

Tommy tapped the walking stick on the floor again.

"Fuck's sake, Tommy." Jeff wiped the sweat away with the back of his hand. "His name was Tobin."

CHAPTER SEVENTEEN

Malcolm heard Billy barking at the front door and went to the hall to investigate. What was up with that mongrel now? Then the dog half-ran, half-skidded across the wooden floor of the hall to the front room. He jumped onto the back of the settee and resumed his barking at the window.

"What the hell is wrong with..." Billy tore past Malcolm and back to the front door. Still in the front room, Malcolm looked out of the window and couldn't believe what he saw – Emily and young Kevin, who was carrying a satchel over his shoulder. Bloody hell. That was quick work. Let's hope, anyway. He got to the front door and opened it as Emily was raising her hand to knock.

"Come on ahead in. The room off the left there." Billy had stopped barking and had flattened his ears in submission. If Malcolm was not mistaken, there was a slight wag of the tail starting as well. Jesus, was Malcolm the only one this dog wouldn't take to?

"Och, a wee Cairn Terrier." Emily had bent down to pat Billy and the tail-wagging took on a greater speed. "Isn't he just lovely? What's his name?"

"Billy. And you must be…" Harriet had come into the hall from the kitchen, still wiping her hands with a tea towel.

Emily took her extended hand. "It's Emily, from the IT class. We spoke on the phone."

"Of course, yes. Lovely to meet you in person." Harriet nodded at Malcolm. "You must be very patient."

"And this is Kevin." Emily ushered Kevin forward to stand sullen and silent beside her.

"Kevin?" Harriet looked at Malcolm. "This is the lad you told me about..."

"Harriet, could you put the kettle on? Emily and Kevin here have kindly agreed to give me a few booster lessons and some advice on a laptop to buy."

"Really?" Harriet furrowed her brow, then shrugged. "Well, whatever it takes to drag you into this century."

When the tea and coffee orders had been made – water only for the lad – Emily, Malcolm and Kevin settled in the sitting room. Somehow Billy had sneaked in and was lying across Kevin's feet, with Malcolm's glove – now so well chewed it could hardly be called a glove at all – in his mouth. Kevin opened his laptop and began to type. After a while, Malcom put down his cup, anxious to get an update.

"So are yeh making progress?"

"Wait a minute. I think we should have ground rules." Emily put her hand on the laptop.

Jesus, more rules. "What would they be?" asked Malcolm, forcing a smile.

"Kevin, this is a project to help some people who have been very distressed by past events. This does not give you the green light to go any further than what we are asking you to do. Clear?"

Kevin sighed and shrugged. "Yessss." He couldn't have put more insolence into the word if he tried.

"The consequence in that case will be," Emily said, "I will... what's the phrase? Grass on you. And don't think that'll get me into trouble as well. Who will believe that with my background, I'd ever get involved in hacking?" She pronounced the word with distaste.

Malcolm frowned. He had known from the start that Emily was a force to be reckoned with, but by God, she was good. Kevin shifted in his seat. He'd probably realised he'd met his match.

Malcolm coughed. "Any rules for me?"

"Just don't get him into anything that I will regret." Then she smiled. "Underneath, he's not a bad lad."

Kevin started to redden at the backhanded compliment. Clearly, he wasn't used to even mild praise.

"So, Kevin, what have you found?" asked Malcolm.

"Well, I used your password – Jesus – Philomena? She your daughter?"

Malcolm bristled. "She is a very talented Tyrone-born singer, young man. You want to listen to her stuff."

Kevin raised his eyebrows. "Whatever. Anyway, as you told us, you were blocked from the Holmes system."

Malcolm's closed his eye momentarily. "So, no joy?"

"Please." He glanced at Malcolm with a withering look. "The front door may be bolted, but there was a back window slightly ajar. I got in through there."

"What?" Malcolm looked at Emily, seeking an explanation in plain English.

"What he means," she explained, "is that he found a small chink in the firewall and was able to get into the system that way."

Malcolm was now really confused. "There's been a fire?"

"Good lord!" Emily exhaled. "Look, we will cover this in the next session in the course. In the meantime, all Kevin means is that he got into the Holmes system. And a few others."

"Oh. OK. And?"

"I've information on all of the people you mentioned," Kevin said. "But you have to remember that most of this is from the dark ages. For example, online tax-return information doesn't go back to 1989. And social services records are even worse." He shook his head. "No wonder social workers are crap."

Malcolm guessed that Kevin didn't have the best support from statutory services. "What have you got?" Malcolm moved to sit next to him on the sofa so as to be able to see the laptop screen. There was plenty of room, but still Kevin moved along. Malcolm was happy about the space between them.

"OK," Kevin said. "Let's start with the easy ones. Duncan Gallagher. Clean as a whistle. One driving offence – speeding just off the Ballygawley roundabout. Straight up with his tax returns. Nothing in social services records. Practically doesn't exist."

Malcolm wasn't surprised but, in his experience, it always paid to check out everyone, no matter how unlikely a suspect. "Next one?"

Kevin moved the cursor to another window on the screen. "Trevor Mulholland. Not much more information on him. Not surprising, seeing as he died in 1989. There was a bit about him on the Holmes network."

Malcolm leant closer to the screen.

"Trevor Mulholland was questioned about a young girl murdered in 1986," Kevin said. "Her body was found in one of his quarries. The report was written up by one DI Robinson."

No mention of that in his conversation with the man. Maybe Robinson would say he had memory problems, but the old bastard had seemed as sharp as a pin.

The sitting-room door was opened by Harriet carrying a tray of mugs, a glass of water and a plate of Malcolm's second favourite, Malteaser cake.

Emily rose from the chair. "That's wile kind of you. Here, let me help." She moved a table from a nest of the things to a position in the middle of the room, so that all were in arm's length of the refreshments.

"Are you making progress?" asked Harriet.

"Yes, love," Malcolm assured her. "We won't be much longer. Billy looks like he needs a walk."

Billy looked up at the word "walk".

"Don't yeh, Billy. A wee walk?" continued Malcolm.

Billy stood, gave an expectant woof and wagged his tail.

"OK, I'll leave you to it. But Kevin..." Harriet said.

Kevin looked up at Harriet but was unable to reply due to having a mouth full of Malteser cake.

"My preference would be one that I can Facetime with."

Kevin looked confused for a microsecond, then nodded vigorously.

With Harriet safely out of the house, Malcolm turned to Kevin. "You mentioned a report by DI Robinson."

Kevin took a swig of water and wiped his mouth free of chocolate crumbs. "Yeah. It seemed to be a standard witness statement from Mulholland. Saying when the quarry had been locked up. Who had the keys? And his wife confirmed that he had been at home all evening."

Mulholland had been a witness not a suspect.

"Anything more about the murder of the girl?" asked Malcolm.

Kevin bit his lip. "You just gave me a list of names to dig up about."

"I know, but maybe if you have another wee look…"

Emily put down her mug of tea. "This was one-time only. That's my laptop. He's not allowed one until his placement and probation are finished, and as soon as we're done here today, that laptop is getting a factory reset. Everything will be deleted."

Malcolm knew he wasn't going to change her mind. "All right. Next one? The barman who was there when Mulholland was shot. Tony Muldoon."

Kevin again moved the cursor to another window. "A lot more on this one… suspected of low-level crimes – handling stolen goods, that sort of thing…" Kevin moved the cursor down the page. "Questioned by the police loads of time. But never done for anything. Mostly questioned about who was meeting who in the pub he worked in. Kealey's Inn. The place where Mulholland got shot. Looks like Muldoon worked there until about ten years ago."

By Malcolm's calculation, Muldoon would be in his late seventies by now. "Is he still alive?"

"Hang on." Kevin checked the screen again. "Yup. No death certs registered for him or his wife. There's a recent address here. He's been on benefits since retiring."

Malcolm reached for the notepad and pen his wife kept next to the landline, and wrote down the address displayed on the screen.

"OK," Kevin continued. "Then there's an Edward Daniels. Was a police officer, but left the force in 1987. Died in 1994. Death cert says liver failure. Not much there either. Survived by wife and one child, a boy. There was a visa application for her and the son to go to Canada the following year."

Malcolm drew a breath. A Canadian accent sound like an American one? The man he'd seen bothering the Gallaghers would be about the right age. But, if it was Edward Daniels' son, what was his beef in all this?

"Then there was Paul McGonigle," Kevin said. "That one's strange."

"The drayman?" Malcolm said. "He was there when the shooting happened. Saw nothing, heard nothing. Claimed he was with Tony Muldoon the whole time. What's strange about him?"

Kevin pointed at the screen. "McGonigle seems to have been in and out of trouble. Prison in 1984 for processing a weapon. A handgun. Admitted to being a member of the UVF. Out of prison in early 1987. No more terrorist convictions. He moved around a bit in rented accommodation – but still in the same area. A number of convictions for non-payment of rent and diddling benefits. Seemed to be on his uppers for a year or so. Took occasional jobs driving. Then from late 1989 on, nothing. No problems with money, it would seem. On disability benefits now. Bad back, uses a wheelchair for outside, can barely walk inside – that's what it says on the forms he filled in to get the benefits. But no money-related court orders or convictions after that. Maybe he learnt his lesson." Kevin looked up from the screen and smiled at Emily. "It happens!"

Emily smiled back. "Sometimes."

Kevin went on. "Looks like this McGonigle stayed put once he got his money problems sorted. Here's his address." He pointed to a scanned copy of the latest letter sent to Paul McGonigle from the Department of Work and Pensions. Malcolm copied the address to the notepad.

Emily turned to him. "So that's the list complete. Right, Kevin, give me the laptop." She extended her hands, clearly keen to finish this.

"Emily?"

"Yes, Malcolm?" Her hands were still held out, waiting for the laptop.

"Please, just one more search," he said. "Here. Right now. I don't even think he needs to hack anything. I'm sure I could do it at the library after a few more of your lessons, but Kevin could get the information for me now, today."

Emily sighed. "Just one more. But then I get the laptop back. It will take a miracle to get you up to Kevin's standard."

Malcolm felt Emily was being a bit harsh. He could learn when he put his mind to it. If he wanted too. He turned to

Kevin. "The girl that was murdered and found in Mulholland's quarry. Liza Tobin. What can you get on her?"

"Give me a minute." Kevin started to type quicker than Malcolm thought possible. "OK. The girl was the daughter of a single mother. Elizabeth Tobin."

Poor Elizabeth Tobin. The woman Hannah had mentioned. The one with mental health problems. The one with the possible son searching for her.

"Any more details on the Tobin family?"

"There's a Samuel Tobin," Kevin said. "He died in 1992."

"Can you tell if he was definitely linked to Elizabeth Tobin?" Malcolm interlocked his fingers. It was great when pieces started to fall into place. Sam Tobin would be old enough to be Elizabeth's father.

Kevin shrugged his shoulders. "Dunno. Sam Tobin's death was registered by a George Tobin."

Damn. That would have been too easy. Still, it wasn't to say there was no connection at all.

"Keep going."

"We need to look at Companies House," Kevin said.

Emily opened her mouth to say no, but Kevin got down to it.

"Seems that Sam Tobin was sole owner of a plant and farming machinery hire business in Tyrone," Kevin said. "But it stopped trading in 1990." He stared closer at the screen and looked puzzled.

"What?" Malcolm asked. Judging from Kevin's expression, there was more information to come.

"The company stopped trading but there is another Tobin Ltd registered at about the same time. Although it never filed accounts. It was down as a dormant company. Still is. Why would you keep a company dormant all these years?" he muttered, as if to himself." No financial returns, just a dormant company. For thirty years?"

"Who owns the company?"

"George Tobin. Date of birth 23rd October 1956. Maybe the same one as the guy who registered the death of Sam? Let's see what I can find on this bloke."

Malcolm considered this. It still didn't mean that Elizabeth wasn't connected. Tobin wasn't such a common name and how many of them could there be in Tyrone? Kevin typed furiously again, then stopped. Malcolm saw him smile in satisfaction.

"Well, would you believe it? Mr George Tobin is a solicitor at Hancock and Belfy. It says here they specialise in property law." Another few rapid clicks on the mouse. "Graduate of Queen's. Started off as a defence solicitor in Thomas and Oliver. Was there about four years, according to his CV."

Thomas and Oliver. Malcolm recognised the name instantly. The company had branches all over and represented many of the ne'er-do-wells and thugs he had nabbed as a police officer. The firm was discerning, though. Tended to only represent those with loyalist leanings. Messrs Thomas and Oliver must have made a fortune over the years of the Troubles.

"There's even a photo here." Kevin turned the laptop towards Malcolm. He looked at the image of a middle-aged, dark-haired man with a patronising smile. Hair neat and short, suit expensive, tie sober. The standard solicitor attire Malcolm had been familiar with throughout his past career.

That was enough for Emily. She held out her hands again. Kevin obediently handed over the laptop.

"I am so grateful," Malcolm said. "This has been really helpful. Kevin, you've some talent there."

"That's good to hear, Malcolm." Emily hesitated. "But you'll understand, I can't ask Kevin to do any more. This is risky enough."

Malcolm knew he had asked more than he should. "I understand." He held out his hand to shake Kevin's and then Emily's.

He showed them to the front door. Emily paused. "Kevin, just wait for me at the gate. I need a word with Malcolm."

"Everything OK?" asked Malcolm. He suspected there was something up.

"I know it seemed that I was less keen to help today, after being so gung-ho before. It's just that I had time to think. That lad." She gestured to Kevin. "He's had a rough time of it. Some kids just don't get the break they deserve. I can't risk making things worse for him. This is as far as it goes with us helping you. OK?"

"It's absolutely fine. And with what you pair have done today I'll be able to help two other good people. You don't need to be involved anymore. I'll take it from here."

Malcolm watched as Emily walked down the path to meet up with Kevin. He was just about to shut the door when Kevin came bounding up the path again.

"Can I ask a favour?" Kevin said, breathless with exertion.

Malcolm rubbed the back of his neck. "Suppose it's only fair." After all, Kevin was still a convicted felon. There was no way he was going to do anything by way of a favour that would upset Emily.

"Your wee dog, Billy. Do you think I could take him for a walk now and then? If you don't mind, that is."

Malcolm smiled broadly. "I don't mind at all. Any time yeh like."

This had indeed been an afternoon of results.

CHAPTER EIGHTEEN

Malcolm was barred from the kitchen and treated to a threatening look from Harriet if he dared dent a cushion in the sitting room.

All this because William and Hannah were coming for tea. It wasn't as if they were strangers. But when Harriet got set on a meal, Malcolm knew from experience he was best out of the way. He retreated to the bedroom with the newspaper.

He'd just settled down with the Tyrone Chronicle – Harriet had arranged with that so-called journalist, Alfie Hamill, to have a copy posted to them each week to keep them in the loop – when the door to the bedroom was pushed open. Billy padded into the room.

"You've been banned too."

Billy flopped down but kept his eyes on Malcolm.

"Come on, then. Let's go visiting. Neither of us will be welcome here for the next few hours."

Billy stood quickly, trotted out of the room and returned with his lead in his mouth.

* * *

"Oh," Pat said on seeing Malcolm. "Hello. I wasn't expecting you." She smoothed down her skirt and pushed her hair from her forehead. There were black shadows under her eyes again and her face was pale.

"I won't keep you long," Malcolm said. "I just thought I'd give you an update."

Pat's face brightened. "Really? Come on in."

After putting Billy in the back garden with Bella, Pat ushered Malcolm into the sitting room where Duncan was dozing in the chair.

"I shan't wake him. We had another sleepless night." She indicated for Malcolm to sit in the chair opposite her. "What have you found out?"

Malcolm kept his voice low so as not to wake Duncan. "First, Trevor Mulholland definitely had money – a lot of money – with him that day."

"I knew that from what Duncan always insisted. Is that it?" Pat seemed to sag into her chair.

"And I know what happened to that money. It was returned to Mrs Mulholland by the Detective Inspector in charge of the case."

Pat looked down at her skirt and brushed off some imaginary fluff. She sighed, then looked up again. "Why?... And why lie to Duncan, put him through all that upset?"

"DI Robinson, the officer in charge, he didn't want to cause Mrs Mulholland any more grief. He thought she had enough to cope with. Didn't want it coming out that Mulholland was paying protection money to terrorists."

"Really. How considerate of him." Her bitter tone belied her words. Pat reached over to the coffee table and pushed a magazine so that it was in line with the one underneath, and then studied her work. "I often wondered if it was anything to do with the family connection."

A family connection? Robinson had kept that quiet. "What family connection?"

Pat looked up in surprise. "Didn't Robinson mention that Mulholland's wife was his cousin's daughter?"

Malcolm shook his head. "No, it wasn't mentioned."

"Just makes you wonder if it was all a bit convenient how it worked out. Nobody wants to wash their dirty laundry in public. Instead, Robinson lied and my Duncan had to live with that burden all these years. There were rumours, despite that Robinson man trying to keep it quiet. People thought Duncan was trying to ruin Mulholland's name. Some even thought he took the money himself and was making a fuss about it to put the blame on others." She took a paper tissue from her skirt pocket and started to smooth the creases, folded it again and held it tightly in her hand. "I hope Robinson got his comeuppance."

DI Robinson's current misery came to Malcolm's mind. "Yes, you could say he did in the end."

"What about the man who's been hounding us? Have you found out who he is?"

"Not yet, but there's an outside chance he may be the son of the other police officer present on that day."

"The other... Do you mean that young PC who brought Duncan home after the shooting? I'll never forget that day. He looked just as shook up.

"That's him," Malcolm said. "Edward Daniels. He left the force – was asked to leave – soon after Mulholland's murder. It seems that Robinson was happy for everyone

145

to believe that if there had been money there, Daniels took it."

Pat rubbed her forehead, studied the carpet and frowned. "The poor man. What happened to him?"

"He died about six years after the shooting. Liver damage. His wife and son emigrated to Canada."

"That Robinson man has a lot to answer for. Is he still alive?"

"Just about."

"I think I need a moment." Pat stood up. "I'll make us some tea." As she left the room, she dabbed at her eyes with the tissue.

Malcolm studied the still sleeping Duncan. All the creases on his face were gone and a slight smile played on his lips. Malcolm hoped he had added to that peacefulness. He stood to help Pat as she returned with the tray of mugs.

"Do you think this man with the American accent could be the son of that poor soul Edward Daniels?" Pat said. "If so, what does he want from us?"

Malcolm sipped his tea. "I'm guessing the same as you. He probably wants to know what really happened." He warmed his hands around the mug. "But at this time, I can't be certain. Do yeh have a mobile phone?"

Pat frowned. "Of course." She reached over to a side table and lifted the mobile that looked nothing like Malcolm's circa-2006 Nokia model. "My sons bought this for me to make sure I can contact them if, you know." She nodded towards Duncan. "If things get too difficult. I know how to use it to phone them. Apparently, it does all sorts of other stuff."

Malcolm laughed. "Well, I certainly couldn't help you with that. But could you put my number into it? And promise you'll ring me if Edward Daniels' son turns up again. Straight away." He stood. "I've taken up enough of your time and," he looked at his watch, "Harriet will be wondering where I am."

With Billy on his lead at the front door, Malcolm turned to Pat. "Trevor Mulholland. What did you think of him?"

Pat frowned and went back to close the sitting room door. "I never took to him. Duncan thought he was a great laugh. I had a notion it was because he was the opposite of Duncan. Where Duncan was honest and decent, Mulholland was always on the make. Always had an angle." She shrugged. "Maybe it was a yin and yang sort of thing. They say opposites attract."

"What about his wife? Did you have anything to do with her?"

"Good heavens, no." Pat laughed. "She was half my age. What would we have in common?"

Billy was straining at the leash. "I'd best be off," Malcolm said. "But remember. Ring me if Daniels' son appears."

* * *

Malcolm opened the door to find William and Hannah on the doorstep. The cold evening air mingled with the tasty smells from the kitchen.

"Bout yeh, William."

""Bout yeh, Malcolm," replied William, holding out a bottle of white wine.

"Ah now, son, you are very welcome to this house. And Hannah!" Malcolm tensed, waiting on the usual hug and kiss from this girl. He would never get used to this continental nonsense.

But Hannah knelt down and stretched out her arms. "Billy!"

The dog rushed past Malcolm into her arms. She carried Billy into the bungalow, letting him lick her by way of a greeting. "Hi, Malcolm."

Malcolm was both relieved and put out.

William smiled at him. "I think you might have to get used to playing second fiddle!"

"Bloody dog," muttered Malcolm. "Never mind. Come on, William, let's get this opened!" He held a bottle of wine aloft.

The meal was terrific. Harriet was praised by her guests. She received the congratulations gracefully and set about clearing up. When she had collected the dirty plates and taken them to the kitchen, Malcolm opened the button of his trousers and let his stomach expand with relief. Harriet knew how to put on a spread. He looked across at William, who had struggled manfully with that second portion of pavlova. Hannah had stood firm, citing some nonsense about joining Weight Watchers last week.

"How is the amateur detective work going?" asked William.

"Less of the amateur, if yeh don't mind." Malcolm punched William gently on his shoulder to show no offence was taken. "I think I've sorted out a few parts of the puzzle." He went on to explain what he'd discovered about the missing money and the probable identity of the man hassling the Gallaghers.

"Job done, then?" asked William.

Malcolm shot a sideways glance at Hannah. "Well, there may be something else."

William looked between Hannah and Malcolm. "What else?"

Malcolm tilted his head to one side. "It seems your man Tommy Smith might be..."

"Who's Tommy Smith?" William asked.

"Just a man who wanted information that I couldn't give him," explained Hannah. She turned to Malcolm. "What about him?"

"The woman who may be his mother, Elizabeth Tobin, has the same surname as a family who owned a farm equipment hire business near Ballygawley."

Hannah raised her eyebrows. "So? There could be a good few people called Tobin."

Williams held up his hands as if in surrender. "Hang on a minute. It's seems I'm not in the loop. Anyone care to fill me in?"

Hannah smiled at her husband.

"This Tommy Smith came to my office demanding information about his birth mother." She frowned. "I couldn't give it to him – procedure and all that – but we have this long-standing client, Elizabeth Tobin, who's been in and out of mental health care for most of her adult life. She always claimed that she had a second child. A boy." Hannah studied her hands. "But as there was no evidence of that, she was treated as delusional. She'd be sectioned when she started on about it. And then later discharged from hospital after she had agreed there was no second child."

"And you think this Tommy Smith could be her son?" William said. "The poor woman." He reached over and squeezed Hannah's hand.

Malcolm apologised. "Sorry, William, should have told yeh. "The thing is, I've been digging deeper and some more information has come my way."

"Where from?"

"It's best I don't say." Malcolm shifted in his seat. "Anyway… my source has found possible links between the murder of Elizabeth Tobin's daughter, Liza, and Trevor Mulholland. He was questioned at the time, as a witness. And my source also found information on the other people present at Mulholland's murder." He sat back in his chair and spread his hands on the table. "I have a notion there's a thread that links the murder of Liza Tobin to Mulholland's murder, and that Tommy Smith is somehow in the mix. And there may be a link to the Tobin family who owned the hire business."

William cleared his throat. "Exactly how much of this are you intending to pass on to official sources?"

Malcolm looked up at him. "If I'd been handed this information when I was a DI, I would've been scratching me head. At the moment, It's all smoke and mirrors. I just need to get a few more facts and then I'll pass it on." He registered William's sceptical look. "Promise!"

The door was pushed open by Harriet, bringing coffees to round off the meal. "What's he promising yeh now?" She laughed. "He's promised me he'll get a laptop."

William looked at Malcolm. "I thought you said when you left the force that the last thing you would..."

"Aye, well, things change," mumbled Malcolm. He turned to Harriet. "I was just telling them about sorting out a few things for the Gallaghers."

Harriet sighed. "I wasn't that keen for him to get involved, but I suppose some good has come of it. He assures me that he has just a few loose ends to tie up and then we can get on with our retirement."

Malcolm tapped his fingers on the table. "Yes, just a few loose ends. I'm thinking it would be a good idea to go visiting."

CHAPTER NINETEEN

Philomena sang out clear and loud from the CD player in Malcolm's car. Of course, Harriet was the centre of his life, but on occasion it was just grand to be alone with his other love. After all, Harriet had Billy to dote on.

He had explained to Harriet that he just needed to visit one or two people to make sure that he'd given Pat Gallagher the correct story. So, Belfast first, then on to a few addresses on the outskirts of Ballygawley. Hannah had arranged to meet him at the last address late in the afternoon he'd better get a move on. He checked the address of Hancock and Belfry Solicitors on the Malone Road, then punched the postcode into the satnav with his sausage fingers. One hour twenty minutes. And if he left now, the school rush would be over by the time he got there.

* * *

The entrance to the offices was through a wooded drive off the Malone Road which ended at a gravel car park more reminiscent of one belonging to a stately home. Signage at the entrance to the drive informed visitors that the solicitors were specialists in property law. The red-brick raised flower beds that edged the car park contained carefully planted spring flowers, which no doubt would be replaced by a gardener when the season changed.

The building was as far from Malcolm's old stomping ground as you could get. There were no less than three series 5 BMWs in the car park, along with a smattering of Porches. The number plate on the Cayenne read TO1 BN. Not a wasted journey then.

Malcolm parked his five-year-old Vauxhall Insignia between the matt-black Cayenne and a lipstick-red GT4. He looked up at the glass façade, a modern addition to this old three-storey stone building. Nothing like the functional, modest solicitors' offices with unsavoury clientele hanging about that he'd had occasion to visit in his professional career. There must be more money for solicitors in property law than the rest of the fraternity that populated the towns of Tyrone.

Malcolm pulled down the back of his jacket and picked some dog hairs from his suit trousers as he walked up to the glass front entrance. How did that animal get his mark on a suit hanging in the wardrobe? There was a ramped access at the side of the building – clearly, they kept on the right side of disability laws, but no unsightly portable ramps cluttered the corners of this smooth-looking place.

Beyond the glass doors, a receptionist sat behind a minimalist grey desk. He raised his eyebrows when he saw Malcolm push the door open, and then painted on a smile. His name badge announced him as Graham.

"Good morning, sir. Have you an appointment?"

"I've come to see Mr Tobin."

"Certainly. Your name?" Graham moved the mouse of his computer to wake it up.

"You wouldn't have my name."

The receptionist looked confused. "He doesn't see anyone without an appointment."

"Oh, he'll see me all right. Tell him it's about his sister and his niece. My name is Malcolm Bell."

Graham couldn't look more confused. "I'll see if he's in." He picked up the phone and dialled.

Malcolm looked around the reception area. Trendy chairs for the waiting customers that were not designed to be used, but he sat, shifting to get into some semblance of a position of comfort. He failed. He reached over and moved the newspaper on the coffee table to a position that allowed him to scan the headlines. Not much to take note of. Graham smiled at him, his handset still jammed against his ear. Clearly no answer yet.

Malcolm felt the metal uprights of the trendy chair dig into his back, and quickly sat straight again. The dark grey marble floor tiles merged with the light grey walls, with only the photos of the senior partners on the wall to give relief. One was familiar from the web page young Kevin had found. The sun streamed in from the floor-to-ceiling windows of this added-on reception area – the original stone façade evident towards the rear.

Graham replaced the phone handset. He looked over to Malcolm and re-adopted his smile. "Mr Tobin has another appointment due soon, but he can see you for a few minutes. Through the glass door on your left. The lift will take you to the first floor. His secretary will meet you there."

Malcolm nodded. The bait had been taken.

When the lift pinged open, a woman was waiting for him. Malcolm guessed she was around forty. But really, with that amount of makeup, she could have been five years either side. That bloody painted-on smile must have been company standard.

He followed her as instructed and was led into a room occupied by a middle-aged, expensively-suited grey-haired man. He was seated behind an imposing wooden desk with carved legs and a leather surface. The walls were lined with glass-fronted bookcases that held sober-looking publications. The carpet had a rich feel to it as Malcolm walked towards George Tobin, who rose from his black office chair to greet him his hand extended.

"Mr Bell." Tobin's smile of greeting didn't reach his eyes. "I don't think we've met. Please, sit down." He extended his hand. His handshake was confident.

"No, we haven't met." Malcolm settled himself in the chair on the other side of the desk. "It's about your sister and niece. I'm looking at a cold case that may involve them."

Tobin gave a brief laugh but shifted in his chair. "You have me confused here. My sister left the province some thirty years ago. A cold case, you say? You're with the police?"

"I'm acting as a consultant. Recently retired DI. They often bring us back. Can't do without the old expertise!" Malcolm felt there was enough truth in that.

"Sorry, I can't help you. A bit of a dead end for you, I'm afraid."

"Oh." Malcolm rubbed his chin. "Now we're both confused. You see, my information is that you're the son of a man who had a farm machinery hire business near Ballygawley. It went bust in around 1989 or thereabouts, but you, according to the records, are registered as the sole company director."

Tobin nodded. "That's correct. My father was in very poor health at the end. My mother, God rest her soul, looked after him. He died in 1989. She tried to keep the business going, but..." He shrugged his shoulders.

"It must have been wile difficult. You didn't want to carry on with the business?"

Tobin spread his hands. "My talents lay elsewhere. I left the family firm registered as dormant. I suppose it was sentimental. But I have children, and you never know. They may want to restart it when they come of age."

"Your sister..."

"Like I said. She's in England. Has been for thirty years." His tone was suddenly cold, the words clipped.

"Oh, I see. It's just that there's an Elizabeth Tobin who lives near Ballygawley whose daughter was murdered in 1986. I thought, you know, with the name and that..."

Tobin stood and looked at his watch. "I am sorry, but it's been a wasted journey for you. Tobin is a common enough name in that part of the world."

Not that common, thought Malcolm. Maybe lies came easily in this man's trade. "Well, I've taken enough of your time." He stood. "You know, this woman, this Elizabeth Tobin, she had a sad enough life, by all accounts. And lately we've found out that the poor woman had a second child after her daughter was murdered. This child, a boy, was adopted somehow, but the authorities had no idea. She's been in a wile state all her life. In and out of psychiatric hospitals."

Tobin produced what looked to Malcolm to be a forced sympathetic smile. "Sounds terrible. I am so sorry I can't help you anymore. And now, if you could excuse me, my appointment..." He extended his arm to show Malcolm the face of his watch. Was it to show him the time or to let him see the Rolex branding?

"Of course. An absolute pleasure to meet you, Mr Tobin."

* * *

Malcolm made his way down to reception. Why would the man get so uptight when asked if he had a sister? The strong denial had sounded fake. And he'd heard enough false denials in his time. It would have been easy enough for Tobin to admit the connection. Whose family was perfect, for goodness sake? But there was almost a panicked reaction in his response.

Malcolm walked through the reception to Graham, who pasted on his smile again.

"Graham, could you do me a favour?"

"Er... Certainly, sir." He didn't sound too certain at all.

"Can you give Mr Tobin my phone number? He may need it, and I forgot to leave it with him." It always helped to leave a door open. Never knew what might come of it.

Malcolm recited both his mobile and home numbers. Graham dutifully typed them directly into an email and clicked the on-screen button with a flourish.

"Many thanks." Malcolm smiled, turned and walked through the reception to the front door, thinking over the conversation with Mr George Tobin.

There was a sudden jolt at his side.

"Sorry, I..." Malcolm's automatic apology was interrupted by the sight of a man in an ill-fitting, shiny light-blue suit. The type Malcolm had seen so many times outside courts, the wearer hoping to give an impression of respectability. This man wasn't waiting for any apology. He continued marching towards the reception desk, placed both hands on it and leant towards Graham.

"I've come to see Mr Tobin," he snarled.

Malcolm shook his head, smiled to himself, and walked out through the external doors. Mr George Tobin wasn't having a very pleasant morning, what with Malcolm's awkward questions and now an appointment with that character. But all sorts could have property problems. Maybe Tobin deserved it after denying his sister's existence. Malcolm was sure poor Elizabeth was George's sister. His visit to her later might resolve the issue once and for all.

As he pulled open the door of his car, Malcolm heard the crunch of hurried steps behind him. He turned to see George Tobin rushing across the drive from the opposite direction of the main entrance. A back exit, Malcolm guessed. He clearly wasn't stopping for his 10 o'clock appointment. George got into his car and sped out of the car park. The conversation with him must have spooked Tobin more that Malcolm had thought.

CHAPTER TWENTY

In the end, it had been easy enough for Tommy to work out that there was a probable link between the Tobin who had helped the cause and received a favour in return, and the solicitor Tobin of Hancock and Belfy solicitors, Belfast.

After Jeff had given him the name and the location, he had typed "Ballygawley", "Tobin" and "machinery hire" into Google. The third result was a suggested page on Companies House. Tommy had no idea that sort of information was so public. In his life he had no call to wonder about the financial status of any company. He was a working man with a good job in a sound engineering works. This was another world. Admittedly, he had fourteen pages to sort through, but finally, there it was. Tobin Agricultural Hire, Ballygawley.

What was a dormant company? Tommy had no idea what that meant. A further Google, and then it was clear. But why keep a dormant company on for thirty-odd years? He had clicked on the "People" tab. Only one name – George Tobin. A click on the name, and a list of the companies this George Tobin was involved with had popped up. There were two. Tobin Agricultural Hire, and Hancock and Belfy solicitors.

The company website showed him the face and history of this George Tobin. Round-faced, serious, with an attempt at a knowing smile. Hair grey and well styled. He was around the right age to be the son of a man who helped the volunteers in the Troubles. And he originally came from near Ballygawley. Yes. Tommy was certain.

The only solicitors he had met back in the days were the duty solicitors when things had got a little out of hand. He had learnt to hate the bastards. Their smug resigned looks when they came into the interview room, their sighs of impatience when Tommy explained that the other guy was asking for it, their polished shoes and suits that cost more than his weekly wage. But he knew what they were about. Expensive education, never from the secondary school he graduated from at the age of fifteen. Biding their time doing duty work until the big jobs came their way, at which point they wouldn't dream of looking at the likes of him.

Tommy remembered once, when he was about twenty-four or maybe twenty-five, he'd persuaded a group of his mates to head for the city centre for a change from the usual dives round their neck of the woods. On the previous occasions he'd ventured further afield on his own, he'd found a few places he hoped would impress them. Some of the places he'd happened upon had stirred an uncomfortable interest in him. He'd known better than to take his friends to those places, but there was one that would suit them all.

The drinks in the city bars had cost a fortune, and a couple of the lads had faces like Lurgan spades when they handed over their hard-earned cash. Still, Tommy had reasoned, they'd all just received a bonus, so what the hell. The queue for the nightclub, the only one worth going to, was endless. As he had told the lads, in for a penny. It must have been around January or February. They were getting fecking freezing in the queue and the boys were getting pissed off. Anger rose from the pit of Tommy's stomach, at them, at the queue, at the cold, at fecking everything. His fists were clenching and unclenching of their own accord. That's when he spotted him, about four people from the front of the queue. Roy Clements. The guy who, the previous year, had seemed to be the most decent of the solicitors that rocked up at the police station – and there had been a few over the years.

"Hang about, boys. I think I can get us in quicker. Hold my place." Tommy ran up to the man he recognized. "Mate, it's me. You were my solicitor last year." Tommy pushed the man – gently, he thought – on the shoulder, just to make sure he had his attention. "Do yeh not recognize me?"

Roy looked at Tommy with disgust and turned away.

Roy's friend stepped forward and pushed Tommy hard on the chest with the flat of his hand. "Piss off – mate." He managed to both slur his words and inject them with contempt.

"I wasn't talking to you."

The double-handed push from Tommy had the man fall against the brick wall, stumble then drop to the ground. It got the bouncers' attention. One walked down the queue to where Tommy was standing, his fists once again starting to clench and unclench.

"Everything all right here?" The bouncer's tone was firm and loud enough to get everyone's attention.

"Just been assaulted. Got witnesses." The man scrambled up from the ground, his words still sliding into each other.

The bouncer turned towards the accused with a growing look of recognition.

Tommy rolled his eyes. He knew what was coming. He had been there enough times.

"You Tommy Smith?" asked the bouncer. "Yes, you are. Right, I don't want no trouble here, so move along." He nodded towards Tommy's friends, who had now left the queue and were walking slowly towards the two men, unsure what was going on. "You and your mates won't be getting in here tonight."

The bouncer was bigger than him, but Tommy was confident he could take him. It was the other three bouncers now taking an interest that he wasn't so sure of. He turned on his heel and walked towards his friends.

"Fucking crap place full of wankers. Let's go." He continued to march away from the club. They could always go to the Crown.

Then he heard the shout.

"Lowlife!"

Tommy turned in the direction of Roy and the wankers. His friends tried to hold him back, their voices nearly breaking through his rage. But not quite.

He smashed Roy's head against the wall with a satisfying crunch and kicked his mate in the nuts with a force that he had honed to perfection on the football field, and on a few other occasions as well.

"I fecking knew you'd be causing trouble." The other bouncers were behind him, pushing on his shoulders, forcing forced him to kneel, his arms yanked behind his back. But by then he was done.

His mates were on the case and handed over to the bouncers what money they had left. Who would believe Tommy up against two respectable solicitors? Who was going to listen to his side of the story? They all thought they were better than him.

It had been a long walk home that night, and it was a long time before his mates would go clubbing with him again.

* * *

For the trip to see George Tobin, Tommy had dressed in his suit, the one he had worn for court appearances and, more recently, at the funerals of first his father, then his mother. The mid-blue colour had been what everyone was wearing when he bought it. It would have to do. There was no way he was turning up to some swanky solicitors' offices in jeans. He knew they'd look down their noses at the likes of him. If he was to make any headway in finding out who his parents were, and why was he rejected, if he was to have any chance of speaking to this George Tobin, then he would have to look the part.

Sweat trickled down Tommy's back as he drove into the entrance to Hancock and Belfry solicitors. He had been fine until he'd turned off the Malone Road. But now he was going into another world. Even the solicitors that Tommy's dad had used to get him out of bother over the years hadn't looked as grand as this. Jesus. The cars.

Only one was as humble as his, squeezed in between a Macan, and, if he wasn't mistaken, only a bloody GT4. Tommy wiped the sweat from his face with the palm of his hand and then wiped his hand on his thigh. He parked as far away from the entrance to the offices as he could, then sat for a good five minutes, breathing deeply to get himself under control, as his counsellor had taught him. It was a fear he hadn't had since his father died.

He hit the steering wheel with the flat of his hands, took a deep breath, got out of the car and slammed the door shut. He walked up to the front entrance quickly so as not to lose his nerve. He headed for the reception desk, focusing on the man seated there. He felt a bump at his side, and heard a vague "Sorry", but he walked on. He couldn't afford to stop. The man at the desk looked up and smiled a smile that didn't reach his eyes. Tommy noticed the name badge. What sort of name was Graham? He put both hands on Graham's desk. Mostly to steady himself. The blood was rushing to his head.

"I've come to see Mr Tobin."

Graham leant backward and his smile turned to a frown. "Have you... have you an appointment?"

What the fuck was up with this eejit? "No. But I need to see him. About his sister."

Graham the eejit looked from side to side, like he was checking if someone was watching him. Then he grabbed the phone from the desk and punched numbers. The frown deepened. He punched more numbers. Maybe different ones? Tommy wasn't sure. A look of relief momentarily crossed Graham's face. Then annoyance? He replaced the handset, took a deep breath and looked up at Tommy, the smile even more forced than before.

"It seems Mr Tobin has left for the day. Can I take your name? Maybe he can see you another time."

Tommy turned from the desk. For fuck's sake. There was no way he was leaving his name. Who would trust these bastards? Or maybe he should. Slowly, he turned back to Graham. "Tell him... tell him it's about his sister. Make sure he knows that. And I will call again. Soon."

Tommy walked quickly from the building. The bloody pretentious place was suffocating him. He paused at the matt-black Macan and the GT4. There was a space where the only other clapped-out old car had been – enough space for a good keying.

Then he walked back to his own car at a more contented pace. As he got in, he glanced back at the line of scraped paint on both cars and smiled.

CHAPTER TWENTY-ONE

The decent weather – cloud, with the occasional appearance of sun – had changed to driving rain as Malcolm took the motorway towards the west of the province. His visit to George Tobin had been useful. Mainly because of what he hadn't said. There was definitely plenty more to find out there. Now it was time to get another angle on what had happened in Kealey's pub some thirty years ago. He had already put Paul McGonigle's address into the satnav – his second call of the day. The route seemed straightforward enough.

After a quick coffee stop at the services outside Dungannon, Malcolm reached the Ballygawley roundabout just before midday. It was a nondescript sort of place to the unknowing visitor, but to Malcolm is was an important crossroad. Take the eastern exit and you'd find yourself on the road to Belfast, the place the rest of the world knew about because of the thirty years of violence. To the south was Dublin, the vibrant, metropolitan face of Ireland that attracted all of the tourism and plaudits. Straight ahead was the road out west, rural and rugged, and the land of lakes with islands enough for every day of the year. If you took the road to the north, of course you would eventually get to Londonderry or Derry, depending on your political allegiance. But before that was Tyrone, with its gentle rolling hills, and Omagh, the small rural town that suffered that last deadly bomb. The place that would be forever remembered for the worst of reasons. Maybe, thought Malcolm, if the Northern Ireland Assembly was relocated from Stormont to this roundabout, they might make some progress in understanding all the people of this land. He indicated right and grunted. Some hope.

McGonigle's place was about twenty minutes from the roundabout, just off the Omagh road. Malcolm reached over and gave the satnav a small shake. It had been a retirement present from the control-room boys, but Malcolm was sure it was meant as a joke, given his reputation with all technology. What was wrong with using a map? And now the damn satnav was taking him a wile strange route. He hadn't seen some of these roads for many a year. Not since the police had been hunting down men who felt safer on the other side of the border.

But thirty years ago, just after he had joined the force, Malcolm had developed an ally in the Garda Síochána not many had known about. In fact, it wasn't that far from this country lane where he and that ally had first met. On a wee bridge, on one of the many roads between Northern Ireland and the south, blocked in an effort to force everyone through the checkpoints. Malcolm snorted as he remembered.

Weather much like today. Miserable driving rain that came and went. The RUC had been tipped off that guns were about to be moved. The armoured jeep had been parked at the junction of the road that continued on north across the border. Nothing but rolling green fields either side, a good four miles from any civilization. The hedges that lined the road were bending in the wind howling around them. DI Robinson had stayed nice and dry and safe in the jeep and instructed Malcolm and two of the other constables to check the other road that led to the blockade. One look at his colleagues' faces and Malcolm could see they were even more scared than he was.

"Let's go!" Giving them no more time to think, Malcolm jumped out of the jeep, his rifle cocked and ready. He led the way up the road, checking from side to side with each step he took. Although he couldn't see them, he knew that squaddies from the local battalion, already dropped by helicopter, were somewhere in the fields, hopefully covering the pitiful trio as they progressed up the road. They had almost reached the bridge where a four-foot-high concrete block reinforced with steel had been dropped to block this road some four years earlier.

Crack!

Malcolm dropped to the floor. He looked back at the other two. They'd done the same.

Crack!

This time a spark of tarmac jumped up from the ground between Malcolm and the others.

"Go back!" Malcolm shouted. He saw their faces now chalk-white and their eyes like saucers. "Fuck's sake, go back!"

Another crack and another spark of tarmac between them. They turned and scrambled back to the jeep.

Malcolm was pinned down. There was a gap in the hedge behind him, in line with where the bullets had come from. And there was a rise in the field that bordered the lane, with a copse of trees in the middle. The concrete block was five yards in front of the bridge. Malcolm dropped low as his mates had, and moved as fast as he could, holding his rifle in a white-knuckled grip.

Crack!

Malcolm didn't look behind him, but that one had sounded closer. He dived for the block and gasped as he rested his back against the cold, hard surface. It was only five yards, but it had felt like a marathon.

"Hey you!"

Malcolm looked to the right but saw no one. Maybe the noise of the gunfire was making him hear things.

"You! Fuck's sake. You deaf?"

There was a very definite southern twang to that accent. Malcolm peered around the concrete block and saw a Garda officer, same grade as himself, crouched down, his back against the bridge wall, gun in his hand. The man's face was glistening with sweat. Either he had just run there or he was as happy as Malcolm.

"What's going on?" Malcolm asked.

"You serious? We're getting shot at. Do they teach yeh nothing in the RUC?"

Malcolm rolled his eyes. Stuck with a smart aleck. Great. "We had a tip-off guns would be moved. Looks like they set us up."

"Same here. It'll be good and handy if my boss would talk to your boss sometimes. Then even an eejit would work this out."

Crack!

This time the concrete block was hit on the far side.

"Come over here," the officer said. "There's a gap in the trees in front of the block. They'll have yeh if yeh don't move. There's more cover over here."

Malcolm didn't have to be invited twice. He scrabbled over to where the Garda officer crouched.

Malcolm drew deep to catch his breath. He moved his gun to his left hand and extended his right. "Malcolm Bell."

The Garda officer laughed and did the same. "Sean Cahill. Please ta meet yeh."

Sean was about the same age Malcolm guessed, and maybe a little slimmer. His dark eyes had long eyelashes and practically a monobrow, it was that thick. But the eyes were dancing like they were having great craic.

Another shot.

From his new position, Malcolm could see where the bullet had hit the concrete block.

"We've got soldiers in the fields around here," Malcolm said. "It'll only be a matter of time." His words sounded much more confident that he felt.

"Aye, us too." Sean shook his head. "I can't figure out who they're after. Why're they having a pop at me?"

"It could be either lot. Those volunteers, as they call themselves, might have savvy leaders, but most of them are as thick as champ."

"Let's find out."

"Find out what?"

"Who they're after, your lot or mine. Give us your hat."

Malcolm looked at Sean in disbelief. Yes, he was in a desperate situation, but this clown seemed determine to make it worse.

Sean elbowed Malcolm. "Com'on. I've seen this done in the movies."

To this day, Malcolm didn't know why he did it, but he took off his dark green RUC hat and handed it over. Sean put it on top of his gun and raised the gun up over his head. The movement was answered by two gunshots.

"There ye are. It's your lot their after. I'll just be on my way." Sean laughed and handed back Malcolm's hat.

Malcolm smiled. "Hang on. Let's do this methodically. Give us your hat."

Sean handed over his dark-blue Garda hat, grinning. Malcolm put it on his gun and raised it up.

Three gunshots this time.

Sean laughed and shook Malcolm's hand. "Fair play. Fuck knows who they're after."

It took, they estimated afterwards, about an hour for the situation to be controlled by a combination of the Garda and the army. In that time, Malcolm and Sean shared cigarettes and confidences – after all, who knew if it was going to end well for them? That time, thank God, it had.

And their long association began. It hadn't been official, of course. Couldn't be. But at critical times, Sean would deliver, and Malcolm would return the favour. There was something about what happened that day on the bridge that seemed to make a lot more sense than any of the political nonsense over the years. At the end of it, flesh and bones weren't green or orange.

* * *

Sean Cahill... Of course. He might be able to iron out the wee niggle about paramilitaries being involved in the Mulholland shooting. The official case was that they had been, but with no claim for responsibility? That rarely happened. As Malcolm pulled up outside the end of terrace house that was Paul McGonigle's home, he resolved to phone his old friend when he got a moment.

A red Fiesta was parked directly outside the house. The car had seen better days, and would need a substantial amount of good luck for the next MOT. The house wasn't in bad condition. Certainly not at the squatters end of the scale, but it, like the car, could have done with some tender loving care. The windows were frosted with road muck and the linings of the curtains had patches of mould. The house door was black UPVC, in contrast to the wooden windows with their peeling paint. Malcolm knocked on it.

The door opened, giving a gap of just six inches. A narrow, grey old face peered out. "You the council? Taken ye long enough. The windows are about to fall out."

"Mr Paul McGonigle?" asked Malcolm. No need to dissuade the old man from his assumption. He put his hand on the door and applied some pressure. "Can I come in?"

"Suppose ye had." Paul McGonigle opened the door fully and turned towards the sitting room. He reached for a walking stick leaning up against the staircase. When he walked, he held it in his right hand, leaning heavily on it.

Through the open door to the kitchen, Malcolm could see a sink piled high and cans of various brands of lager covering most of the worktop.

Paul turned towards him. "The home help didn't turn up this week. Lazy cow."

He gestured for Malcolm to sit on the settee, and took the armchair opposite. The room smelt as if fresh air was a rare visitor. Malcolm couldn't say it was for lack of funds, just uncared for. The settee was firm and comfortable, but the scatter cushions were stained. The carpet had a new look about it. It was just as well it was grey, with the overfilled ashtrays next to the armchair and one on the fireplace. The dining table in the area behind the armchair looked to be solid wood, with good quality chairs. It was piled high with letters in brown envelopes on one side, and on the other was a place set for one.

"Have ye the forms for me to sign?" asked Paul, leaning forward. "Bout time. I was starved with the coul this winter. Ye wouldn't want a death on your conscience, would ye?" Paul gave a crooked half-smile.

"I'm not here about the windows."

"You're not?" Paul's smile disappeared. He looked at Malcolm with suspicion. "What then? If you're from the benefits, sure ye can see the state I'm in. What's that oul biddy from next door been saying? I could tell you a few things about her too." Paul seemed to shrink into the chair.

"Look, pal, I'm not from the benefits either. I'm investigating a cold case." Malcolm rested his elbows on his knees. Despite the walking stick, it was clear that

174

Paul had overstated his disability for the benefits claim. There was no sign of a wheelchair for a start. Not that it was unusual. Malcolm had come across many that over-emphasised their disability in order to get the meagre amount that was on offer.

Paul started to rise from his chair. "Fuck's sake. A peeler? I've been as clean as a whistle these long years. You can just..."

"Whoa now." Malcolm held up both hands, palms out. "You were a witness to this case. I'm just going over the witness statements and visiting to see if there's anything else." He shrugged his shoulders. "A bit of a long shot, but somebody has to do it."

Paul looked... was it puzzled, or worried? Malcolm wasn't sure.

"What case?" Paul asked.

"The Mulholland murder. You were the drayman that day. Do ye remember?"

There was an almost imperceptible pause. But it was there. "Aye. Suppose." Paul stopped, his lips tight.

"Just tell me what you remember. It must have been a wile shock." Malcolm waited.

A longer pause and then, "I was there, but in the stockroom. Must have got to the pub about fifteen minutes before it all kicked off. I told them back then. Saw nothing. Heard nothing. The walls were dead thick. Check it out for yourself. You've wasted your time coming to see me." Paul clasped his hands together. His left leg was trembling.

"Where were you delivering from?" Malcolm asked. His questions were having an effect, that much was sure.

This man knew more.

Paul frowned. "From the normal place. The brewery lorry came down from Belfast, stopped at the depot, just off the Ballygawley roundabout, and us draymen took whatever'd been ordered for the pub."

"That's great, Paul. All I need to know. Thanks for your time, and I hope ye get those windows done soon." Malcolm stood up to leave. Paul let out a breath.

They reached the door, Paul still leaning heavily on his walking stick, but now holding it in his left hand.

"So, Paul – it's all right if I call you Paul?"

Paul nodded.

"You've always lived round here?"

"Mostly, on and off."

"Ever heard of a man called Tobin? Had a farm machinery hire place around here."

Paul's eyes narrowed. "No," he snapped.

Malcolm cocked his head to one side. Paul clearly seemed under pressure.

"You sure?" asked Malcolm. "Seems he had a big business here for a long time. Funny you never heard of him. Look, if you do remember him, or anything else that might help me, can you ring me? Here."

Malcolm reached into his coat pocket and pulled out a notepad and pen and wrote down his mobile number and the landline. "My numbers."

He held out the ripped page to Paul, who snatched it and threw it onto a side table. Then straightened from his stoop and pulled the door open with a force that his previous posture and mobility belied. "I think I've given you enough of my time. Goodbye."

As the door was slammed behind Malcolm, he heard a mobile phone ring. Too far away to be his. He walked to the front window and peered in. Paul was standing with his back to the window, holding a phone to his ear, the walking stick nowhere near him.

"What the fuck is going on? First no money, then some fucking eejit asking me questions. And now, a visit from the peelers!" Paul shouted. There was a pause and then, louder, "Why the fuck would I say anything to anybody after all this time?" Another pause, longer this time. "Right. OK. Just get the money here. I'll sort it." His voice was now a degree calmer. He threw the phone onto the armchair and left the room. No walking stick needed.

CHAPTER TWENTY-TWO

Malcolm chuckled to himself as he drove out of Augher and reached the main road to Ballygawley. Two visits today and both of them had caused upsets. That Paul McGonigle seemed a slippery character. His walking difficulties seemed to come and go, and why so angry about money not arriving? And from whom? Was his other visitor that Canadian who had been bothering Pat Gallagher? Or maybe the young fella that had given Hannah a hard time? The names of Mulholland and Tobin were definitely linked. But how and why? Oh yes, a bit of stirring was always good. Got the game on the go again.

Paul McGonigle was right about one thing. It would be good to check out Kealey's pub. Bit late in the day – thirty years too late – but an investigation was never complete without a visit to the scene of the crime. Malcolm's best guess was that the pub wouldn't have changed too much. Not many of them had around here. Change was never seen as too much of a good thing in these parts.

He pulled into a bus stop and looked at his notes left on the passenger seat. He punched the postcode of the pub into the satnav, and was surprised at the route suggested. He would have thought the best way would have been through Omagh, but no. This bloody satnav had other ideas. Malcolm sighed and completed a quick U-turn to drive back towards Ballygawley. A left turn had him once again travelling long single-carriage country lanes, with metaphoric fingers crossed there would be few others on this road. The satnav told him it would be just twenty minutes to his destination – it felt a lot longer.

He had just got to the top of what could at a push be called a hill, when he saw, on the right-hand side of the road, a boarded-up entrance with a faded sign. He pulled to the side of the road. The weather had clearly done its best to damage the sign over the years, but the wording was just about legible – Tobin's Machine Hire. The wind had torn down part of the wood covering the gates. Beyond them Malcolm could see the remnants of a large outhouse. The corrugated roof had come loose and was hanging over the side of the building. Behind that was a detached two storey double fronted house, typical of the farmhouses in the area. A little too far away to see if it was lived in but, given the rest of what Malcolm could see he very much doubted it.

As well as keeping the family firm on, albeit in a dormant state, George Tobin might also have kept the family homestead. But that would have been a hell of a sentiment after all these years. The heavy-duty chains, padlocks and bolts would make it impossible to get in, and Malcolm had nothing with him to even try.

He drove on, tapping the steering wheel in time to Philomena's dulcet tones. It helped him think. She always did. There was no evidence that Tobin had anything to do with the Mulholland murder, no mention in any of the documents either William or Kevin managed to get access to. So why did Malcolm have a gut feeling that it was all linked? Surely it was just a coincidence, the Tobin place being on the way to Kealey's pub through these back lanes?

He pulled into the car park of the deserted pub. The signage was in marginally better condition than the one at the Tobin place. A "For Sale" sign was attached to one of the boarded windows. Not being sold as a going concern, then. In front of the pub, a man brushed away blown branches from the entrance. He didn't look up.

Malcolm got out of his car and called, "Excuse me?"

No response. The man carried on sweeping. There seemed despondency in his slow strokes. He was bent over, concentrating on the ground. Malcolm walked up and tapped him on the shoulder.

The man jumped. "Jesus fecking Christ!" He was shorter than Malcolm and thin. Grey-haired with a comb-over that was lifting in the wind. He was maybe around seventy, and not a well-looking man at all.

"Sorry. I did shout."

The man squinted at him and cupped his hand to his ear. "Eh? What did ye say? Hang on." He fiddled at his ear and there was a whistling sound. "Bloody thing." He fiddled again and the whistling stopped. "That's better. What did you say?"

"Sorry if I frightened yeh."

"I turn the damn thing off most of the time." He gestured to his ear and the beige, old-fashioned-looking hearing aid attached to it. "The other one is completely gone. Makes for a peaceful life." He gave a half-grin.

"You looking to buy this place?" he asked hopefully.

"No. I'm investigating a murder that happened here." Malcolm pulled his coat around him to keep out the cold wind.

"A murder? I think you've got lost. There's been no murder here. I check on the place every day."

"A murder that happened about thirty years ago. A man called Mulholland?"

The man frowned, turned away and started his slow sweeping again. "I hear coppers are getting slow, but after thirty-four years you're checking it out? Huh."

Malcolm walked around to stand in front of the man. "It's a cold case review. And you are?"

"Tony."

"Would that be Tony Muldoon?"

Tony stopped brushing, leant on the broom handle and peered at Malcolm through narrowed eyes. "What do you want?"

Malcolm shrugged. "Just checking some facts, that's all."

"Check away," replied Tony, still peering at him.

Malcolm was now getting chilled to the bone. "Any chance we can go in there?" He nodded towards the building.

Tony walked towards the dilapidated pub and reached into his pocket. Malcolm heard the jangling of keys.

"This place been closed long?" Malcolm asked as Tony sorted through the keys on his keyring.

"Bout three years. But in my view, it was the Good Friday Agreement that did for this place."

"How so?" asked Malcolm.

Tony put a key in the lock and yanked at it. It wouldn't turn. He pulled the handle towards him with a jolt and tried again. This time it worked.

"That's got it. After the agreement there was no need for this place. No need for a place to do quiet business."

Just as well, thought Malcolm. "I can see that would have an effect on the business. The place carried on for quite some time though."

Tony snorted. "Aye, I suppose the boss hoped the whole peace thing would collapse and normal business would resume."

Malcolm looked around. Perhaps business would have improved if a bit of investment had been made. The décor and furnishing were certainly 1980s. A smell of building decay hung in the air. Tony indicated a nearby table. Malcolm wiped the dust of the chair with his hand and sat down.

"So, what's the interest now?" asked Tony.

"Och, ye know. The old retrospective investigations."

Tony frowned and studied Malcolm. "I thought that was more to do with the British Army. Yeh know, the oppressors."

Malcolm wasn't there to argue past politics. He shook his head. "That's for the press. We're looking at all sorts. So… Tony. I understand you were here that day, when Trevor Mulholland was killed?"

Tony sighed. "I was."

"And?"

"It was over in a flash. I was with the drayman when it all happened. Out the back. Saw nothing. Heard nothing." He studied his hands.

It was the second time that day Malcolm had heard that phrase, saw nothing, heard nothing. "Ah yes. The drayman. Paul McGonigle, wasn't it? Bit of a character, from what I've heard."

"Bit of a dick, more like."

"Sounds like yeh didn't get on."

"He wasn't in the job long. He was never in any job long. From what I remember, he started the drayman job just after he was sacked from Tobin's place. And the boss wasn't too happy about the likes of him being here at all. Could have been a spy for the other lot. There was talk he was linked to the UVF." Tony spat on the floor.

Another link. Another piece of the jigsaw. Malcolm was getting closer to finding out how it fitted together. "Why was he sacked from the Tobin business?"

"Never heard. God knows why Tobin gave McGonigle a job in the first place. He was certainly hopeless as a drayman. Never on time. Stuff always missing from the order. None of us were comfortable with him around. With his connections."

"What did you see that day?" asked Malcolm.

"As I said, for the most part nothing. I did feel wile sorry for the bloke Mulholland was with. I'll never forget the state he was in." Tony shook his head. "He seemed to be a dacent sort."

Malcolm shifted in his seat. "Tony, why did Mulholland have that amount of cash with him? Was he meant to be meeting someone?"

Tony squinted and adjusted his hearing aid. "Let's pretend that you have a hearing aid too. And that it's turned off. Or else my memory has just turned to mush."

"Go on."

"That Mulholland was a regular. Not just at the bar – meeting people, too. But I was surprised he was there that day. I'd got word when a deal was going on. To make sure they had peace and quiet. But there was no word that day. Just Mulholland rocking up with a fat envelope. I thought there might have been a breakdown in the usual communication – there hadn't been before, but stuff happens. And it was a busy time for the volunteers."

Malcolm stayed quiet. But it hurt. The volunteers from both sides had caused so much pain and destruction back then.

"I had to improvise," Tony went on. "Just lucky for me that prick McGonigle turned up and I had to go out to the back to let him in. So I didn't have to lie. I really didn't see anything. Well, not much anyway. I came back into the bar when I heard the shots, and the shooter was on his way out by then."

"The money?" asked Malcolm.

"It was there, it was definitely there, and then it was gone."

"Gone where?"

"Could have been any of the fuckers. Not that chap who came with Mulholland, poor sod." Tony sniggered. "And obviously not Mulholland himself."

"Who, then?"

"Could have been that police constable or the DI. You could tell he was a git."

Malcolm glanced down briefly. DI Robinson would have had an opportunity. He looked up at Tony again.

"What about the gunman – did ye recognize him?"

Tony stood up. "Look, pal, all that's gone now. The volunteers are either dead, gone down south or in a nursing home."

"Tony, relax. Like I said, it's a cold-case review. Ye know yourself no one has an appetite for raking over coals. I just need to fill in some details, for my own peace of mind."

Tony cleared his throat. "Look, nothing gets back to me? There's still some about that would hold a grudge. Call me a grass. And that never ends well."

Malcolm shook his head and held out his hands. "Look, no notepad. Nothing gets back to yeh."

Tony stared at Malcolm for a few seconds, then rubbed the back of his neck and sat down again. "The shooter, that was strange an' all. He must have been from another brigade. Like from away. Maybe Belfast? I know he was masked, but ye can still recognise people. The way they walk or whatever." He shook his head. "But I didn't recognise that shooter at all."

"Was there any chat about it afterwards?"

Again, Tony shook his head. "Not a peep to me. I was too low down in the pecking order. But there were some heated discussions in the back room with some of the local big boys getting wile upset. Got the impression they were blaming each other." He shrugged. "Not great business sense when ye think of it, shooting the cash cow. That Mulholland was known for delivering when asked."

So, no claims for responsibility, no advanced warning to the pub to clear the decks, and the shooter not from the local battalion. Not to mention the poor business decision. That opened up the possibility the shooter might not have been from any battalion.

"Thanks, Tony. That was really helpful."

"Was it? God knows how."

"Look, if anything else comes to mind, ring me." Malcolm pushed a slip of paper with his two numbers on it towards Tony.

Tony took the scrap of paper. "PSNI cutting back? Not much of a calling card."

"Something like that. Just one other thing." Malcolm gestured at their surroundings. "Why are you still here? I mean, the place is finished."

Tony brushed at the table with the flat of his hand as if cleaning it. "You won't understand, but this place – I had a home here. Better than in my own home. Feck sake, it's just that I loved the place, loved the work. Loved the craic. Aw, bollocks."

As Malcolm walked out of the derelict pub, he reflected that he knew just what Tony Muldoon meant.

CHAPTER TWENTY-THREE

Tommy slammed the front door behind him and reached up to his tie. There was a rip as he pulled at it. He threw the torn tie on the floor. Much bloody good dressing up like a prat had done. That receptionist bloke had definitely sneered at him, stuck up prick. And Tommy didn't believe that man Tobin hadn't been in. A completely wasted journey.

Everyone was hiding something. That stupid social worker with her snobby English accent. That Paul McGonigle lying through his fucking teeth. Only Jeff had given any information and even then, Tommy had to threaten him to get anywhere.

He sat at his dining table and surveyed the paperwork. He pushed it this way and that. Then he grabbed it and ripped it all to shreds. He held his head in his hands, elbows resting on the table. He was going to explode. He reached for his wrist band but there was nothing but bare skin.

He poured whiskey into a mug. Neat. He took a swig. It made him wince, but the burning in his throat led to warmth spreading through him and he was able to take a deep breath. Slow it down. Think. That's what he needed to do. Yes, there had been doors shut to him but Jeff's door remained slightly ajar, and his da had always said it was better to push at a half-open door than to try to break down one that was shut. Maybe with a bit more persuasion Jeff would cough up more information.

* * *

Tommy knocked hard on Jeff's door. No sound came from within. A harder knock, his knuckles stinging. Still no answer. Tommy drew his breath to shout. A tap on his shoulder made him pause. He turned to see a vaguely familiar woman of around sixty wearing a housecoat, thin carpet slippers and a woolly beanie hat, wisps of steel hair poking out around the edges.

"You looking for Jeff?"

"Yes." Tommy bent down to shout through the letterbox, "Open up, ye old bastard."

"I'm his neighbour. Had to call the ambulance last night. You'll have to shout brave and loud for him to hear ye in the Royal."

Fuck's sake. What next? "What's wrong with him?"

"Huh. Sounds like you're wile concerned." The woman shrugged her shoulders and turned to go into the next-door terraced house.

Tommy grabbed her arm. "I said, what's wrong with him?"

"Oww…" She tried but failed to shake off his hand. "Since you've asked so politely. It's his heart. That's all I know."

Tommy dropped her arm and she stepped away. She shouted as she closed her front door.

"I know you. You're Tommy Smith. Everyone round here knows what you're like. You're a disgrace to your ma and da!" The door slammed shut before Tommy could attempt to reply.

Everyone knew what Tommy Smith was like? They knew fuck all. He picked up an empty bottle that the woman had left out for the milkman and smashed it on her front doorstep.

* * *

"I'm looking for Jeff Henry. He was admitted last night. I'm his nephew."

The nurse at the desk of the Medical Assessment Unit of the Royal Victoria Hospital smiled sympathetically at Tommy. "Let me check." Her index finger slid down the list of names on the page. Another smile, this time sadder. "He's been transferred to high dependency. Go left when you get to the end of this corridor. That's where the lifts are. Third floor. The nurses there will help you."

Tommy walked so quickly it might have been described as jogging. He pushed past a young couple to get into the first lift. High dependency wasn't good. He knew where the ward was. The same place his da had been before he died.

Tommy checked the side rooms as he walked into the ward. He stopped at a windowed bay. There was the small figure of Jeff, tubes into and out of him. Tommy had never seen him so shrunken, so vulnerable. So beyond any use.

"You are?" A male nurse had arrived beside Tommy. He had short hair, clear blue eyes and chiselled features. Tommy was angry with himself for noticing.

"He's not in good shape," the nurse said softly.

"Jesus!" Tommy slammed his hand on the window glass.

The nurse looked at him sadly. "I know it's a difficult time. He's not conscious, but he's not in pain or distressed."

"That's good," lied Tommy. What good was Jeff to him unconscious? "Can I go in?" Might just be able to rouse him. Get even a sliver of information from him. Before it was too late.

"Sorry, no." The nurse shook his head slowly. "If he gets through the next twelve hours, then maybe..."

Tommy turned on his heel and walked out of the ward. Walked out of the hospital. Kept walking. On Botanic Avenue he paused outside one of those trendy student pubs, just down from Queen's University. He realised he was still wearing the blue suit. Good enough to be acceptable here.

Tommy sat in a quiet corner of the bar, nursing the over-priced beer. Jeff was no use to him now. He pulled out his phone. Scrolled down to a contact his so-called father had insisted he kept. The old network was still available. Long dead, and lying bastard though he was, the old man's name could still pull in a few favours. There was a plan formulating in Tommy's mind – and some new documents were going to be needed. A passport and bank account in a false name would do for starters. He dialled the number and explained his requirements.

It was after the third or maybe fourth whisky – he couldn't remember – when he knew what he needed to do this evening. He knew where to go, where the club was. He'd been a few times, but never plucked up the courage to do anything but sit and watch others dancing, touching, then leave. That was back when he was trying to work things out, think things through. When his mother was still alive, when there would have been greater consequences. Now? He didn't give a fuck.

* * *

The club was off the main street in the Cathedral Quarter. When the bouncer stopped him and gave him a cursory search, Tommy laughed. He didn't need any weapons.

The bouncer stepped back and studied Tommy, "You some sort of nutter?"

Tommy stopped laughing, but kept the smile. It felt tight on his face. Tonight was going to be good. "Naw, pal. Just happy. No problem in being happy is there?"

The bouncer smiled back. "Go in and enjoy yourself, pal."

Tommy ordered a Peroni and sat at the back of the club in a semicircle booth. It gave the best view of the bar, where the single fuckers perched. It didn't take long to spot him. Slim and neatly dressed in smart casual. Nervous. Sipping his lager, not drinking it. Checking out the room, but too scared to make eye contact. Like Tommy used to do. He picked up the Peroni bottle and walked to the bar. Slim Jim had his back to him, elbows on the bar, turning his lager round and round.

"Anyone sitting here?"

The man started and turned towards Tommy. "No."

Tommy could see the concern in his eyes. He knew what he was feeling. Not sure if he was brave enough to take the next step. Tommy sat on the bar stool with his back to the bar, his elbow on the counter. "Not too many here tonight."

The man kept looking forward, determinedly focused on the display of spirits behind the bar. "Naw. I mean, isn't there? I don't come here usually."

Tommy smiled at him. "Sure you don't." He turned and mirrored the man's posture.

"The name's Sammy." Tommy held out his hand. "And you are?"

The man stared at Tommy's hand for a second and then shook it. "Josh."

"Josh? Like The Joshua Tree?"

"Not really." Josh nervously smiled back. "Me ma was wile keen on the Joshua in the Bible story."

Tommy held onto Josh's hand a moment more, then released it. "I guess your ma wouldn't be too keen about you being here." He gestured around the room with his Peroni bottle.

"No." Josh's reply was so quiet Tommy could barely hear him.

Tommy slapped him on the back. "Well, you're here now." He waved his now empty bottle at the barman. "Hey, pal, same again here for me and young Josh."

* * *

Afterwards, Tommy stood back and looked down, disgusted, at Josh's unconscious body lying in a foetal position amongst the bins at the back of the club.

It had taken only three more pints for Josh to relax enough to be persuaded to leave with Tommy, who had put an arm firmly around him as they went through the main door. The bouncer had the decency to look away. Josh had been small enough and weak enough for Tommy to drag to the back of the club and kick the living shit out of him. Every kick into Josh's soft body felt good. Felt like he was kicking away the part of him that had made everything go wrong.

Tommy stood with his hands on his hips for a while, surveying his handiwork. The fucker was breathing – bubbles of blood had appeared at his nose and his legs were twitching, jerking. Time to go.

CHAPTER TWENTY-FOUR

At the petrol station on the Omagh road Malcolm grabbed a sandwich from the "food to go" section. This was one thing he didn't miss about working for the PSNI: crap petrol-station food to satisfy the hunger pains but not the appetite. He sat in the car outside the final address on his list, trying not to get crumbs on his suit, and grimacing as he washed down the sandwich with the brown liquid the petrol station had the cheek to call coffee. He looked at his watch. 4.05pm. She'd be there soon. He'd better get a move on.

The street off the main road through Seskinore was a line of terraced houses, most of which appeared well looked after. Except the one Malcolm was waiting on Hannah to enter. The top street-facing windows were almost black with dirt that had accumulated over the years from the passing cars. One of them was boarded up. The street-level windows were nearly as bad. Paint had peeled off the front door. Malcolm could at least see some curtains hanging haphazardly.

A knock on the car window made him jump and almost spill his coffee. Hannah smiled at him through the glass.

"Jesus, ye frightened the life out of me!" He opened the window and smiled back.

Hannah looked at her watch. "We're late."

"Only five minutes or so, and you're a busy woman." Malcolm held up his disposable coffee cup. "Catching up with a bit of hydration." He put the cup in the cup holder and got out of the car.

Hannah frowned as they made their way over to the house. "No, it's not that. It's just that Elizabeth doesn't cope with changes to plans."

Malcolm checked his watch again. "But it's only five minutes."

Hannah shrugged. "Sometimes that's all it takes."

Malcolm raised his hand to knock on the front door.

"Malcolm, you've got to let me lead this."

He dropped his hand and took a small step back. "Of course. Whatever you say."

"This woman isn't very well. If that Tommy Smith turns out to be her son... when I think of the treatment she's had over the last three decades... There might be a lot of repair work. We have to take this slowly."

The door opened a crack in response to Hannah's knock. A thin, birdlike face peeped out at them past the door chain.

"Elizabeth, it's Hannah. Can you let me in? I've brought someone to meet you."

"You're late!"

The door slammed shut. Malcolm was relieved to hear the sound of the chain being undone. The door opened slowly to reveal a pile of junk mail and brown envelopes pushed to one side. Malcolm followed Hannah down a hallway with a lino floor cluttered with a small, battered suitcase, a pile of clothes that may have been on the way to a washing machine, and a vacuum cleaner used as a coat stand. The terraced house was similar in size to Paul McGonigle's, but that's where the comparison ended. Elizabeth Tobin's home was poor, tired and cluttered.

Elizabeth was already in her sitting room, curled up in an old faded armchair with a back cushion that had partway collapsed through regular use. Hannah made for a settee on the opposite side of the room but had to push some blankets aside so that she and Malcolm could sit down.

"You sleeping down here again?" Hannah asked Elizabeth. "It's much better for you to sleep in your bed."

Elizabeth shrugged her shoulders in reply and folded her arms.

"How have you been keeping? Did you manage to go to the day centre?"

"Naw. Full of oul people," replied Elizabeth.

Malcolm was willing to bet there wouldn't be many there that looked older than this woman, with her lined face, her long grey hair tied back with a plastic band at the nape of her neck. Elizabeth's grey cardigan that she wrapped around her thin frame drew even more colour from her. Malcolm admired Hannah's patience even more than he had before. He could not do her job.

"That's a shame," Hannah said. "Maybe if I took you one time?"

"If you want. What's he here for?" Elizabeth nodded towards Malcolm. "Another psychiatrist trying to work me out?"

Hannah smiled. "No. he's... he's looking into some historical crimes."

"A peeler?" Elizabeth's voice started to rise. "I've done nothing. Hannah, you know…"

Hannah quickly went over to her and knelt at the side of her chair. She placed her hand on Elizabeth's arm and looked up into her face.

"Elizabeth, listen to me. He just would like to speak to you. About your daughter, Liza. Would that be OK?"

Elizabeth's eyes darted in Malcolm's direction and then she returned her gaze to Hannah. "OK."

Hannah turned to Malcolm. "What would you like to ask?"

"Elizabeth," Malcolm said quietly. "I don't want to upset you, so we can stop whenever you want."

Elizabeth kept her gaze on Hannah and said, as if replying to her, "Yes. Stop anytime."

"Can you tell me about Liza?"

There were tears building in Elizabeth's eyes but she smiled. "Liza was beautiful and clever and funny and I loved her." She shook her head. "But she shouldn't have gone that night. Not as far as Ballygawley. I shouldn't have let her go. She begged me. Said it wasn't fair, everyone was going. All her friends. A friend's dad would give her a lift home from the disco. She never came home."

The tears were now falling freely down Elizabeth's cheeks. Hannah reached for her hand and squeezed it gently.

"She was only fifteen. They found her in the quarry." Elizabeth looked up at Malcolm. "Who would leave her in a quarry? Who?"

Malcolm didn't know what to say to this woman. "Elizabeth, what happened afterwards? I mean after Liza died?"

"Afterwards?" Elizabeth's voice grew louder. "There was no afterwards. Nothing." She gestured at the room. "All these years, I'm just waiting to die!"

"Elizabeth," Hannah said, trying to draw the woman's attention. "Was there another child?"

Elizabeth snatched her hand away from Hannah and looked down into her lap. "No. No. I'm not falling for that. You're trying to trick me." She looked from Hannah to Malcolm in fear. "I'm not going in again."

"I promise this isn't a trick," Hannah said softly. "No hospital. I just want to know."

Elizabeth's tears started again and she rocked back and fore, her chin on her chest.

"Elizabeth, you can tell me. It'll be OK," Hannah assured her.

There was a silence and then... "They took him away. First, they hid me in the house. Wasn't allowed to go out. Then they took him from me." Elizabeth's words fell over themselves as if a dam had burst.

"Who hid you?" asked Hannah.

Elizabeth looked up at her in surprise. "My parents, of course. They kept me in their house. Didn't let me out." She looked down again. "They're gone now."

She started to pick at the sleeve of her cardigan. Her actions became quicker. She stared into the distance, her body rocking, almost imperceptibly at first, then growing ever quicker.

Hannah looked at Malcolm. "I think that's all we can expect from Elizabeth today." She turned to Elizabeth and gave the sobbing woman a hug. "You've done great.

Malcolm's going to go now, and you and I are going to have a cup of tea. I'm going to stay a while."

Malcolm stood. Parts of this story were beginning to fit, but he had a guess that needed to be confirmed. "Can I ask just one more question?"

Hannah shook her head. "Not about the child."

"It's not," assured Malcolm. "Elizabeth, have you a brother?"

The sobbing stopped immediately. Elizabeth looked up, her eyes wide, her knuckles white as she gripped the side of her chair. "No. No brother."

There was no sadness in her eyes now, but there was something else there. Was it fear?

* * *

Malcolm rang Harriet to let her know he was on the way home. Should be there in two hours, if there wasn't too much traffic on the way. Irish stew and a wee slice of wheaten was waiting for him. He was very pleased to be heading home to Portrush. Although, if he was honest enough with himself, the first three calls of the day had been enjoyable, that last one with Hannah had been harrowing. Malcolm was much more comfortable with hoods and criminals. You knew where you stood with them.

Once more, Hannah had gone up in his estimation. Malcolm was more certain than ever he couldn't have done her job. She had clearly a huge amount of work to do with that woman who had lived a life with such loss and a story no one believed.

The road towards Portrush was quiet. Philomena sang and helped him think. Mulholland's murder looked less and less like a paramilitary operation. Like Tony Muldoon had said, why would they kill the man that was funding them? Neither side of the conflict was that stupid.

Malcolm needed more information. He pulled into the next lay-by and fished his phone from his pocket. He scrolled down and found Sean Cahill's name. As he pressed the call button, Philomena stopped singing and the sound of a ringtone filled the car.

"Jesus H Christ!"

Then Malcolm remembered. The last time that William had visited, the lad had hooked up Malcolm's phone to the car's system, God knew how. Some trick that Malcolm neither knew nor cared about. He saw Sean Cahill's name on the screen in the middle of the dashboard, which he usually didn't much bother with. The one that offered all sorts of information about the car and the journey that didn't make the journey quicker or easier. The ringtone was replaced with Sean's voice.

"Bell, what about yeh?"

"Aye I'm doing all right. Yourself?"

"Struggling on," Sean said. "Filling my days with this and that. Retirement's hard work. I spend most of my time avoiding doing repairs about the house. Anyway, this a social call, Bell? Not like you."

"Listen, I'm checking out a cold case. One you'd remember."

"Jesus, they're not that desperate they're getting yeh back into uniform?"

Malcolm smiled. They would need to let out the seams of his uniform he used to wear, big time. "Naw, just doing a favour for a friend. Do yeh remember the Mulholland murder? In Kealey's pub?"

"Oh aye. That's the one they tried to say was a paramilitary murder but neither side would claim responsibility for it?"

"That's the one. Have you still got contacts in work?"

"Course I bloody do! Hah, they were begging me to stay when I retired. God knows how they're managing without me. Why d'yeh ask?"

Malcolm smiled again. He would bet his last pound Sean Cahill's boss would have been as pleased as his that he was retiring. Being bloody-minded was a trait they had in common. "Do yeh think you could find out if your lot ever did nail it on one of the paramilitaries in the end, even if they didn't have enough to hand over to the RUC?"

"What's this? Disturb the peace of my retirement would yeh, yeh cheeky bar steward? Suppose I could try. But it's a bit far back. I'll need to call in a good few favours."

Malcolm could hear the pretend reluctance in Sean's voice. But there was interest there too. "It would be wile decant of yeh, Sean. Make a big difference to my friend. Sure, I had to come to the best." Bit of flattery would swing it.

"Aye, all right then." Sean laughed. "Anyway, it'll give me another excuse for tomorrow. She has me down to wash out the guttering of the house and I'm getting stuck for ideas to get out of it."

Malcolm pulled out of the lay-by and carried on towards Portrush. Philomena's song about an ill-treated woman had him back to thinking about Elizabeth Tobin. Why had she lied about having a brother? Of course, he could ask Emily or Kevin to check the birth register to absolutely confirm it, but he was sure the woman had lied to him. Lied because she was frightened.

CHAPTER TWENTY-FIVE

Tommy woke to the sound of the first bus of the day passing his house. He hadn't made it to bed but had drifted to sleep on the settee in a whiskey-fuelled haze. He sat up, stretching out the stiffness in his body. His head hurt. His tongue was dry. He looked down at his blood-soaked shirt and trousers. And remembered.

He knew the neighbours would be unhappy about a fire in the back garden at this time of the morning. But he also knew they wouldn't complain. Wouldn't dare. Tommy pulled the brazier out of the shed at the back of the garden. He knew how to set a good fire. His father had showed him. Dried leaves to act as kindle. One firelighter, small sticks on top. Then, once it got going, larger sticks and logs.

But that was in the past. Tommy had no time for the past or that man who had lied to him all his life. No time for anything he had told him. He threw his bloodied shirt and trousers into the brazier and sprinkled petrol from the can kept to fuel the lawnmower. When he lit and threw the match into the clothes, the garments caught immediately. He poked them into the centre of the fire to make sure they burnt. That prick from last night would probably be too embarrassed, too afraid, to go to the police, but it was best to make sure there was no evidence.

It had felt good last night. Kicking the shit out of the man he had been, once. But now? Nothing had changed. He didn't know who or what he was, and the anger burning a hole inside him just kept getting worse. He knew there must be answers in Tyrone, but every bloody attempt he had made had ended in nothing. That Paul McGonigle knew something, Tommy was sure, but he didn't even know where the man lived. Couldn't be far from that pub on the Omagh–Ballygawley road. Paul didn't have money, so he wouldn't be able to afford to go any distance in a taxi. Still that area had more sheep than people. That barman might know something, but Tommy knew the type. No way would he give out information, and the size of him would make it unlikely Tommy could use any of his usual forms of persuasion. He could try that social worker another time, but, again he had come across them before. All regulations and rules.

So, who? He flipped open his smart phone. The news app popped up automatically.

News. Newspaper. That was it. A local journalist.

They definitely weren't all regulation and rules, not in Tommy's experience. He remembered the ones that came to the door to talk to his da when he was a youngster. He was never allowed in to hear what was being said, but there was always a bit more money to spare in the house when they'd left.

He googled newspapers in Tyrone and picked one from the results. He rang the number and asked to be put through to a journalist.

"Hello, Alfie Hamill. How can I help you?"

"Hi, I was wondering if... I mean do you do, like, investigative stuff?"

Silence.

"Hello? Are yeh there?"

"We can do." Another pause. Then, "Look, is this some sort of wind up? You've rung the Tyrone Chronicle. We're more birth, deaths, marriages and a few punch-ups at the council meetings."

"Well, if you're not interested!" Who was this plank he was talking to? This had been a bad idea.

"No, now houl your horses. Not so fast. What's this all about?"

"I think," Tommy said, "I mean, I believe that I was subject to an illegal adoption thirty-four years ago."

"You were what? Like the convent scandals?"

Tommy had a strong impression he had this man's full attention now. "No, not a convent job. It might have been arranged by a man local to Ballygawley."

"Go on."

"Naw, not until ye meet me."

"OK, when? We're a bit busy here today. We go to press tomorrow. What about, say, Friday?"

"If you want the story, you'll see me today." Tommy wasn't waiting anymore.

A pause. "All right. Today. When shall I expect yeh?"

"Couple of hours." Tommy slammed the phone down.

Wherever this was leading him, he wasn't going to finish until he got the answers he was looking for. He looked around the room. This used to be his home. Not now. Tommy was disconnected from it. It was a place he used to know, when everything made sense to him.

What was he going to get from this journalist, Alfie Hamill? Tommy knew he was born near Ballygawley to someone who didn't want him. He was connected to a man called Tobin. Was that his father? Or was Tobin just the man who arranged favours when there was inconvenience? That Paul McGonigle knew more, that was for sure. He'd been involved in the volunteers, but not a central man – some crap driver, if Jeff was to be believed. But who could he believe, when everyone had lied to him?

Tommy grabbed the empty whiskey bottle from the table and threw it at the wall. It shattered over the floor. He stared at the pieces of glass but had no inclination to pick them up. Why should he? This house was now meaningless to him.

He packed more clothes for this trip. The gun was still securely in the bottom of the bag. It just felt right to have it there. He determined not to come back to his home city until he had the answers he was looking for. Whatever it took.

* * *

Tommy made better time than the two hours he had suggested to Alfie Hamill. The newspaper office was in the middle of the town, with a large window at the front. Maybe its location was useful, to catch the town gossip. Tommy pushed open the main door and the ring of a bell announced his arrival.

Three people. One man, and two women. A counter stretched the width of the room, separating Tommy from them. No corporate shiny office here. There was even the distinct smell of cigarette smoke, despite large No Smoking signs on the pale green walls.

The man looked up. He was in his late fifties, maybe early sixties, slight, wearing a tired-looking cardigan. His face was lined, his hair short. He got to his feet and approached the counter.

"Can I help you?"

"You Hamill, the man I was talking to on the phone?"

The man smiled and leant on the counter. "Aye. That's me. You never mentioned your name."

Tommy hesitated. It didn't feel right to give information so soon, but if he wanted the truth... "Tommy Smith."

"Pleased to meet you, Mr Smith."

Tommy ignored the outstretched hand. "Can we talk in private?" He could see the two women paying more attention to him than he liked.

Alfie frowned for a second, then smiled again. He lifted the hinged section of the counter and stood to one side to let Tommy through. "We have an interview room at the back. Mostly used for the bereaved when they want us to do an obituary piece. You know how it is – it can take some time and tears."

Tommy followed Alfie to the small office. He felt the eyes of the two women burn into him as he walked past them.

Alfie gestured for Tommy to sit at one side of a battered desk. "Coffee? Tea"

"Naw." Tommy studied Alfie. "Look, I haven't much time. I need someone to do a bit of digging. I've met journalists before. I know you lot can get information that others can't. But to be honest, I'm not too sure you're the man to do it." He gestured around him. "I mean you look like an amateur operation."

"Now just hold on a minute." Alfie sat up straight. "We might be small, but this paper goes back over a hundred years. If you're looking for local knowledge, you couldn't come to a better place. And I've done some very extensive investigative work. I'm well known for it in these parts."

Tommy looked at the dark-haired, washed-out man with the hopeful look in his eyes. His heyday must have been some time ago. But local knowledge was what he needed just now. "All right. Like I said on the phone, I was adopted. But my adoptive parents are both dead."

Alfie frowned. "Sorry to hear that. But aren't there official ways of getting that information? Through social workers and that?"

Tommy slammed his hand on the desk, making Alfie jump. "Don't you think I've tried that? Apparently, it takes time. I don't have time."

"You mean you're... Jesus, I'm wile sorry..."

It took Tommy a moment to figure out what Alfie meant. This could work to his advantage. "Shocking, isn't it, that they wouldn't help? But that's not all. I believe the adoption wasn't done right."

Alfie rested his elbows on the desk. "Go on."

"I understand that the correct procedures weren't followed, and for all I know money may have exchanged hands, or I may be linked to someone of importance."

Tommy couldn't think of anything else to embellish his story, but he could see it might be enough.

Alfie licked his lips and ran a hand through his hair. "A scandal involving the local government that led to a son being torn away from his parents. A son whose time..."

Tommy wasn't sure if Alfie was reiterating his story or formulating a headline for the paper. "That's about it, he said, looking down at his fingernails in what he hoped would pass for sadness. "I have a son myself, and I just want to be able to tell him... you know, before it's too late."

"Right, Tommy – OK if I call yeh Tommy?" Alfie took out a notepad and pen.

Tommy nodded.

"So," Alfie said, "what do ye know? Ye seemed to have made some inroads if ye have got this far."

Tommy smiled in relief. Alfie had gone for it hook, line and sinker. Progress at last. "I have two names. The first is Paul McGonigle."

Alfie wrote the name down. "What's his link?"

Tommy still wasn't sure, but he had to give this clown something that fitted with the story. "He may be a relative. His name was mentioned by my adoptive parents once. I just don't know where he lives. But possibly near Ballygawley."

"Should be easy enough to track him down. Anyone else?"

"There was just one other name – Tobin."

"Okey dokey." Alfie wrote the name down. "How does the Tobin name fit in?"

"Again, just someone my parents mentioned. A friend of theirs from Ballygawley."

"Not the most common name, but there's a few of them about," Alfie tapped the table with his pen and focused on the wall behind Tommy. "If I recall rightly – and it's a good time ago, so I may have got this wrong – there was a farm machinery business owned by a man named Tobin. About five miles from Ballygawley." He shrugged his shoulders. "I'm talking about thirty years ago. I'll check it out. Might be linked or it might be a wild goose chase."

This country hick had told Tommy more than he realised. A farm machinery hire business near Ballygawley would be the ideal place to hide the volunteers' hardware. Plenty of space and away from prying eyes. But he needed the address. If Tobin junior had kept his old man's company, then maybe old man Tobin was still around, still living somewhere nearby.

Tommy fought to keep his expression neutral. "When do you think you'll have addresses or any other information? Sometime today?"

"That would be stretching it a bit." Alfie flicked the pen over and under his fingers in his hand. "Look, from what you've told me so far, I'm dead keen to crack on with this, but I've other responsibilities as well. The publishing train slows for no one."

Alfie was making himself sound a tad more important that the run-down office led Tommy to believe. But at this stage, he needed to keep him on side. "OK. Where would you recommend I stay, here?"

"Depends on your pocket. There are a few decent bed and breakfasts around."

Tommy wanted anonymity, not the close attention of some B and B host. "Any hotels?"

Alfie smiled. "I'm pleased to say we have an excellent one here. Oh yes. Great entertainment too. This place is quite the up-and-coming town." He closed his notepad. "Look, pal, I know you want – need – to make progress fast. Give me till tomorrow."

He gestured through the glass panel in the door to his colleagues in the next room. "Like I said, we have our deadline today, but I'll get cracking on this first thing tomorrow."

CHAPTER TWENTY-SIX

Malcolm woke still tired. That "grand tour" of the province had been productive, no doubt about that. But when he had gotten back to Portrush he had nearly fallen asleep in his stew. He had thought Harriet would be cross with him, leaving her to her own devices all day. But no. She had been very sympathetic, ushering him away to bed as soon as he'd finished the meal.

An early night and sleeping like the dead hadn't improved anything. His tiredness annoyed him. Could Harriet be right about his need to get fit? Something about strength and stamina. Perhaps he'd try that running around the park thing, or as they did it in Portrush, running on the beach. Maybe not running. A brisk walk until he got the hang of it. For now, he was content to sit in the conservatory and think things through with a cup of tea and slice of lemon drizzle cake. He had woken to the smell of it baking this morning.

George Tobin had lied and had panicked. If he was in any way related to Elizabeth Tobin, he didn't want to admit it. A quick look at the phone book confirmed there weren't many Tobins in Tyrone. Would have been different if the name was say, Johnston. Malcolm had met a fair few by that name in his career, good, bad and indifferent.

He remembered his Paul McGonigle conversation with some distaste. The man was definitely a blamer, a manipulator and probably a more practised liar than Tobin. But he, too, had been spooked by Malcolm's visit. And there was the phone call he had overheard. Someone else was involved with Paul McGonigle, that was certain. He had been reassuring someone that he would smooth things over. Well, Paul, don't make promises you might not be able to keep.

Despite Tony Muldoon's dubious past as a facilitator of meetings that shouldn't have occurred and were later denied, Malcolm had warmed to the man who loved his job as much as Malcolm had loved his. There was a kind of straightforwardness in the man that he had appreciated.

And lastly, poor Elizabeth Tobin. What sort of life had that woman experienced? If Hannah's suspicions were true, so much of it had been undeserved. Malcolm couldn't even begin to guess at the turmoil she had suffered, firstly when her daughter was murdered, and then being denied the son she knew she had. He hoped Hannah would be able to make a difference there.

Malcolm heard a familiar yapping. Not a bark, more of a playful sound. He looked at his watch. Damn. Billy's morning walk. He sighed, put down his half-eaten cake and looked around for his shoes. Then the front doorbell rang and there was more barking, this time louder.

"Come on in," he heard Harriet greet whoever it was. "Great timing. Look, Billy recognises yeh. I'll get his lead."

Malcolm dared to be hopeful. It sounded like he wouldn't be needed for walking duties. Happy days. He opened the door from the conservatory to the corridor.

Billy had his lead in his mouth and was jumping up at a kneeling Kevin.

Harriet spotted her husband. "Kevin came round yesterday. Do yeh remember he mentioned that he would like to walk Billy? Look." She pointed at Billy, who was now on his back. On his face a look of doggy ecstasy as Kevin rubbed him behind his ear. "They're getting on like a house on fire."

"Great stuff," said Malcolm. Bloody absolutely fecking fantastic stuff! Reduced or, if he was really lucky, no dog-walking duties at all in the future. Probably until Billy showed his true colours or Kevin did the usual teenage thing of moving on to another interest. Meanwhile, he wasn't going to look a gift horse in the mouth. For as long as it lasted, this was very good news indeed. "Enjoy yourself."

Kevin looked up and smiled. It suited him better than that snarl he usually wore.

"I've suggested that Kevin meets up with the Gallaghers on their usual walk at the East Strand," Harriet said. "Just in case he can't manage."

It's hardly rocket science, thought Malcolm, just as long as the lad knew to keep the lead on. Heaven forbid the bloody animal would run off and get lost. Still, no more walks, no more chewed gloves and no wee nips from the animal when Harriet wasn't looking. But that, Malcolm chastised himself, would break Harriet's heart.

He watched from the front window. Kevin had a sure spring in his step and Billy pulled at his lead, anxious to get going. Malcolm turned back to his cup of tea and half-eaten lemon drizzle cake. As he did so, he noticed a small red car drive off. He was by now very familiar with all the usual cars in his street, and not one of them was red. Grey, black, silver, but none red. He'd had always fancied having a red car. But it would have had to be a Ferrari. Pity his policeman's salary made that impossible. Never mind. There was always Harriet's lemon drizzle cake. No one could ask for better.

The next half hour was a treat. The spring sun making an appearance and streaming in through the conservatory windows. Harriet back and forth with tea. And the Chronicle was a decent enough read this week. Malcolm even had the opportunity to enjoy a mean, silent chuckle when he saw the by-line of the journalist who had been covering what was clearly a council committee meeting that had gone nowhere. Alfie Hamill. Malcolm could just imagine Alfie sitting at the back of the meeting, bored and trying to see how he could make an article out of not very much. They had been good friends once, but a mistake by Malcolm had given Alfie an opportunity to do an exposé, Alfie thinking it would advance his career. It had been satisfying to Malcolm that it hadn't. But it had ended their friendship back then and in truth, and despite Harriet's best efforts to get both of them to see sense, it was still on shaky ground now.

The phone rang. Malcolm heard Harriet answer it. He looked at his watch. Ringing at this time of day, it was probably some con artist hoping to catch out pensioners.

"Malcolm?" Harriet called. "It's Sean Cahill."

Jesus, the man hadn't let the grass grow under his feet. Sean had grumbled a bit, that was for sure. But

Malcolm had heard the keen interest in his voice. Maybe retirement wasn't suiting Sean too well either.

"Bout yeh? Sean. Any news?"

"The Garda was always a step ahead of the RUC."

Malcolm smiled. He would have been disappointed if Sean made it too easy. "Stop fecking about. You wouldn't be ringing if yeh hadn't something to say."

"Yeh might be right. And I think me turning grass for the RUC deserves some sort of payment. What's on the table?"

Malcolm had been going to buy the old bastard a good bottle of Irish whiskey as a thank you if he came up with anything – Jameson's was Sean's favourite. But now Malcolm had a notion that he would buy him a bottle of malt Bushmills, just to annoy the man. Sean would never admit the quality of Bushmills just because it was from, as he would call it, "the north".

"Just give me the goods and we'll chat about that later."

Sean laughed. "All right, ye tight git. Our sources were well confused about this one. The attack on Trevor Mulholland had the hallmarks of the IRA. The meeting was arranged at one of their safe places. The shooter did the standard routine. But there was mayhem afterwards amongst the ranks. No battalion commander would own up to giving the order, and no one had any idea who the shooter was."

That confirmed what Muldoon had said.

"Could it have been from the other side?" asked Malcolm. "Would the other lot have been annoyed that Mulholland was funding the opposition?"

"Could be. There was a Paul McGonigle who was there at the time, and who had some tasty loyalist links. But all low-level. We believe they didn't trust him with active service, so he wasn't someone we ever needed to concern ourselves with. Anyway, given where the shooting took place, it would have been a hell of a risk for a single loyalist shooter. Can't see it meself. Our sources had McGonigle down as someone in the wrong place at the wrong time."

"Yes," Malcolm agreed, and at the same time nodded to Harriet who, through mimed actions, was asking if he wanted a fresh cup of tea. "I met him recently. McGonigle. Didn't take to him. But he didn't come across as a player – now or then. No involvement from either side? That would've been rare for those days."

"Rare enough, but where does that leave yeh? A shooter who wants to look like a player but isn't."

Malcolm snorted. "A novelty, that's for sure. Thanks for that, Sean – really helpful. At least we know who it wasn't."

"Malcolm, what's the interest in this particular case?"

"Suppose it's a bit of a retirement hobby. Someone here in Portrush was there at the time. Duncan Gallagher. He was with Mulholland that day. He was looking for answers."

There was a pause, and then, "We all were, back then."

Harriet had come out with Malcolm's fresh cup, and, oh yes, another slice of lemon drizzle cake. No mention of the diet today, then. Must have done something right. He couldn't think what.

"Sean, That's great, thanks for your help."

"Aye, all right. But that Mulholland man... you know he wasn't a great loss."

Malcolm waved at Harriet, indicating for her to take his tea and cake into the conservatory.

"What d'yeh mean, not a great loss?" Seemed Sean wanted to tell him more.

"Nothing concrete, but I remember a few years before his shooting there was the death of a wee girl. The body found just your side of the so-called border."

Malcolm started to get a little irritated with his old friend. Christ, even when he was helping, Sean couldn't let go of his beliefs about a united Ireland. "That's right. Liza Tobin. Body found in Mulholland's quarry."

"You weren't in post at that time, were yeh?" Sean asked.

"No. I started three years afterwards."

"There were rumours, about Mulholland."

"And?"

Another pause. "He seemed to have a fancy for young girls."

"Go on, for Christ's sake. Since when have you been stuck for words?"

"There were just rumours," Sean said, "that's all. But Mulholland's wife, she was barely eighteen when she married him. That was what the talk was about. That didn't stop him coming our side of the border. There were a few almighty cross fathers came to have words with us. But the usual. Nothing yeh could prove. Nothing yeh could link to that wee girl that got killed. Things were different back then."

"Yes, they were. Look, Sean, thanks for the info. It's mighty appreciated. Really useful." Malcolm would have to work through this and decide how useful it was, how it fitted with what he already knew. "So, when can yeh visit? I know it's a long way, but ye know you're always welcome. We have a lovely bungalow here." He smiled. "I'll vouch for yeh when ye get to the border."

"No need for that," Sean said. "The missus has always wanted to see what all the fuss was about in the Troubles, so she's booked us on an Ulsterbus tour. In a couple of weeks we'll be staying in Portrush. Somewhere called the Northern Counties?"

"That is some hotel. I hope your credit card can take it. But we'll be over for a few jars."

"Grand," said Sean. "Looking forward to it."

A bottle of Jameson's it would be. Possibly a litre.

Malcolm swallowed his last piece of drizzle cake and checked the clock. An hour and twenty minutes had passed. Kevin should have been back by now. Maybe that bloody dog had run off – Malcolm wouldn't put it past him. You had to have your wits about you with that creature.

"Harriet?"

"Yes?" she called from the kitchen.

"Do you think they..."

A ferocious knocking at the front door, followed by the door bell ringing like someone had their finger constantly on it.

Harriet and Malcolm arrived at the front door at the same time. When they opened it, Billy trotted in without a care in the world, but Kevin was red-faced, tears streaming down his face as he thrust the lead at them. He looked a million miles from the belligerent youth Malcolm had first met. He looked scared and young.

"Kevin, love, what's happened?" asked Harriet.

Malcolm scowled at Billy, who continued into the hall, his lead trailing on the floor. What had that bloody dog done now?

Kevin was shaking his head, tears continuing to flow, his words running like a torrent. "There was a man. He tried to take Billy. I had to push him. He fell but I didn't mean it. He was going to take Billy!"

"Kevin, love..." Harriet said, her voice softened by concern. She reached out to him.

"I… didn't… mean it!"

"Kevin." Malcolm spoke firmly so as to get through to the lad. "I want you to tell us what happened. Now."

Kevin took a deep breath and walked into the bungalow, but the tears continued to fall silently.

"Sit down," Malcolm said. "Now, calm yourself down."

"If that man goes to the police, I'll go to jail!" wailed Kevin.

Malcolm could see the boy was distraught, but at this stage kindness would get them nowhere. "Kevin, I want you to start at the beginning."

"I met with Mr and Mrs Gallagher at the East Strand. Like you told me too. She's really nice, Mrs Gallagher. We took the dogs on the beach. She said it was good to do today, because when the summer season comes, they're not allowed."

"That's right." Harriet placed a hand on Kevin's shoulder. He looked up at her.

"It was when I was coming back. We had walked together until they had to turn off. I said I would be OK. I thought I'd be OK. They'd only be gone a few minutes when this man came up to me."

"What did he look like?" asked Malcolm.

"Hard to say. He had a hat and scarf on. His face was sort of pointy."

"Was he short, tall, fat thin?"

Kevin looked around the room as if to find something that would jog his memory. "Thin, I think. And tall. A bit taller than me, anyway."

"His voice. Did he sound American?"

Kevin frowned. "American? No. He sounded ordinary."

Malcolm pressed him. "What else can you remember?"

"He was old."

Any age over twenty would be old to Kevin. "As old as me?"

"Maybe older. Yes, definitely older. I don't know. It happened so quickly."

So, a thin older man, about five-foot-seven with a Northern Irish accent. Clearly not the same man who had been worrying Pat and Duncan.

Harriet knelt beside Kevin and took his hand. "Perhaps the man just wanted to pat Billy. Sure, he's the cutest wee dog. Was that it? Maybe you misunderstood."

Kevin shook his head. "No. He wanted to take Billy. He said he was a friend of yours. Said you'd told him to take Billy home. But that was the thing. He didn't know Billy's name. He grabbed the lead and he nearly had

221

him. So I pushed him." Kevin looked down at his hands. "I pushed him as hard as I could. I saw him fall. And then I ran back here."

Malcolm stood and looked out of the window. He knew dognapping happened, but surely not in broad daylight, and he would have thought it a young man's game.

"Should we ring the police?" asked Harriet.

"And say what?" replied Malcolm. "Look, get the boy a cup of tea with plenty of sugar. I think he's come off the worse. Billy just looks tired." He gestured towards the dog who was stretched out on the rug, eyes shut. "You did good, Kevin. Don't go worrying about pushing the man. Sounds to me like you acted in self-defence."

Malcolm's mobile phone rang just as Harriet left the room. He looked at the name on the phone. Pat Gallagher.

"Malcolm? Can you come quick?"

"What's the matter? Is Duncan OK?"

"Duncan? Yes, he's fine, well not really. He's getting upset. It's just… we have a visitor. The man is back. He arrived just after we got back from our walk. He's at our front door. I can see him from here. He's been shouting through the letterbox. He says he won't go until we talk to him. Malcolm, I'm scared."

"I'll be right there."

CHAPTER TWENTY-SEVEN

Malcolm stopped his car a few metres from the Gallaghers' drive. A man was sitting on the front doorstep, his head in his hands. Pat and Duncan were standing together inside, peering through the window of their sitting room.

Malcolm got out of the car, closed the door quietly, and walked without haste up the drive. At the sound of his footsteps, the man looked up and stood quickly. He was, Malcolm guessed, in his mid-thirties, tall with a large frame, and was wearing what was clearly an expensive wool overcoat, a Barbour scarf tucked around his neck. His expression was both wary and distraught.

Malcom got straight to the point. "Who are you?"

"I'm Ted Daniels."

"Edward Daniels' son?"

"That's right. Who are you?"

"Malcolm Bell. Friend of the family."

Malcolm knew this man was Canadian. The accent was from somewhere in that direction. He should really find out what the difference was. Maybe from across the Atlantic, they felt the same about accents in Ireland. Malcolm couldn't get that. There was a world of difference between accents from Northern Ireland and the south. Everybody knew that.

He pointed though the window to Pat and Duncan. She was guiding Duncan gently away, out of sight of Malcolm and Ted. "They've been upset by your visits."

Ted shook his head as if in disbelief. "Upset? How would you like a lifetime of not knowing? How would they like it," Ted waved at the bungalow. "They've been able to carry on with lives, retiring to this place." He got to his feet. "I've come to get answers for my mother. She had to leave her home all those years ago, and she never understood why. I'm just trying to give her some piece of mind before it's too late."

Malcolm studied Ted. He, too, had been deeply affected by the events of that day thirty-odd years ago. By the actions of that old bastard Robinson thinking he had the right to decide who would be protected, and who would be sacrificed.

"Duncan Gallagher isn't going to be able to give you the answers you're looking for," Malcolm said.

"Of course he is." Ted spat out the words. "He was there when it happened."

"Look, come with me. I'll explain. I'm doing a bit of investigating into the Mulholland murder. I have more information than the Gallaghers will ever be able to give you. There's a wee café a couple of minutes" walk from here."

Malcolm could see Ted weighing him up, working out if he could be trusted.

"I'm police – well, ex-police anyway," offered Malcolm.

The man sighed. "OK."

Clearly Malcolm had passed muster. They walked in silence out of the cul-de-sac to the main road.

"The café's just across the road, over there, on the East Strand. The views are lovely." Malcolm knew they would have to get settled in the café before he could start the story, but a bit of small talk now could get them going. "So, do you live..."

At that moment, Ted grabbed his arm and pulled him back onto the footpath. A flash of red went past. The car carried on at a pace Malcolm knew would get the driver at least three points on his licence.

"Jesus!" They were certainly keen on their red cars around here. But two in one morning?

Ted gave a wry smile. "That would be something. Just as I was about to get some answers, you get knocked down. I've noticed the driving in this country can be... interesting."

"Yes, well, thanks."

Malcolm left the small talk well alone and they reached the café without any more drama. The white and pale-blue place was empty, except for the bored woman behind the till. She brightened up when Malcolm pushed open the door. He chose a table overlooking the almost white sands of the East Strand – a beach as empty as the café.

Malcolm got straight to the point. "How did you find Duncan Gallagher?"

"The usual way. Private detective. I use them all the time in my line of work. Insurance."

Coffee arrived. Ted took a sip and winced. "Not the same as Canadian coffee."

"Your private detective can't have been that good. He wasn't able to tell you that Duncan has... memory problems."

"I paid for the best. He was able to get access to medical records." Ted shook his head. "Nothing there to say he was anything but fit and well."

"Not too sure that sounds legal, access to medical records."

Ted laughed. "I only used the best. Let's just say nothing was too much trouble for my contact. I know when to invest in services. It could be why I did all right business-wise."

Two things came to Malcolm's mind. First, a career idea for that young Kevin, with his skills in accessing information. Kevin the private detective. He tried to imagine what Emily would think about that that. Second, Pat couldn't have sought help from her GP yet. What Duncan was suffering from would have been on his medical record and Ted would have been informed. It was all right being determined, struggling on alone, but she needed help.

When this was all sorted, Malcolm would have a good chat with her.

He turned his attention back to Ted. "I can assure you," he said, "the man's not well and all you're doing is making him upset. I have been making enquiries about the Mulholland murder. So, ask me what you like."

Ted took a deep breath. "My mother emigrated to Canada with me after Dad died – after he drank himself to death. But she never settled. She was never content there, even though I did all right. She would have come back but she was scared the abuse would start again. Mum was hounded out of the country by the rumours that Dad had taken the money, and she was too frightened to return. It's too late for her now. Stage four cancer. I just wanted to get the truth for her. It's the only thing left I can do. She's deteriorating, so I can't stay away from home any longer." He took another sip of coffee. "I was getting desperate."

"There was money the day Mulholland was murdered." Malcom said.

"I knew it." Ted looked into Malcolm's eyes. "So who took it?"

"DI Robinson."

"Robinson? I was sure it was Duncan Gallagher." Ted shook his head in disbelief. "Why would Robinson do that? He was a Detective Inspector for God's sake. Why would he need the money?"

"He gave it to Mulholland's widow," Malcolm said. "He wanted to make sure the Mulholland name wasn't sullied by an association with paramilitaries. Felt she had been through enough."

"Great. He sacrificed my dad instead? I visited Robinson but couldn't get any sense out of him. I didn't realise what a bastard he was. I even felt sorry for him. You could see he wasn't happy." Ted studied Malcolm again. "Did you know Robinson?"

"Aye, I did. He was my commanding officer for a short time. Never got on with him."

"You were in the RUC too? Did you come across my father?" Ted looked hopeful. "It would be good to know more about him."

Malcolm didn't want to add any more emotional turmoil to Ted. What good would it do for him to know that in career terms, his father's loss was Malcolm's gain?

"Sorry, no. We weren't serving at the same time."

227

"Pity. Too much to hope for." Ted sighed. "Which side did it? Did they ever find out?"

"At the time they thought it was a paramilitary murder, but no one claimed responsibility. I've being looking at it as a cold case. Bit of a retirement hobby, you might say. I think there was more to it."

"It would be interesting to hear what you come up with. So I can have the whole picture." He reached into his coat pocket and handed Malcolm a business card.

"Yes of course." Malcolm took the card and turned it over in his hands. "I don't know if this helps, but there were also rumours that Duncan took the money. He got on with life, but it was always there at the back of his mind. And now his memory is going, he gets upset about it. Very upset. Makes life very difficult for his wife. They say that, don't they, that when the recent memories go, people tend to think of things in the past? Pat, his wife, she has had a lot on her plate."

Ted rubbed his eyes. "Can you tell them I'm sorry? Can you explain?"

"Of course. Pat will understand. She's a good person. Duncan too."

Ted looked at his wristwatch. Malcolm asked him what he was going to do next.

"I'll go back to Belfast today. I have a flight back to Vancouver tomorrow." He stood and pointed out of the window. "I would like to come back – for a holiday. This country is as lovely as Mum said. I was too little when we left to remember much about the place."

Malcolm thought of something else. "Before yeh go, and don't take this the wrong way, but earlier, before yeh got to the Gallaghers" place, did you come across a lad with a wee dog?"

Ted wrinkled his nose. "Me? No." He gave a half laugh. "I'm allergic to dogs. Stay well clear."

* * *

Malcolm watched Duncan as he stroked Bella. He wasn't sure who looked the more contented. Bella didn't seem to move on Duncan's lap. She even whimpered when Duncan attempted to adjust his position. Duncan's eyes grew heavy and he was soon breathing the deep breaths of peaceful sleep.

Malcolm had summarised his meeting with Ted. He wasn't sure how much Duncan had taken in, but as for Pat, it looked as if a weight had been lifted from her shoulders. She seemed slightly taller, somehow.

"That's it, then?" Pat asked. "He's going back to Canada?" She handed Malcolm a cup of tea and sat down next to Duncan.

"Yes." Malcolm smiled. "Off to Belfast today. He flies home tomorrow."

"From what you said, I feel sorry for him. And his poor mother. We weren't the only ones who were blighted by Robinson's lies."

"He did say he would like to come back for a holiday. I think that would be after, yeh know, his mother..."

"Of course." She paused. "I think, if he does come back, it might help him if we met. Properly, this time."

"Entirely up to you." Malcolm handed her Ted's business card. She studied it and then placed it carefully on the side table.

"Pat, I was wondering." Malcolm paused. "Could you help me with something?"

"What is it?"

Malcolm leaned forward. "It's about Mulholland. You started me off looking at the case, but I believe there's more to find out. The more I learn, the more I feel the whole truth didn't come out. It's not just about the missing money."

Pat frowned. "Go on."

"You mentioned that Mulholland wasn't a great sort."

Pat stiffened. "I didn't think so, anyway. I could never work out why Duncan thought he was so wonderful."

"What was his wife like? You said she was young?"

"Very. It was a hurried marriage. The poor girl was only eighteen when the baby was born. The same year they found that girl in the quarry. Duncan told me Eileen Mulholland was very upset with the police coming round. Another year and she was pregnant again. Then she was a widow. All before she was twenty."

"I didn't realise there was such a big age difference."

"It was the talk of the place at the time," Pat said. "I thought you knew. Nineteen years between them. Ridiculous. I don't know what her parents were thinking of. Even for the look of the thing and the sake of the children, how could any couple cope with that difference? And what did she know of life, especially what life would be like with that man? No wonder she moved to England soon after Mulholland was killed. I think she went as soon as the estate was settled. I can't tell you more than that, really."

Malcolm tapped his fingers together. Another piece of the jigsaw was falling into place.

"Pat, did you ever come across a man called Paul McGonigle?"

Pat smiled wryly. "Oh yes. Now there was a man we hated to see coming into the post office. Always some complaint. He was forever claiming for something or other. I couldn't believe it when he was awarded the disability payments. He might've put on a limp now and then, but more often than not, I saw him skip from the post office to his car after he lifted his money."

"Did he have anything to do with Mulholland?"

Pat shook her head. "No, not that I knew anyway. And there's not much you miss in a post office. It's like exchange central for local information. There was only the most tenuous link between them."

"What was that?"

"The girl found in Mulholland's quarry, Liza Tobin, was the granddaughter of Sam Tobin. The Tobins were God-fearing, church-twice-a-Sunday types. And then they employed Paul McGonigle? Couldn't understand it myself. It didn't last long, though. When the Tobin business folded, McGonigle was out of a job again." Pat shuddered. "Horrible man."

Malcolm couldn't disagree. "God-fearing types, yeh say? Was there ever word about Liza's father? I mean, I can't imagine God-fearers being too happy about a wean born out of wedlock."

Pat nodded. "You're right there. Especially Mrs Tobin." Pat sucked her teeth. "She was some woman. If anything, she was the more fundamentalist of the two. Mr Tobin wasn't so bad. In fact..." She frowned.

"What?"

"Well, erm... I'm not supposed to say. People's finances should be confidential, but..."

"I believe they're both dead, and any information would be a help." Malcolm said gently. He knew it was difficult for Pat to put her principles aside.

"I could see Mr Tobin wasn't so... hard as his wife. He deposited money for Elizabeth every month in a post office account, for as long as I can remember. Of course, it all stopped when he got ill. He had his first stroke about four years after Liza was killed. He died a couple of years later. Mrs Tobin didn't last too long after that. It was one tragedy after another with that family."

"Did the Tobins have a son?"

"That was one bit of good news for them. He did well. Did law at Queen's. But sure, like the rest of them, when they go away to university they tend to stay away."

So the good, upstanding solicitor definitely is Elizabeth's brother. Malcolm felt sorrier than ever for the rejected woman.

Duncan began to stir from his nap, but Bella was still fast asleep. Malcolm stood. "I have taken enough of your time, Pat. Thank you."

"No, I need to thank you." She gestured towards Duncan. "I'll let him come around from his nap and then tell him what you've found out. That poor Daniel's family. But at least it will be something we won't need to worry about."

Malcolm glanced back at the Gallagher's home as he walked to his car. Hopefully his investigation would give that couple some peace.

* * *

When Malcolm parked in front of his home, he could see through the sitting-room window that Kevin had been joined by Emily. Probably contacted by Harriet. Good call. The boy had been an emotional mess when he left.

Malcolm had got his key positioned in the lock, when Harriet opened the front door.

"All sorted with Pat and Duncan?"

"Yes. They won't be bothered again."

"Thank God for that." Harriet gestured down the hall. "Bit of a to-do in there."

Malcolm sighed. "What's up now?"

"Emily wants to call the police and Kevin is terrified they'll find something to blame him for. God knows what. But I suppose given his background... He thinks whoever it was will say Kevin assaulted him. I was wondering, you know of any sympathetic police officers here? You know, have a word – tell them the boy's not to blame for anything. That would reassure Kevin and satisfy Emily."

Malcolm hung up his coat. He'd never had much contact with officers in Portrush.

"I could ring William, get a recommendation from him."

"Yes, good idea."

Peace descended on the bungalow again once Kevin and Emily had left, both having been reassured. Malcolm sat in his armchair in the conservatory and picked up the newspaper. He tried to focus, but then put the paper down again. He didn't even have enough energy to continue his enjoyment of another of Alfie Hamill's attempts to make council meetings relevant or interesting. So much had happened since Malcolm had enjoyed the lemon drizzle cake first thing this morning. Lemon drizzle cake. That was the ticket.

"Harriet, love," he shouted out to the kitchen. "Can I have a bit of that drizzle cake? Just to keep me going."

Harriet came into the conservatory, wiping her hands on a tea towel. "Sorry, love. All gone."

Gone? He hadn't eaten that much. Harriet explained.

"Well, Kevin was so upset, I thought he needed a bit of something to cheer him up. It was so cute."

"Cute?" Malcolm spluttered the word. What was cute about the boy eating all his cake?

"Yes." Harriet smiled. "He insisted on sharing it with Billy."

Malcolm sighed. Harriet turned to go back into the kitchen.

"Harriet?" He put a hand on her arm to stop her.

"Yes?"

"I'll ring William tomorrow. First thing."

CHAPTER TWENTY-EIGHT

Tommy leant on the window sill of the newspaper office and peered in. Alfie had texted him last night to say he had made progress. Tommy knew the journalist would be able to access information by fair means or foul. Sod the official channels. But the bastard was late. They had agreed 9am and it was now five past. Out of habit, Tommy reached for his wrist to pull the band. Nothing. Fuck it. He didn't need those tricks anymore. If he got angry, there was a reason. Sod the consequences.

Then he saw the stooped, wiry figure of Alfie ambling up the street, a fag hanging out of his mouth.

"Sorry, sorry, sorry. Car wouldn't start." Alfie held up his hands in apology, then reached into the pocket of his trench coat and pulled out a bunch of keys. With practised ease he turned the keys in the lock, then half-turned to Tommy. "Do yeh want a coffee or anything before we head out?"

"No. I"m fine." Tommy followed Alfie into the office. "So, what have you found out?"

"Well, we have a few places to visit and a couple of people to have a wee chat to." He looked at the wall clock. "Those women are always late the day the paper goes to print." He tutted. Shook his head in despair. "No urgency for the next week's stories."

Tommy looked around the room – a drab, empty space. It hardly suggested that this was cutting edge journalism. Even their computer monitors were the old boxlike type.

"What addresses? What people?" he asked.

The door was pushed open and a rotund, dark-haired woman in her mid-twenties came in. Her delay getting into work could have been caused by the vast amount of makeup she'd felt necessary to apply.

"Ah, here she is. Come on, Claire." Alfie tapped his watch. "You know I have a big story on the go." He nodded towards Tommy.

Claire rolled her eyes. "Yeh. Right. Whatever." She walked past Tommy and Alfie to an untidy desk. She unwrapped her scarf, opened the buttons of her coat, sat down heavily and sighed like it was the end of a hard-working week.

Alfie seemed not to have registered this insolence. Or possibly he was well used to it.

"Right." He rubbed his hands together. "We'll be off. Your car or mine?"

"I think mine."

"Yes, well… you might be right. Don't want to be stuck in the back of beyond, do we?"

Tommy thought of the hotel he had stayed in, its posters advertising the upcoming country and western night this weekend, the excitement of the bar and reception staff. The headliner was somebody called Philomena Begley, along with her Rambling Men. He'd asked if it was a joke band and had got astonished looks in response. Apparently, she was some sort of local celebrity. The staff even played him some of her music to see if he recognised it. Country and bloody western? No, he was already in the back of beyond. And he was determined to leave as soon as he had his answers.

"Where first?" he asked when they reached his car.

"Right, well you mentioned the name Tobin. The place isn't overrun by them, but there are more than one or two. However." Alfie emphasized the word and then paused dramatically.

Tommy's hands tightened on the steering wheel. He sighed heavily. "Yes?"

"There were rumours, way back during the Troubles. When you wouldn't have been a twinkle in your parents" eyes." Alfie elbowed Tommy gently.

Tommy rolled his eyes. What a prick. He forced a smile. "Why don't you give me the address and then tell me about the rumours."

When he had the address safely in his satnav and they were on their way, he turned expectantly to Alfie. "So? The rumours?"

"Oh aye." Alfie clunked his seat belt into place. "Right. Well, on the face of it, the Tobin's were decent churchgoing folk. But old Mr Tobin – let's just say he had his allegiances."

Tommy already knew Tobin had helped the cause, storing the hardware for the volunteers. Maybe this idiot journalist wouldn't be as useful as he had hoped.

"You know." Alfie dug him in the ribs again. "Paramilitary allegiances. But his daughter was a bit of a let-down to the family."

"A daughter?" This was new.

"Yes. Poor wee girl got pregnant and the fella ran off. Old Mrs Tobin wouldn't have her in the house, wouldn't have any talk of her. It was if as if the girl stopped existing." Alfie shook his head sadly.

"The baby. Wasn't a boy?" That would have made sense. The Tobins would have been able to get rid of the embarrassment. Used the paramilitary links, like Jeff had told him.

Alfie looked at Tommy and shook his head. "Naw. It was a girl. Poor wee thing. She got killed."

"What? How?"

"Murdered. Years later. She was at a Blue Light Disco. Yeh know, the discos the police ran in the Troubles? Community engagement and all that. Nobody saw her leave and the next thing she turns up, you know, violated, and dead in Mulholland's quarry. She was only fifteen."

Tommy hadn't expected this. Maybe there was another woman that Tobin had organised a "favour" for. He pondered…

Twenty minutes late, Tommy's satnav announced they'd arrived at their destination.

"Here we are." Alfie pointed to a boarded entrance to what seemed to be a large yard.

A weather-beaten sign identified it as Tobin's machinery hire. Part of the boarding had been blown down. Through the gap, Tommy could see dilapidated buildings and, in the background, a house that appeared abandoned. Grass was growing through gaps in the concrete driveway.

"The empire that was once the thriving business of Tobin Machinery," announced Alfie theatrically. "Now, for the story, yeh know, for the paper, I thought maybe a few photos outside the family home? You looking sad?"

Tommy glared at Alfie.

"If you wouldn't mind looking just a wee bit sad? For the look of the thing. Gets the reader's interest..."

Tommy got out of the car, pulled more of the boarding down and wrenched open the gate.

"Hang on." Alfie followed him. "Don't do no damage. The paper can't afford a claim."

Tommy ignored him and kept walking. Alfie trailed behind.

They reached the out buildings. So this was where the hardware, the guns, the bullets and the bomb-making paraphernalia had been hidden. Tommy pulled open a door. There were the remains of a rusted red tractor, and other parts and bits that meant nothing to him.

"I was going to tell you more," mumbled Alfie.

Tommy walked around the tractor and opened the door to peer in. "Go on then."

"Well, after the wee girl was murdered – that was 1986 – old man Tobin got ill and the business started to go downhill. Their son George had no interest in it."

"George? George Tobin? Is he a solicitor in Belfast?"

"That's the one!" Alfie frowned. "Hang on, how did you know that?"

"Never mind." Tommy slammed the door of the tractor. Alfie jumped at the sudden noise. "That's it? All you've got to tell me?"

Alfie looked hurt. "No. I was going to say about the daughter, Elizabeth. Naturally, she took the death of her daughter wile bad. I mean, real bad. Yeh could say she lost the plot good and proper. But here's the thing. Another two years after the wee girl got killed, she started ranting on about another child she had. A boy. Nobody ever took her seriously, for no one saw any sight of this baby she's supposed to have had. She used to ring us at the paper, say this wean had been stolen, that her father had done it. But nobody believed her. In fact, she was in and out of the loony bin after that. I've been putting it all together, and maybe, just maybe, you might be him." Alfie rubbed his hands together. "It's going to make quite a story. Any chance of a photo now?"

Ignoring him, Tommy walked out of the building and towards the two-storey house beyond. The place had an unforgiving frontage, like the house was staring him down. So here was the home of the people who had discarded him like he was rubbish, shit under their shoes. Someone was going to pay.

"What about now? You know, you beside the family homestead?" Alfie had followed Tommy and now was waving his mobile phone hopefully. "Come on. It'll help the story. You know, long-lost son returns to family home."

"You can fuck off! No photos!"

Alfie's hopeful smile faded and he slid his phone back in his coat pocket.

Tommy turned, walked quickly to the car. "Get in. Where next?"

Alfie sighed. "We're going to Elizabeth Tobin's house. The woman who could be your birth mother."

The car journey to the next address was quiet, with Alfie giving only muttered instructions to Tommy when the satnav tried to take them the wrong way. They pulled up outside a run-down terrace house. Tommy reached for the door handle.

"Wait!"

Fuck's sake. What was with this prick now? "Yes?" Tommy couldn't keep the impatience out of his voice. This could be the key. The key to who he was and why he was rejected. Maybe it wasn't her fault. She mightn't have had a choice. Maybe she had been looking for him all these years.

"Look," Alfie said, "if she is, I mean, if we're guessing right... you know she's not well. I'm not sure..."

But Tommy was out of the car. He wasn't going to stop now. In that house could be his mother. His real mother. She would have been searching for him. For sure she would. Those things happened. By the time he reached the door, Alfie was at his side.

"Look, Tommy, let's take it easy. Maybe we should involve Elizabeth's social worker," he pleaded.

Tommy turned to face him. "Social worker?" He spat the words out. "Like that stuck-up English bitch I asked for help? I don't think so."

He banged on the door.

"OK, OK, but just let me talk to her. She knows me."

Tommy stepped back as the door started to open. His heart was pounding. Hands sweating. He wiped his palms on his jeans, then motioned for Alfie to stand in front of him.

"Who's there? Who are you?" The woman – Elizabeth – had opened the door only enough to let her peer out.

Tommy took a step back in horror. Even at the end of her life, his adopted mother hadn't looked this ill. Elizabeth's clothes seemed to be a mixture of charity-shop donations. She pulled her faded cardigan around her thin form. Greasy grey hair fell over her thin, lined face, her eyes sharp and suspicious.

"Elizabeth. It's me, Alfie. From the paper. Just called round for a wee chat. Yeh haven't been in touch for some time."

The woman's face relaxed into a weak smile. "I remember. Alfie. Nice Alfie. You're always nice to me." She left the door and shuffled into a sitting room. Alfie followed her. Tommy stayed by the sitting room door, not wanting to get closer, wanting to keep his distance from this disappointment.

"Can I sit?" Alfie asked.

Elizabeth nodded. She was already sinking into her chair and pulling her legs up into a seated foetal position, wrapping her cardigan around her even more tightly.

"Elizabeth, do yeh mind that you told me years ago that you had another wean. I mean after Liza..."

Elizabeth frowned.

Alfie glanced at Tommy and then pushed on. "Didn't yeh, Elizabeth?"

"No!" Elizabeth started to rock slowly in her chair.

"You sure? Because many's the time you've told me." Alfie said quietly. "Do yeh want to tell me again?"

"Who's he?" Elizabeth pointed at Tommy.

Tommy stepped back a fraction into the hall, out of Elizabeth's view.

"Him? Och, sure, he's just someone who's working with me. Don't mind him."

Elizabeth's rocking paused for a moment and then started again.

"Every. Time. I. Tell. People…" Then she screamed, "THEY TAKE ME AWAY!"

Alfie stood up. "Elizabeth, sorry, love, we'll go. I… look, love, stop crying. I'm wile sorry. I didn't mean…"

Tommy had had enough. This was crap, getting him nowhere with this madwoman. A bloody wild goose chase. He came into the room and grabbed Alfie by the arm. "For fuck's sake, come on. Let's…"

Tommy was stopped by a violent shriek from Elizabeth. She was pointing at him, her hand and arm shaking. Crying. Trying to get words out. He couldn't make out what she was saying.

Alfie pushed past him to the front door. "For Christ's sake, let's go! Look what we've done."

Then Elizabeth's words came loud and clear. "You're back! You said you'd stay away. George promised me!"

Tommy stared at her. "What the fuck are you talking about?" He moved towards her. "You stupid cow. I've never met you before." He grabbed her shoulders and shook her. "Listen to me!"

"No, don't. Please, please, please don't touch me…" Elizabeth folded her arms over her head as if to protect herself. She drew her legs up, still rocking, still crying.

Tommy left the house, raging at the nonsense he had just heard. Alfie was waiting by the car.

Tommy glared at him. "What the fuck was that?"

"I think we should go back to town," Alfie said, his face ashen.

"No. There's somewhere else I need to go. I met a man called Paul McGonigle. Connected to Tobin, way back. And he wasn't straight with me. You know him?"

"As I said, I think we've done enough." There was a tremor in Alfie's voice now.

"Then, as I said I'll take you back. When I'm good and ready. Do you know this man? I think he lives near Ballygawley."

"No!" Panic in Alfie's response now.

Tommy lowered his voice. "OK. Here's the deal. You get the man's address. We'll take a quick visit there and then we'll head back."

Alfie made a phone call to the newspaper office. They sat in silence for a long five minutes. Alfie studied the street through the side window. Tommy tapped his fingers on the steering wheel. George Tobin, bloody stuck-up solicitor George Tobin who refused to meet with Tommy, he was this woman's brother. Tommy had been sure Elizabeth Tobin was his mother. It had all fitted together. And now? Now he wanted desperately to be wrong. That weak pathetic woman, his mother? But maybe that was it. Maybe she was so weak that she couldn't or wouldn't fight for him. Maybe she was to blame for all of it.

Then a text came through. Alfie showed it to Tommy who tapped a third address into the satnav. As he drove, he didn't want any small talk or conversation, and judging by the silence from the passenger seat, it was clear Alfie didn't either.

* * *

Tommy parked the car on a street similar to the one they'd just left. Not much difference in the layout of these villages.

He let Alfie get out before reaching across to the glove box, where he'd left his handgun. McGonigle would need a bit more encouragement to talk. He pushed the button and the glove box fell open – just as Alfie opened the car door again.

"You coming or..." Alfie's eyes widened as he looked inside the glove box. As he saw the gun. "What the fuck is going on?"

Tommy grabbed the gun. "Nothing you need to be concerned about. Just a bit of protection."

Alfie slammed the door and leaned against the car. Waited for Tommy to get out and join him.

"Look, pal." Alfie ran a hand through his hair. "This is getting out of control. I was meant to be helping yeh find your birth family. Write a feature. Not... I mean what the fuck is this?"

Tommy tucked the gun into the back of his trousers and pulled his jacket around to hide the bulge. "Like I said, nothing you need be concerned with. All you need to do is show me Paul McGonigle's house. You knock and I'll be just behind yeh."

"Jesus, this isn't some sort of... I mean, you're not going to... Jesus." Alfie looked up and down the street, his face flushed, beads of sweat on his forehead.

"Alfie, calm yourself." Tommy had never felt so in control, and it was good. "Just walk over to the front door and knock. I just want a wee chat with the man. That's all. Now move."

Alfie walked over to the last house in the terrace. He knocked on the door without conviction, then turned to Tommy. "There. He's not in."

Tommy shook his head slowly. "Not good enough, Alfie. Try again. Louder."

Sweat was now running freely down Alfie's face. He knocked harder. Still no answer.

"You the social?" The door of the next house had opened and a woman with black hair that didn't match her lined face was standing half in and half out of her hallway.

Tommy turned and smiled at her. "We are looking for Mr McGonigle. Do yeh know if he's in?"

She spat on the pavement. "I knew you'd catch up with him some day, the slimy git. He's gone out. Oh, I know he told you lot he could barely walk. But he can do more than that. He's been gone all day in his car. I can ring yeh when he gets back. So yeh can catch him, like."

"That isn't necessary. We can just call another time." Tommy smiled again. "And you don't need to mention we were here." He tapped the side of his nose.

"I can houl ma whist, don't you worry."

Tommy walked back to the car, Alfie trailing in his wake.

"Look, I don't know what this is about, and I don't want to either." Alfie's voice trembled as he fastened his seat belt. "Just drop me at the office."

"Alfie, you have been very helpful." Tommy reached into his waistband and withdrew the gun. No need to hide it now. He placed it back into the glove box and slammed it shut.

Alfie stared at the glove box door and then looked out of the side window.

Alfie was hanging on to the door handle as they approached the newspaper office. He practically fell out of the car in his haste to get out.

"Thanks again for your help!" Tommy shouted after him. He watched the pathetic fool rush to get into the office. He had done what Tommy needed him to do.

Now, time to think. He couldn't bear to go back to that hotel. Not with that shite country music everywhere. He looked at his watch. 5pm. The pub he'd stayed at the first night he was here would do the trick. Not too far away. And close to where McGonigle lived. He might not be there today, but he would be back. And Tommy could wait.

CHAPTER TWENTY-NINE

Malcolm had slept well. It was hard to consider getting out of the warmth and comfort of his bed. Harriet had left him a cup of tea on the bedside table. He reached across. Cold. Damn. That would have been perfect. He pulled back the duvet, rolled onto his side, dropped his legs to the floor and levered himself into sitting up. He looked around for his slippers and dressing gown.

"Malcolm?" Harriet called. There was an urgency to her voice that worried him. "Come quick!"

He forgot about his slippers and dressing gown. In the hallway, Harriet was holding the phone out to him, her face stricken, her eyes filling up.

"What's happened?" Malcolm took the phone from her. "Hello? Malcolm here."

"Malcolm? It's Bella. She's…" Pat Gallagher stopped.

"Jesus, has Bella been taken?" asked Malcolm.

"She's dead." Her voice cracked. "She wouldn't leave Duncan all last evening. Then she started to be sick, just when we were going to bed. I put her in her basket and hoped she would be OK. I was going to take her to the vet this morning, but when I got up… I wish I'd taken her last night… but I was tired… I'm always tired…" Her voice cracked again. "I've told Duncan that Bella's just sleeping. I need to take her… to dispose of her, I suppose."

Malcolm looked up. Harriet was mouthing something, but he couldn't get it. He mouthed back What? She threw up her hands and mouthed again. This time he could make it out.

"Look, we'll be over shortly. We can take Bella to the vet. They usually do it."

"Thanks. I am so sorry to bother you. I just didn't know who else to ring."

"That's no bother. Be with you in fifteen minutes."

Harriet insisted Billy came with them. She reasoned that a persistent dognapper wouldn't give up easily, and maybe they knew where Billy lived. Maybe they'd followed Kevin. As Malcolm pulled away from the kerb, he looked in the rear-view mirror to see the dog lying down with his head pushed into the back of the seat. It was Harriet's opinion that he was a nervous traveller. More like bloody rude. Such was the rush to get out of the house Malcolm hadn't had time to put a rug on the back seat to save the later job of vacuuming the hairs Billy would be sure to leave.

"Thank you so much for coming over." Pat didn't look her usual neat self. Her hair hadn't been combed, her trousers and top were mismatched, and her eyes were red.

"Like I said, it's no bother," replied Malcolm. "Where's the..."

"I've left her in the basket, in the kitchen. I've kept Duncan in the sitting room. He keeps asking for Bella."

"I'll keep Duncan company." Harriet gave Pat's arm a gentle squeeze. "Is it all right if I take Billy in to him? Might be a distraction."

"Yes, of course."

Malcolm followed Pat into the kitchen. There was an acrid smell of vomit and diarrhoea. Pat stayed at the far end of the room while Malcolm knelt beside the dead dog. There was blood around her nostrils.

"Pat, this doesn't look right. I mean, I'm no vet and I don't know much about dogs, but there's something —"

Pat put her head in her hands. "I know. I know. But I just can't think straight. First all the business with that man chasing us and now this?" Her voice started to break. "Jesus, there's only so much I can cope with."

"OK, Pat, it's OK. I'll sort it out. Have you something that I can carry her in? Would this blanket in the basket do?" He reached down to take it.

"Yes."

Malcolm looked up at her. There were tears flowing down her face. She dabbed at them with a sheet of kitchen roll.

"Why don't you go into the sitting room with Harriet and Duncan? I'll get Bella into my car."

Gently, Malcolm wrapped Bella in the blanket, taking care to cover her entirely, and carried her to the boot of his car. A drizzle had stared to blow in from the west, painting a greyness into the morning. It seemed fitting.

When he returned to the house, Billy was at the door waiting for him. Damn. In the rush to come over to the Gallaghers, he hadn't walked Billy. The last thing Pat needed now was for this mutt to do its business on her cream carpets.

"Pat, would it be all right if I let Billy have a wee run around your garden? I think he's getting desperate,"

Malcolm asked when he joined them in the sitting room.

"Of course."

Malcolm took Billy's lead. "Come on." There was no way he was going to let Billy run free in Pat's carefully maintained garden. "A quick wee and that's your lot."

He opened the door and Billy strained at the lead across the patio which ran the whole width of the bungalow, towards the four steps that led to the lawn bordered by a wooden fence. As soon as he reached the grass, Billy cocked his leg for what seemed to Malcolm an impressive length of time. "Quite the bladder there!"

When Billy was done, he pulled again at the lead towards the carefully planted border in front of the fence.

"Hang on a minute. It was a quick wee stop only."

But Billy was pulling harder than ever, his front legs wide for extra traction.

"What's up with—" But then Malcolm could see what Billy was so anxious to get to. Strips of meat on the grass next to the fence. It looked like beef. Malcolm pulled Billy closer to him. There was no way Pat would throw meat into her perfect garden.

Malcolm and Billy returned to the sitting room. "All done." He handed the lead to Harriet. "Pat, do you have a plastic bag I could have?"

"Yes." She frowned. "I thought you used the blanket."

"I have. It's... could you just come into the kitchen a minute?"

In the kitchen, Malcolm closed the door behind them. "This might sound like a very strange question, but have you thrown meat out on the grass?"

"Have I what?"

"I've found some meat on the grass. Beside the fence. I might be putting two and two together and getting five, but…"

Pat leant back against the worktop. "Are you suggesting Bella was poisoned? Oh my God." Her eyes welled up again.

"Look, Pat, I don't know. I'm going to take Bella to the vets and I'll take the meat too. We'll see what they say."

Malcolm and Harriet left, Bella's blanket-wrapped body in the boot and Billy taking up his usual position in the back seat. Harriet had promised that she would pop in later to see Pat and Duncan.

"When you see her, do you think you might suggest that she gets some help? I mean with Duncan?" asked Malcolm. "I know she's determined to carry on caring for him, but we all need help from time to time."

Harriet reached across and stroked the back of Malcolm's hand. "I was thinking the same myself. I'll have a wee word with her when we've been to the vets."

"I need to have a chat with the vet."

"Why? I thought we'd just leave poor wee Bella with them."

"There might be more to it. Bella might've been poisoned."

"What?" Harriet turned to look at Billy. "First Billy nearly gets stolen and now this? Malcolm, what is going on?

What indeed? If Bella was poisoned, the two incidents were too close in time. Malcolm was not a believer in coincidences.

* * *

He explained his suspicions to the vet – the diarrhoea, the vomiting, the blood around Bella's nostrils. The vet promised to ring Malcolm when he got the results of tests on both Bella and the meat.

Afterwards, Malcolm dropped Harriet at the Gallaghers" bungalow and drove home. He agreed that it wouldn't be a good idea for Billy to stay with Harriet. There might still be poison in the garden he hadn't spotted. And he needed time by himself. To think. He needed to run through what he'd found out, try to make sense of what had happened over thirty years ago, what had really happened when Mulholland was shot. He needed to put the jigsaw together.

He turned the key in the lock and pushed open the front door. Billy trotted in and skidded on some junk mail delivered since he and Harriet had left earlier. Malcolm bent to pick it up, cursing at the unnecessary rubbish that got pushed through his letterbox seemingly every day. At the bottom of the pile was a hand written card. It read "LET SLEEPING DOGS LIE".

CHAPTER THIRTY

Malcolm picked up the card and turned it over. Just a card, like you would have in an old-fashioned Rolodex. He didn't recognise the writing. He looked out of the door. Glanced up and down the road. Nothing. Not even a passing car. But this hadn't been posted just now, not with the junk mail on top of it. The postman usually came between 10.30am and 11am. This had arrived before then.

Malcolm slammed the door closed. He was suddenly cold, despite the warmth of the house. Sweat ran down the back of his neck. He went into the kitchen where the dog was finishing off the breakfast from which he'd been pulled away from earlier.

Should he ring Harriet? No. No need to cause more alarm. Not yet.

As he watched Billy eat noisily, he considered the events of the last few days. Surely it was too much of a coincidence not to link it to his investigations. Bella had been poisoned – he would bet his pension on it – and now there was this delivered threat. From where? Yes, he had earned a few enemies during his career, but he'd been retired some six months now. And there had been no word of trouble from any other source, from any of the good number of low-life's he had help to put away over the years. His ex-colleagues would have told him.

So… Assuming this was related to his current digging, which of the three he had spoken to about the Mulholland murder would have felt worried enough to try to scare him off? And how had they found out where he lived, and so quickly? He had only given them his telephone number. The landline code would have narrowed the search down, but still, Portrush was a big enough place.

George Tobin had been panicked, that was for sure, and possibly his practice may have contacts that could trace someone. After all, Ted Daniels did. But Tobin had seemed to want to shut Malcolm's interest down. Would he really have done something like this? Threatening a police officer, even a retired one, wasn't the cleverest thing to do. And if nothing else, George Tobin was a bright spark.

Tony Muldoon hadn't come across as worried. Couldn't care less about things in the past. Only concerned about the pub, looking after it like a custodian. No, Malcolm couldn't see it being important to him.

That left number three. The man who was reluctant to tell him anything, but who looked like he had plenty to hide. Paul McGonigle. And that phone call Malcolm had overheard. McGonigle had said that he would "fix it". Yes… Paul McGonigle would be Malcolm's guess for the person who had both sent the card and poisoned Bella.

Billy finished his food and padded away for a post-meal snooze. Malcolm bent to lift the dog bowl in order to wash it, when he heard the front door opening.

"I thought I would walk back," Harriet called from the hall. "Put the kettle on."

Malcolm left the dog bowl where it was and went into the hall. "Why didn't yeh ring me?" Jesus, with all that was going on… "I would've picked you up."

Harriet took off her coat and hung it up.

"Duncan started to get agitated. Pat said it was best if I went, but I did get her to promise to go to the GP, to ask for—" Harriet came into the kitchen and then stopped. "What's the matter?"

"Nothing," Malcolm lied.

"Malcolm Bell. I can see from the look on your face something's up." The expression on Harriet's face changed. "It's not… where's Billy?"

Billy came into the kitchen wagging his tail, and dropped the mangled glove at Harriet's feet. She bent to hug him. "Thank God. Yeh wee dote." She stood. "So, what has yeh so worried?"

"Let's go and sit down."

He explained what he had put together and showed the note to Harriet. She held it between her forefinger and thumb as if it was contaminated, her other hand over her mouth. Malcolm wished he could take her anguish away.

"And this is to do with what happened over thirty years ago?" she said. "And you think the same person, this Paul McGonigle, it was him that poisoned Bella?"

"I think so. I've no other realistic explanation."

Malcolm wrung his hands. His sleepless nights and nightmares had been a drain on Harriet, he knew that, but he had always managed to keep threats away from her, had never let his work directly affect her. And now this, when he was retired. It wasn't fair.

"How could he have found us? How did he know where we live, and for that matter where Pat and Duncan live?" asked Harriet.

"I haven't worked it out yet. I just left my telephone number with him. That's all."

Harriet handed back the note. She looked at her hands.

"Malcolm, I may know." She looked up. "I had a phone call from a delivery firm. The day you went to Omagh. The man said you had ordered something for me. For my birthday."

Her birthday? Oh Christ. He hadn't missed it, had he? No, it was at the end of April.

"He wanted me to confirm our address." Her hands went to her mouth once more, her eye wide. "What have I done?"

Malcolm went over to her, held her close. "It's fine. I'll get it sorted."

Harriet turned her head towards his chest. "How can yeh say that when…" Her sobs stopped the words from coming.

What the hell had he done? Just when he had thought he had gotten some peace for Pat and Duncan, he had managed to rake up the past and brought danger and distress to their door. And to his own.

"Harriet, love, I'm going to make a phone call."

Harriet nodded, wiping her tears with the back of her hand.

Maybe William could help. He might know somebody in the force in Portrush. If so, Malcolm could go through the official channels. Like he should have in the first place. What an old fool he was.

The phone rang as he reached for it. He picked up the receiver. "Hello?"

"Hello Malcolm, Pat here. I've managed to get an appointment for the doctor. For this afternoon. Harriet said she would sit with Duncan? That is, if it's not too much trouble."

Malcolm looked at his watch. Nearly 1pm. "That'll be no bother. I'll bring her over shortly." Maybe some good would come out of this mess if Pat got some help.

* * *

Malcolm wanted to leave Billy in the house, but there was no way Harriet would have it. Not after everything that had happened. There he was, sitting on the rear seat as usual.

When they arrived at the Gallaghers' bungalow, Harriet came round to the driver's side. Malcolm wound down the window.

"I'm going to persuade Pat to go and have a break after the doctor's appointment. Yeh know, have a walk around the town, or go shopping. Anything. She needs it. So don't hurry back to pick me up." She made to go, but then turned back again. "Here, Billy will be annoyed if he doesn't have this."

She handed him the ripped and soggy form of what had once been one of Malcolm's favourite gloves. He took it between his thumb and forefinger and shoved it in his coat pocket. There was no way that animal was going to make a mess in the back of his car.

What now? He could go back home and ring William, but even if the lad did know someone, the local police here in Portrush would think he was overreacting. An old retired policeman with more time than he needed on his hands, that's how he would be seen. He had no proof, certainly not before the vet got back to him. But he could talk through the whole Mulholland story. He might see some other angle that Malcolm was missing. There was definitely a link between Mulholland, Tobin and McGonigle. Had to be. But still there were information gaps. If Malcolm was right, McGonigle had ramped things up, making it personal. But why? Why was he trying to warn him off?

Yes, a chat with William would be useful.

Meanwhile, McGonigle needed sorting out. And quickly before he could get up to anything else. During his career, Malcolm had engaged in numerous wee chats with those who thought they could put one over on him. Unofficial, of course, but the message had always been clear and had always produced the desired effect. It wouldn't take that long to drive to McGonigle's house, put the frighteners on him. An hour at most. Malcolm had dealt with worse than McGonigle before.

"Right, Billy boy, we're going on a wee trip. We'll be back before Harriet knows we've been away.

CHAPTER THIRTY-ONE

Tommy tried to open his eyes. There was a pounding behind his forehead and a sharp pain on the left side of his jaw. He squinted one eye open and raised a hand to touch his face. His jaw was swollen. There was crusting around his nose. He picked a bit off and examined it. Dark, dried blood. He rolled over onto his side and dropped his legs over the edge of the bed, pushing his body into an upright position. Everything hurt. He was still wearing the clothes he'd had on last night.

Last night. Tommy groaned at the pain and at the memories flooding back. He'd got to the Kelly's Inn around 5pm, and immediately started on the beer. That Alex, the barman, had suggested food, to line his stomach. The more Tommy drank, the more it had sounded like a suggestion for something else. Then later, when the world had started to spin, and there was no way Tommy was going to make it to the hotel room, Alex had seemed keen to help. Surely that had been another hint. Tommy felt his jaw again. It hadn't been.

Tommy eased himself upright. He checked his face in the bathroom mirror. Alex had landed a belter on his left jaw. Right-handed uppercut. Bastard. Neither Tommy's pride nor his stomach would let him face breakfast. He could come back. Wait for Alex to return for his shift this evening. Even the score. He looked at his watch. Maybe he'd be able to make time for that later. First, he had to find out more. And McGonigle could give him answers, Tommy was certain.

As far as he could make out, Sam Tobin was his grandfather. Elizabeth Tobin a pathetic excuse of a mother. And that shite of a solicitor, George Tobin, his uncle. Why hadn't Elizabeth tried to keep him? Why had she rejected him? What was so wrong about him? It only made sense that she had loved that daughter of hers more. Must have. And McGonigle was in the thick of it. Jeff had said he was a low life, not trusted with anything substantial by the Brigade back in the day. Just used as a driver. But that meant he was everywhere. That meant he knew stuff. And he had been wile anxious not to spend time with Tommy. It spoke volumes.

He washed and showered, and then examined his chin again. Not so noticeable now. He could get away with just turning up the collar of his coat. Maybe he wouldn't have to shave, either. He checked his nose again. Not broken.

First call of the day, would be the petrol station-cum-hardware store next to Kelly's inn. Tommy was sure he would be able to get what he needed there. Everything he needed. He looked at his watch. 9.30am. Just about perfect. McGonigle hadn't looked the type to start the day early. Besides, he had another visit to make on the way.

* * *

Tommy slammed the shabby door behind him and strode to his car. He glanced round to take one last look at the place that had housed his shambles of a birth mother. The first of the loose ends was tidied up. Why should she live when she had given him up? Not making a fight of it to keep him.

He had known the task wouldn't take long. He had explained to Elizabeth what he believed – that he was her rejected son – and through her crying and wailing, she had confirmed it all.

She had tried to justify everything. To say she was forced into it. He told her she had made a pathetic attempt at being a mother. She had let her daughter die, and she had rejected her son. And still, she wouldn't tell him who his father was. Or maybe, she couldn't.

In the end, she'd almost wanted the option he gave her. A final release from her miserable existence. He had put out on her table enough tablets to end her misery. He had left when he was sure she had taken enough.

The weather suited his mood. Low-hanging clouds that threatened hard rain but delivered driving drizzle instead. He threw his holdall into the back seat, reached over to the glove box and took out the handgun. He checked it was loaded. Today he was going to get answers. Whatever it took. He slammed the glove box shut.

* * *

Tommy parked a good four houses away from Paul McGonigle's end-of-terrace house.

He looked at his watch. He looked up and down the street. No sign of life. Those with jobs would have already left for work. Seskinore. Who would live in this place? Surrounded by bogland as far as Tommy could see. It didn't even have a pub.

He needed to get his business done and get back to civilisation in Belfast. Or maybe further. Maybe he'd outgrown the whole province. What was there in Belfast for him now? Not even a job, not after the time he'd taken off. Emails and texts from work had started to come through to his phone. At first HR were sympathetic, but now they were demanding to know when he would be back, or at least when he'd get in touch with them. Sod them. And with his da no longer around to protect him from the worst that HR could throw at him, the loyalties and legacy of the past were starting to lose their effect. Whatever... It was time for him to get the whole picture of who he was and what had happened. What had robbed him of his real family. And then he would leave. Proper leave. For good. Make a new life somewhere on the mainland.

He got out of the car, the gun tucked into his waistband, his fleece big enough to cover the tell-tale bulge. Another look up and down the street. No one. He walked quickly to McGonigle's front door. A sharp rap. Nothing. Another louder knock.

A voice came from inside. "Houl on. Jesus, I'm coming."

The door opened a fraction. Paul McGonigle peered out, frowning. Then his eyes widened. "What the feck do you want?"

Tommy put his hand on the door to keep it from closing. "Just wanted to finish off our wee chat from the other night."

"I don't know ye. I've nothing to say to ye!"

Paul attempted to push the door shut. Stronger that Tommy expected, but no match for his strength.

"You do know me. Or at least you know about me. It's a bit rude, keeping me on the doorstep."

Tommy pushed hard. The door sprung open. Paul staggered backward, his eyes wide with panic. He turned, ran into the sitting room and slammed the door behind him. Tommy followed and tried the door handle. He couldn't move it. He put his shoulder to the door and pushed. There was immediate resistance, and then the door moved.

Tommy tried a false friendly tone. "Paul, it's only fair to tell you I have a gun. I only want to talk."

He pushed hard at the door again and it gave way.

Paul had his back to the wall at the far side of the room. His thin, unshaven face was ashen. He licked his lips, his eyes darting left and right. There was a damp stain running down his trousers. Tommy smiled. There would be no escape.

He took his gun from his waist band, then motioned for Paul to sit in the armchair. "Just a wee chat. That all right?"

Paul sank into the chair, his eyes fixed on the gun. "What do ye want? Money? Do ye want money?"

Tommy shook his head slowly. "I'm not here to rob yeh." He nodded at the settee. "Mind if I sit?" Not waiting for a reply, he dropped onto it, legs wide, gun resting on his thigh. "So, tell me about the old days. When me da was visiting these parts."

Paul frowned. A drop of sweat ran down his forehead. He wiped it away with the back of his hand. "You're Smith's boy? Smith from the East Belfast Brigade?"

"The very same." Tommy rubbed the gun along his thigh. The cold hardness felt good. "I understand you did a bit of work for him. That right?"

"A driver. I was a driver. Look, what's this about?"

"Oh, I think you know." Tommy pointed the gun at Paul. He pulled back the safety catch with his thumb. Click.

Paul flinched and shrank back in the chair. "I'm telling yeh. I was just a driver."

"Right, driver, tell me. Tell me about the good oul days."

Paul's eyes darted from side to side. Tommy knew the old man was looking for an opportunity. He smiled. It was pathetic, really. Paul had no chance.

"Look, I'll make it easier." He sank back into the settee and stretched his left arm across the back of it. "I know you did a bit of driving for the main men. They wouldn't trust you with the important stuff, so I've been told. But drivers have ears and eyes. And I reckon you saw plenty."

The old man raised his eyebrows before lowering them and smiling nervously.

"I can tell yeh plenty alright. Is that what this is about? You want to know about your old man? He was mighty, that's a fact. We all respected him. Yes, your da was a great man. Look, I have some pictures..."

"That's the problem." Tommy's eyes started to bulge. He pulled at is collar, as if it was suffocating him. "He wasn't me da, was he?" His voice was rising. "And you, scumbag, you know. You fucking know!"

Tommy was standing now. He couldn't remember getting to his feet, but he was looming over Paul, pressing the gun against his forehead. Paul was sliding towards the floor, almost supine in the chair. There was a fresh dark stain on his trousers. The acrid smell hit Tommy. He kicked Paul's legs and stood back. Plenty of time. Needed to get control again. Needed more information.

"Here's what I think. I think there was a woman named Tobin." Paul's eyes widened at the name. "Yeah, Elizabeth Tobin. You know her?" Paul shook his head desperately. "Oh, I think you do. This woman, Elizabeth Tobin, she had a daughter who got killed and then soon after she got up the duff. Following me?"

Paul scrambled to an upright position, his eyes wide, his face soaked in sweat. "All right, all right, I know her. I knew old man Tobin. I helped him out once or twice. That's all."

Tommy studied him. There was something else, he was sure of it. "You helped pass on the wean? Elizabeth's wean? Is that it? I know that child was handed on. That child was me and I was just given away."

Paul licked his lips. "No, I never. I was in prison. Check it out. Look, I don't know what you want, but if it's money? I can get you plenty of money."

"I'm not here for that." Tommy sat down again and lowered the gun. In a quiet voice, he said, "I need to know the truth. Who I am. That's all."

Paul's eyes flitted to the door. "You know your man Tobin? Well, his son. Elizabeth's brother. George. I can get yeh plenty of cash."

Tommy stared at him Paul wasn't making any sense. Tommy pointed the gun at his head. "Tell me."

"I have something on him. He killed a man. Mulholland. Is that what this is about? The man who killed Elizabeth's first child. Mulholland was into young girls. Everyone knew." Paul licked his lips again. "About fourteen was his favourite age. He was well in with a detective by the name of Robinson. So it was always covered up. But he must have gone too far at that Blue Light Disco. George worked it out. Worked out they would never get justice. He planned it himself."

"You helped him?" Tommy lowered the gun, kept his voice quieter now.

McGonigle was warming to his topic. He sat a little straighter. "No. But I was there that day. I was a drayman, delivering to the pub. I was early so had a wee fag break. I saw George passing. Knew him from the brigade work. He was never involved like his da was, but I saw him about his father's yard when we were delivering hardware for the boys. When I ran into financial problems, I cashed in. Told George I would keep his secret as long as he kept paying." He sniggered. "Been a regular income for me ever since." He pointed a shaky nicotine-stained finger at the gun. "Now, if you just could put that away, I won't mention a thing and you can have a cut of the money. What do yeh say?" He bared his teeth in a hopeful but weak smile.

Tommy studied Paul, his hand tensing around the gun. He still didn't have the answer he needed. "But what about Elizabeth? What about the child? The second one?"

Paul shrugged. "Old man Tobin was a patriot, but his wife, she was one of the God squad. Church twice on a Sunday. Bad enough that Elizabeth had the first child out of wedlock, but a second? Old Mrs Tobin put her foot down, big time. There was no way she was going to tolerate a second. Didn't help that Elizabeth had turned to drink after the girl was murdered. That was the end for Mrs Tobin. She told her husband that arrangements had to be made. Like I say, I was at Her Majesty's Pleasure when the wean was born. I only heard through the grapevine. But it didn't turn out too bad for yeh, did it? I mean, you ended up with a da that was a hero."

Tommy smoothed the gun barrel, stroking it like he would a cat.

Paul shook his head. "Christ, you could have ended up with Elizabeth as a mother. Fuck's sake. The woman was a bike." He laughed. "We all had a go."

Tommy stood quickly, took a step forward. He raised the gun and smashed it down on Paul's head.

CHAPTER THIRTY-TWO

Malcolm looked at the clock on the dashboard. Should make it to that eejit Paul McGonigle's house in just over an hour.

Looking in his mirror again, he saw the bloody dog hadn't moved since they'd set off on their journey. Billy's head was down and pushed into the back of the seat, his ears flat to his skull. It was just a dog, Malcolm tried to reason with himself. It was hard not to take offence, though. He'd tried doing a couple of "Billy boy, there's a good dog." But it hadn't made a jot of difference. Maybe the dog could hear the falseness in his voice. Well, the damn beast could suit itself. Malcolm reached to the CD player and pushed the play button. Philomena Begley's soothing tones would keep him company. He glanced again in the mirror. Hang on. Billy's ears were now raised and twitching. Maybe he had a redeeming feature.

Malcolm was sure Paul McGonigle wouldn't be going far. He was more of an early-evening-to-the-pub type. He had come across the like before. Even if he had gone somewhere, it would be no bother to track him down. That curtain twitcher from next door would be happy to help. Malcolm wouldn't be going back to Portrush without putting the bastard straight.

There was no way he was going to let McGonigle terrorise him or the Gallaghers. Just who the hell did he think he was? McGonigle was going to get it, full blast. The nonsense was going to end. Whatever the reason he wanted to scare Malcolm off, it was risky for the man. Very risky. So there must be a powerful reason for trying. Something linked to this digging around in the past. Mulholland's murder, or maybe that of Liza Tobin. Whichever one it was, Malcolm would get to the bottom of it today.

Philomena had nearly reached the end of her tenth song when Malcolm approached the sign for the care home. He looked at the dashboard clock again. It wouldn't take more than five minutes. The roads were fairly quiet. He could make up the time. He needed to know why Robinson had set off this series of events. Yes, the man was a pain in the arse and arrogant with it, but the rest of his career had been exemplary. What had made a good policeman go so wrong? He indicated and turned off the road.

He knocked on the open door of the office-cum-reception. He kept Billy on a short lead. He'd better not lift his leg in this place.

Orla, in her lilac uniform, looked up from the notes she was writing. She frowned and then smiled in recognition. "Oh hello. You've come back to visit him again. That's grand. He's in good humour this morning." She smiled ruefully. "Well, not so crabbit, anyway." Her smile widened when she saw Billy. "Och, and yeh have a wee dog with you. Isn't he a wee dote?" She kneeled beside Billy to stroke his head, and the dog cocked his head to one side. "Your wee dog's lovely." Do you want me to show you to Mr Robinson's room?"

Malcolm shook his head. "No. I remember the way. Orla, would yeh mind looking after Billy when I have a chat with Mr Robinson? I'm not sure he likes dogs."

Orla grinned. "Of course, no bother."

"Do you want me to sign the book?"

Orla's grin faded. "If you don't mind. It's the regulations. We had an inspection last week. Mr Robinson took the opportunity to make all sorts of allegations about us, so they're checking on everything we do here." She shrugged. "Bit unfair, really. I know residents get upset they can't stay in their own homes, but this is one of the best places I've worked in."

"It seems to me you do a grand job here."

Orla smiled and patted the back of her hair. "Thanks. It's a great job." She glanced towards the corridor that led to DI Robinson's room. "Most of the time. "You alright to make your way yourself?"

Malcolm saw Robinson through the open door. The old man was sitting in an upright chair staring out of the bay window of his room. A tartan rug was tucked around his legs. Malcolm knocked on the door frame.

Robinson whipped his head round, a scowl on his face. "Clear off..." He let his mouth hang open for a second before firmly closing it again. "You? What do you want?" he snarled.

"Nice to see you too. Thought you would be glad of a visitor. I doubt you don't get many. Not the way you treat people."

Robinson frowned. "You can't talk to me like that. I'm an oul man." He stretched his neck and tried to look around Malcolm. "Nurse! Nurse!"

Malcolm kicked the door closed behind him. "They're busy."

Robinson stared at Malcolm, no fear in his eyes. "What are yeh back here for?"

Malcolm leaned against the door and crossed his arms. "Just want to fill in some details. About Mulholland. Nice bloke, was he? Salt of the earth?"

Robinson continued to stare at him, his mouth firmly shut and narrow.

"Here's what I think," Malcolm went on. "The man liked young girls. Had a bit of a reputation for it. But let's say he married one of these girls, possibly had to marry because she was going to have his wean. And blow me, straight after that one came into the world, she was pregnant again. He got bored with this perpetually pregnant wife of his. Maybe one night he decided he needed more fun. Maybe he went to a Blue Light Disco – you know all about them, don't you, DI Robinson? – and offered a wee girl a lift home. Maybe she objected to the cost of the lift. And maybe she ended up dead in Mulholland's quarry."

Robinson looked to one side. He rubbed his eyes.

"Still nothing to say? All right. Let's say Mulholland did this terrible thing. A decent police investigation would put it all together. And one thing you were, DI Robinson, was a very clever police officer. Sure, look." He gestured at the framed awards on the wall. "The evidence is there. Wouldn't yeh wonder why yeh never got to the bottom of it?"

Robinson mumbled something. Malcolm couldn't make it out. "What did yeh say?"

"I had to protect her!" Robinson pointed his bony finger at Malcolm. "She was my niece. He was rubbish. A skitter. A bastard. But he was the father of her children." He put his head in his hands. "What would people have said if it had all come out?"

"Jesus, you were a police officer!"

Robinson straightened his spine. "I tried to make amends. I told Tobin. The girl's granda. With his connections I was sure he could arrange something. Right the wrong." He spread his hands. "And he did, didn't he? I just had to get the money back to my niece." Robinson gave a half-smile. "Job done. All sorted."

Malcolm's stomach churned. He shook his head in disgust. This man who had been charged with the protection of his community had twisted the system to his own ends. He could see that Robinson was still convinced that he'd done right. Maybe that was the case for his niece, Mulholland's widow, but what about everyone else?

There was a knock and a slight push at the door behind Malcolm. He stepped forward and Orla's head appeared. There was the sound of yapping behind her. She smiled apologetically. "Sorry to disturb you, gentlemen. I think your dog is getting restless. And I have the medication round to do. Sorry."

"No bother. I need to head on anyway." Malcolm took the lead from Orla's extended hand and started through the door.

He heard Robinson's voice behind him as he walked out to the reception area. "A dog? Sure, I love wee dogs."

273

After giving Billy an opportunity to stretch his legs and lessen the chances of having an accident during the remainder of the trip, Malcolm got back into the car. He looked at the dashboard clock. Shite. Too much time with Robinson after all. Time wasted.

He was clear now about the death of poor wee Liza Tobin. Mulholland's murder had been triggered by the information that Robinson had given old man Tobin, who had plenty of dubious contacts and could have the job done himself. Malcolm decided to hand over all the information he had gathered, as soon as he had sorted out McGonigle. William would have plenty to go on for a cold case review of both murders. He could call in on William on the way back to Portrush.

* * *

He pulled up outside Paul McGonigle's house. Not a soul about. The man's curtains were open, so at least he was up. Billy sat up from his usual position.

"Right, Billy boy. I'll be five minutes – ten minutes, tops. I'll leave the window down a bit. And if any of the dodgier residents of Seskinore try anything, I will be very disappointed if yeh don't bite the hands of them."

Billy did that cute cocking his head to one side. Malcolm had the impression that the dog would be more likely to lick any hand coming in through the open window. He sighed. Ah well, he wouldn't be too long. Just sort Paul McGonigle out. Put him straight.

He walked up to the front door and knocked loudly. Nothing. No twitching of the curtain. No sound of footsteps. He knocked again, this time louder. Still nothing.

He opened the letterbox. "Paul. I know you're in there. I just need a quick chat. To confirm a few things, that's all."

Nothing.

He walked to the side of the house. Fuck's sake. There was the red Ford Fiesta that had nearly knocked him down. Definitely the car he'd seen racing around Portrush. Bastard. The man would get more than a bit of a talking to. Just enough to know he should never mess with Malcolm.

Malcolm went back to the front door. This time, the force of his knocking swung the door open slightly.

Strange.

He pushed the door and it swung open. "Paul?"

He took a tentative step into the hall. The house was silent. Instinctively, Malcolm felt for his handgun.

Shite. No longer a serving policeman with the sidearm benefits. He pushed open the door to the sitting room and looked to the left. Nothing. Then to the right. Paul McGonigle was lying on the floor, trussed up like a chicken, a gag in his mouth. Malcolm took another step into the room. "Fuck's sake!"

He sensed movement behind him. But it was too quick. A blow to his head. Searing pain. His knees started to give way. Then nothing.

CHAPTER THIRTY-THREE

Tommy studied the unconscious man lying where he'd fallen. He had hit him with the heel of the gun. Now he kicked him. In the ribs, for good measure. For fuck's sake. Things had been going to plan before this old lump of lard appeared. So...Now he had a choice. Did he leave the man there or take him too?

He sat on the arm of Paul's chair. This newcomer might have nothing to do with McGonigle. Or he could have everything to do with it. For all he knew, this man could be the go-between. The one who had brought Paul McGonigle his payments from George Tobin. His uncle. Who had killed some man called Mulholland in revenge for the killing of Tommy's half-sister, two years before he was born. Paul McGonigle was Tommy's link to the truth. To his real family.

He sighed. Yes, best to hedge his bets and take both with him.

When he'd secured the unconscious man's ankles and gripped his hands behind his back with insulation tape, he put a strip across the man's mouth. He dragged him to the back door of the kitchen, which led to the side of the house. He looked out to make sure no one was walking past on the street. He dragged the inert body towards the rear of his car and opened the boot.

Paul, legs and hands tied, tape across his mouth too, stared at Tommy with wide, scared eyes.

"Fuck's sake." Tommy thought he'd hit Paul hard enough to keep him out of it for longer. "Right, Paul, you'll need to move up a bit. I have company for yeh."

Paul made a noise and shook his head frantically.

Tommy sighed. He took out the gun from his waistband. "You will move over, one way or the other. Understand?"

Paul wriggled backwards into the recess of the boot.

Tommy replaced his gun. "That's better."

He heaved the still unconscious body of the stranger into the boot. Paul made a noise through the tape on his mouth as the man landed next to him.

"Shut the fuck up. It's not my fault you have some mate calling round." Tommy slammed the boot shut.

As he was about to get into the driver's seat, he heard frantic barking. Surely to God this low life didn't have another caller. Surely, he wouldn't have many acquaintances, let alone friends.

He got out of the car again and peered around the side of the house. No, nobody at the door. But there was a car parked before the front door. It was bound to belong to the mystery man. Christ. The stupid git, whoever he was, had brought a dog with him. Tommy reached for his gun and took a step towards the car.

At that moment, the door of the house next to Paul's opened. A woman came out and walked towards the car. Tommy stepped away and watched, holding the gun behind his back. The dog put its paws on the window of the car and tried to stick its nose out of the space left open. The woman put her hand to the dog's nose. Billy licked it.

"Och, you wee dote. Has somebody left yeh here? Yeh poor wee lamb. She looked towards McGonigle's house. "I bet it's somebody to do with that bastard, has left yeh here. Right, I'll sort that out."

The woman marched to Paul's front door and knocked loudly. "I know you're in there." She knocked harder. "If you don't come out here right now, I'm ringing the police... or the USPCA. I'm tellin yeh. I will." Another banging... "Right, that's it. I've warned yeh." She turned and stormed towards her front door.

Tommy walked quickly back to his own car, started the engine, gunned the motor and raced away. He was sure that the police would consider a dog in a car with the window open on a cool day a low priority, but he had work to do. Information to get. And he wasn't going to be stopped.

On the road to Balleygawly, he kept smiling at the sound of Paul kicking the rear of the boot. There was no way he was getting out of there. He might as well save his energy – he was going to need it. Tommy had plans for him. Consolidated at the moment when Paul made that comment about his mother being the local bike. Tommy had been disgusted by her, disappointed by her. That wasn't what he wanted. He had dismissed her. She would always be nothing to him. But there remained the question of who his father was. Paul knew, Tommy was sure of it. And he was equally sure Paul would be soon telling him his father's identity.

* * *

Tommy pushed open the gate and drove into the lane he had previously driven with Alfie Hamill. He closed the gate behind him, then parked next to the out buildings.

He was about to get out of the car, but stopped. No. He had every right to be in the family homestead. He drove on and parked in front of the dour-looking house. It had been abandoned for over thirty years, but Tommy guessed it would always have looked forbidding. A house where an honest day's work was paramount and church attendance on a Sunday as essential as breathing. The support for the Unionist cause would have added brownie points. This should have been part of his heritage. Why not? Maybe he would need to right a wrong, just as his uncle had. Yes. Paul McGonigle would provide the answers.

It didn't take much force to kick open the weather-peeled front door. He was through to a large hallway. The floor had brown and black tiles and the stairway in front of him had threadbare carpet and peeling wallpaper. A door stood either side of him. Both shut. He tentatively opened the one to the right. A single chair pushed up against a brown flat desk. Maybe used as an office. On the wall was an open wall safe. Two filing cabinets stood adjacent to it but the room was bare of anything else. He went back into the hall and opened the door to the left. This was a much larger room which seemed to run the whole length of the house. A three-piece suite occupied the space near to him. A dining room table complete with six chairs sat at the other end.

A fireplace decorated one wall. A layer of dust covered the room. It smelled damp. Damp and empty. Yes, this room would do just fine.

Tommy placed two of the dining chairs opposite each other by the fireplace. Satisfied, he returned to the car. Collected a full jerry can he had bought from the garage next to the Royal Oak. He placed it by one of the chairs. Yep. Good to go.

He returned to the car and opened the boot. The stranger was still unconscious but behind him Paul immediately started to wriggle and tried to shout through the tape.

"Patience, Paul. I'll be back for you in a second. Won't be long now."

Paul stopped still and drifted into silence.

Tommy pulled the stranger out of the boot and heaved him over his shoulder. "Christ, you need to lose a few stone, pal." He slammed the boot, staggered with the inanimate load into the house and threw him onto the settee. He went back to the car and popped the boot. Paul shrunk back, his eyes wide in fear.

"Right. Here's what I'm going to do. I'm going to take the tape off your legs and you are going to walk all nice and calm into this here house." Tommy pointed. "And in case you decide to do anything different..." Tommy gestured to the gun in his waistband. "That clear?"

Paul nodded, his eyes still wide. Tommy ripped the tape off his legs, then stood back and took out his gun. "Out yeh come, then."

Paul wriggled forward. He dropped his legs over the side and levered himself to sit upright. He tried to stand, but couldn't.

"Fuck's sake!" Tommy levelled the gun in his right hand and grabbed under Paul's armpit with his left. When he was upright, Tommy nudged him with the gun. "Off yeh trot, old man."

Paul stumbled and then righted himself. He shuffled towards the house, looking once or twice over his shoulder at Tommy.

"I'm right behind yeh. Through the front door and the first on your right."

When they got into the room, Tommy gestured towards the dining-room chair facing them. "Sit."

Paul obeyed. Tommy stepped behind the chair, grabbed Paul's arms and yanked them high. Paul screamed though the tape. Tommy pulled the arms down again, over the back of the chair. He moved to stand in front of Paul and leant down so that his face was six inches away. Tommy could smell the fear. Could see the rivers of sweat on the man's face. The tape was blowing in and out with his heavy breathing.

"I am going to take this tape off and we are going to continue our wee chat. Ye see, I am convinced…" Tommy slammed the butt of the gun on Paul's left temple. Paul gave a muffled yell. Blood trickled down the side of his face. "Convinced that you know more. Remember more."

Tommy reached towards Paul's face and ripped the tape from his mouth. Paul screamed.

"I'll tell yeh everything. I can get yeh money. Whatever ye want. Look, I'm an oul man. Sure, I'm half dead," pleaded Paul.

Tommy laughed. "Half dead? I can help yeh go the whole hog. Slowly or quickly. Or maybe I'll be overcome with gratitude and let yeh go. Let's see how we get on, shall we?" Tommy looked down at the gun. Where to start? "You knew my grandfather?"

Paul licked his lips. "Yes. I worked for him on and off. In between a couple of times in prison."

"And you were part of the Tyrone brigade?"

Paul nodded. "Yes. I helped out. So did old man Tobin. I was a driver. I told yeh that."

"And you said you knew Elizabeth Tobin."

"Everyone knew Elizabeth. Good-time girl. Everyone knew that."

Tommy took that in. Elizabeth may have been pathetic now, but he knew she was his mother. Paul had just lessened his chances of leaving here this day. "That so? She had one wee girl who was murdered by this guy called Mulholland—"

"Aye." Paul leant forward, nodding. "And then George Tobin, Elizabeth's brother, sorted him out. I know. I saw him going there that day."

"OK. I get all that. So tell me about afterwards."

Paul eyes darted from side to side. "Afterwards? After what?"

"After Elizabeth's daughter died. What happened to Elizabeth?"

Paul sniggered. "Is that all yeh want to know?" He shrugged. "She went to pieces. Took to drink in a big way. She's still a mess. Back then she was looking for a bit of companionship, if yeh know what I mean. All yeh needed to do was bring a bit of the hard stuff."

"Then what?"

"The inevitable happened. Another wean. Born in this house. The Tobins wanted to keep it quiet."

"You said you were in prison when the wean was born."

"I might have got me dates wrong. Look, you want the whole story don't yeh? Yeh were born here. Upstairs. Back bedroom."

"What happened next?"

"I took you to the Ballygawley roundabout. Your father was waiting there."

"He wasn't my father."

"As good as."

"Who was my father, my real father?"

Paul shrugged again. "Who's to say? We all had a go. Could have been me."

Tommy raised his gun and smashed it down on Paul" head. His head lolled to one side. Then Tommy paused.

They were miles from anywhere. No one to hear anything. He stood back and pointed the gun at Paul's right knee. Crack! Paul's unconscious form jerked with the impact. Then his left knee. Crack!

CHAPTER THIRTY-FOUR

Malcolm heard the first shot as if it was from periphery of a dream. The second brought him immediately to consciousness. He opened his eyes and tried to move his arms and legs. He was lying on his side on a dusty, mouldy settee in a room he did not recognise. Paul McGonigle was bent over, lifeless, in a dining-room chair, blood pouring down his trousers, a mess of bone and cartilage where his knees should have been.

A tall, slight man was standing facing Paul with a gun in his hand. As Malcolm shifted on the settee, trying to get to a sitting position, the man turned round. Malcolm was sure he had seen him before. Recently. The man came over and ripped the tape from Malcolm's mouth. Malcolm winced.

"Who the fuck are you?" He had a broad Belfast accent. "You the money man between that gobshite and George Tobin?"

"Whoa now, I have nothing to do with Paul McGonigle." Malcolm struggled to a more upright position.

"Oh aye, so you just happened to be passing? Just thought yeh would check out a random house? Don't take me for a fool." He held the gun to Malcolm's forehead.

Malcolm felt cold sweat running down his face. "No, wait, wait. I'll tell yeh. I was there to warn him off. He was terrorising a friend of mine and trying to stop me investigating an old murder. A man by the name of Mulholland."

"The man George Tobin killed? What's that got to do with you? You some kind of peeler?" The gun was lowered. The man looked at Malcolm quizzically.

"Yes. I mean I was. George Tobin killed Mulholland?"

"That's what the gobshite said. Reckoned he was being paid off for years. So you're nothing to do with that setup? Pity." He shrugged. "Collateral damage. That's what they call the likes of you." He walked over to the dining room table and placed the gun down. Then he lifted a jerry can and started to unscrew the cap. Malcolm could smell the petrol fumes.

"Malcolm. My name's Malcolm." From somewhere in the depths of his memory, he recalled being told in training that it helped if you were seen as a person with a name in these circumstances. "You know Paul McGonigle? What's he done to you?"

The man put the petrol can down. He lifted the chair, walked over to where Malcolm half-sat, half-lay, and placed it in front of him. He sat down and studied the man on the settee. "I came for answers. About my parents. I've worked out most of it. I thought that bastard..." he nodded behind him "... knew more than he did. I thought he could tell me who my father was."

"Jesus, you're Tommy Smith. The man that gave Hannah a hard time."

Tommy's brows furrowed. "Hannah?"

Malcolm looked between the slumped figure in the chair and Tommy. He could place him now. The man rushing out of Tobin's office that day.

"Hannah is a social worker. You're Elizabeth Tobin's boy."

"You seem to know an awful lot for a has-been peeler." Tommy pointed the gun again. "Talk some more."

He wanted more. That was good. "I knew Mulholland was murdered and now I know why. You've told me by who. I didn't know that bit."

Tommy snorted. "And they call me unnatural. That Mulholland who killed my sister was a paedo. Liked wee girls. Christ. That what it's like in the boglands? Maybe you're all the same." He straightened his gun arm towards Malcolm.

"Yes, Mulholland was a paedophile. Deserved to die. Course he did. But I'm trying to help you. I'm trying to get to the truth. I can get justice for your sister. Even now."

"No need, mate. Good old Uncle George did that. And that was fair enough. But the trouble is, none of them wanted me. Not me ma, George, their parents or me da, whoever he is. So here's the thing. I've had a look at my past and it's crap. Everyone lied to me from start to finish. What I'm going to do is erase it. All of it. And then I'm going to start again. Me ma – me real ma – she was away with the fairies already, so that was easy to sort out. Put her out of her misery, yeh could say. That box is ticked. Then this place." He gestured around him.

"This should have been my homestead. But it wasn't. I wasn't good enough. So it's going. And you and that bastard there are going with it. Can't leave any trail behind, can I?" Tommy lifted the jerry can. "You get that, don't you? You know, with your professional background?"

The petrol smelled stronger now as Tommy sprinkled the fluid around the room. Malcolm thought about Harriet. He couldn't let it end like this. Couldn't give her that pain.

"Look, I can help you. Help you find out who your father is. That Hannah..."

Tommy turned quickly towards Malcolm. "She was fucking useless! Didn't want to help when I asked!" He carried on throwing petrol around the room.

"I'll have a word with her. She was just following procedure. I can get her to access the right records. I can insist. Make sure you find out who your father was. I can help you."

Malcolm tried to keep the pleading out of his voice, but he knew he was failing.

"TOO. FUCKING. LATE!" Tommy threw the jerry can down onto the floor.

Malcolm watched the liquid run out of it. Tommy reached into his pocket. He pulled out a lighter and flicked the flint wheel.

"No. No, you don't want to do this. You'll be caught. Christ, just go. Go now. Start your new life anywhere. I'll never say a word. I'll make sure he doesn't either!"

Tommy walked towards the door. "Like I said. Collateral damage. No hard feelings, eh?" Tommy opened the door, half-turned towards Malcolm and held the lighter out in front of him.

Malcolm scrambled to his feet. "Tommy, wait, Paul's your da! Can't yeh see? You're the spit of him!"

Tommy frowned.

"We can do tests just to be sure…"

Tommy stared at the slumped figure of Paul McGonigle. He looked at the flame of the lighter. Then threw it next to Paul. The petrol ignited with a flash. And Tommy walked out of the room.

Paul's body started to twitch as the flames took hold of him. He was startled into consciousness and began to scream and scream and scream.

Malcolm had to move. To have any chance, knew he had to stay low and get to the door. He threw himself onto the floor, impeded by his taped hands and legs. He rolled towards the door. The flames were still licking around Paul's body, but now there were no more screams.

The flames had now got hold of the carpet and were creeping towards Malcolm. The smoke clawed at his throat. Still he rolled towards the door, coughing and coughing, drawing upon energy he didn't know he had. His eyes streamed. He gasped to get a breath, but all that entered his lungs was smoke. Thick, dense, acrid smoke.

Nearer the door now. The flames were cracking. Louder and louder. The heat burned at his legs, at his body, at his face, the smell of sulphur burned at his nose and mouth. Through streaming eyes, Malcolm could see that the door was ajar. But it was too far. Just too far. His stinging eyes closed. He coughed out smoke but more attacked his lungs.

He had tried. Dear God, Harriet, I tried so hard to stay with you.

CHAPTER THIRTY-FIVE

Tommy swung the Fiesta onto the main road. In the rear-view mirror he could see smoke rising. Good. The fire had taken hold. And he had time to finish this business. He was ahead of events now, not dragging himself up to speed behind them. In total control. He looked down at the gun sitting on the passenger seat.

A second later he was watching a car racing towards him. The Fiesta had drifted into the middle of the road. He swung the steering wheel, swerved to his left and bounced onto the verge. The front of the car dug into grass and gravel, then lifted again as Tommy managed to turn back onto the road. The oncoming car roared past him. Seemed like the driver hadn't even registered Tommy was there.

* * *

Something was dragging him. Across the floor. Pressure under his arms. Is this what it was like? To die in a fire? Were you dragged towards your death?

Then there was a voice.

"Fuck's sake! Keep breathing, Malcolm. Keep breathing!"

He knew that voice. That voice was good. It was safe.

His face still was unbearably hot, but less so now. He coughed and coughed and coughed. There was another heave. And tugging, at his pocket. Then it stopped. He was rolled on his side, and he vomited.

"Over here!" he heard the good voice shout.

His lungs began to expel the acrid smoke. His head started to clear. He found his voice.

"William!" he gasped.

"The very same. Jesus, Malcolm, I thought you were a goner."

There was another voice now. One maybe not so welcome. "Is he alive?"

What was Alfie Hamill doing here? Malcolm tried to ask, but he couldn't stop coughing.

Try as he might, he couldn't open his eyes. They were stinging and swollen shut. His face burned like the worst sunburn.

"Alfie, grab the dog before it runs off," William said.

The dog. Christ, the dog. He'd left it in the car. How had the dog got here?

Now there was a siren.

"Malcolm, the ambulance is coming. You're going to be fine. Try and get your breath. Alfie, have yeh got the dog yet?"

Malcolm heard the siren getting louder. Doors slamming shut and footsteps running. Still the coughing wouldn't stop. Then liquid was being poured on his eyes, washing away the stinging. That was good. Pressure over his mouth. He tried to push it away. He needed to breathe, for God's sake. Then a whoosh of air came through and he stopped struggling. His breath came more easily. He drank in the oxygen. More liquid on his eyes. He attempted to open them a fraction.

"Malcolm, we're going to get you onto a stretcher." An unfamiliar voice, but one that was in control and could be trusted. "I need you to keep the mask in place. You will have a degree of smoke damage, so no silly nonsense like trying to get the mask off. Plenty of time later to tell us what happened. We need to get you safe to hospital first."

Malcolm felt water running down his face mixing with his tears. He knew that at some stage he would be going home to Harriet.

* * *

It all seemed so right, this obliteration of his past life. All of it. He could start again. Away from all this shite. Just one more call to make. To finish the job. Then there would be nothing left of where he had come from, and those who had rejected him. Just one last loose end to tie up. But he was a fair man. He would give his Uncle George a choice. He could do the decent thing, one way or another.

Tommy drove up the now familiar driveway to the solicitors' offices. He parked in a space with a notice that read Reserved for Senior Associates. He opened the Fiesta door and pushed hard – making sure the car door made a satisfying dented line in the black Porsche Macan parked alongside.

Tommy marched up to the entrance. Through the window he could see the receptionist with his head bent over his desk. He pushed open the door, strode up to the desk and put both hands on the documents the receptionist was concentrating on.

"Hey, pal."

The receptionist looked up, startled. He took a deep breath before clenching his jaw.

"Can I help you?" he squeaked.

Tommy guessed he didn't look – or smell – like George Tobin's standard type of client. "Which way to George Tobin's office?" he demanded.

The receptionist reached for the phone. "I'll have to check if he's available. Your name?"

Tommy slammed his fist down on the receptionist's hand and kept it there. "Don't bother warning him. I said, which way?"

"First floor. Second door on the right at the top of the stairs." The man's free hand trembled as he pointed towards the lifts.

"I would suggest that you do not ring him," Tommy said. "But just to be sure you're not tempted…"

Tommy lifted his fist. Reached down to the phone line jack and pulled hard. The connector ripped out of the socket. Tommy twisted the connector off and dropped the lead on the floor.

He didn't knock on the man's door. Sod that crap. He turned the handle and used his shoulder to push it open. The door swung inwards, bounced on its hinges and swung back. George Tobin, sitting behind an imposing desk, looked up from his paperwork with a start.

"Who the hell are you?"

Tommy backheeled the door shut.

"Somebody who's looking for answers." He walked to the desk and sat on one of the seats reserved for clients. He took his gun from his pocket. George stared at it. Speechless. "And you, my friend, are going to start talking."

Staring at the gun, Tobin found his voice. "Look... Erm... I have no idea who you are or what you want."

"I'll help yeh out, Uncle George."

Tobin's expression segued from terrified to confused. "What the fuck are you talking about? I've never met you. I have no..."

Tommy slammed the gun on the desk. "You are my uncle. You are one of the bastards that got rid of me. Wasn't I good enough?"

"You're Elizabeth's... Jesus." George's face paled. "No, no, no. It wasn't like that. Christ, What could I do? I was fifteen, sixteen when Liza... and then Elizabeth was pregnant. My parents, my mother, she was having none of it."

Tommy nursed the gun on his lap. "She must have been a right old witch."

Tobin, shivered, licked his lips and looked toward the door. "She had... principles."

"And her principles meant getting rid of the embarrassment. That was me, was it?"

"No. I mean, yes. It was for Elizabeth's good."

"Looks to me that she turned into a wreck. Not much backbone there. Letting one child get killed and letting another one go."

"You've met Elizabeth? She's not well..."

"Well, let's just say she's at peace now."

Tobin stared at him. Swallowed. "Sweet Jesus, what have you done?"

"I've been righting a few wrongs. Getting rid of a past that didn't want me in the first place. Surely that's fair. But you, George…"

Tommy pointed the gun at his chest. Tobin sank lower in his chair. His hands curled into fists on the desk. Tommy moved on with the story.

"You're interesting. See, I can't work out why you would be paying Paul McGonigle all these years. Why didn't yeh just sort him out? Get rid of him? You killed one man—"

"Christ's sake, be quiet!"

"Oh, I see. Looks to me like you couldn't bring yourself to pull the trigger again. Once enough for you, was it? Well, rest assured, Uncle George, I done it for yeh. You won't be needing to send your cheques or whatever to McGonigle from now on. That account is closed."

"For the love of God, what do you want from me?" Tobin was pleading now.

"I am going to "move on". Isn't that what they say? Draw a line under it. But to do that I need money. Quite a bit of money, in fact. And maybe occasional top-ups. Given your obligation to McGonigle is finished, I reckon that could work out just fine. You see, I was going to include you in my, if yeh like, tidying up the past." Tommy stroked the gun. "But then I got to thinking. You tried, didn't yeh? You tried to do the right thing, shooting Mulholland back then. Like me, you were trying to right a wrong."

Tobin shook his head. "No, no, no. That was different. It was long, so long ago. I was an eejit and I've been regretting it ever since." Colour was creeping back into his cheeks. "But I'll sort you out with money."

Tommy smiled. This was going to be so easy. "I want a guarantee."

There was a firm knock at the door. Tommy glared at Tobin. "Expecting someone?"

Tobin shook his head, eyes wide with fear. "No."

Another knock, louder this time. "Mr Tobin? Everything alright? Reception said there might be a problem?"

Tommy tucked the gun into his waistband, crossed his arms and perched on the edge of the desk facing the door. He nodded at Tobin.

"Come in!" Tobin shouted.

The door was pushed open. A security guard, as broad as he was tall, appeared in the doorway. Another peered over his shoulder.

Tobin waved them away. "No. No problem here."

"Okay." The guard looked uncertain. "It's just the receptionist said—"

"That receptionist is always over reacting." Tobin waved them away again. "Just go. You're interrupting my appointment with my client. Time is money. I'm sure your company won't want to be charged for this interruption?"

The guards started to back out of the room. "No sir. Right. Just let us know...".

Tobin rose to his feet. "For God's sake, get out!"

Tobin's eyes followed the security men into the corridor. The office door closed. Tobin blew out his cheeks. Looked at Tommy.

"See...? I'm not going to say a word to anyone. Why would I? Why would I risk losing all of this?" He waved around the room. "Just tell me how much you want and where to send it."

Tommy's heart started to beat faster. He swallowed the rage building in his stomach. Took a deep breath. Christ, this man must take me for a fool.

"First... Get yourself a pen and paper. I'll tell yeh what to write. Then I'll give yeh the bank details."

Tommy dictated Tobin's confession to the murder of Trevor Mulholland. Tobin's hand shook as he wrote. It was still shaking as he signed and dated the page, folded it and placed it in an envelope. He held it out to Tommy who put the envelope into his jacket pocket next to the gun.

"This is my insurance policy. Nobody gets to see this as long as you keep the deposits coming. After all, you won't need to pay McGonigle anymore. Think of it as keeping the money in the family." He snorted. "You prick, the way I see it, I'm doing yeh a favour. You can just go on with your life... as long as there are no delays in the transfers."

Tommy gave Tobin his new name and the account details he had set up online through Jeff's contacts. Then he watched as the first instalment was transferred.

* * *

Tommy took one last look around the terraced house he had called home until just a few weeks ago. The jerry can was heavy in his hand, but this had to be done. The car was already burning on wasteland two streets away.

He had what he needed in his holdall. Enough to start again. His guarantee was safely in his pocket for now. The new identity paperwork was perfect. And the forged passport. Jeff's old contact still had the requisite skills. In truth, the old man had seemed delighted to use them again as he'd done in his heyday during the Troubles to ensure volunteers could get away. Now, Tommy had a route and tickets out of the province to... he hadn't decided.

He splashed the petrol about, taking care not to get any on his clothes. He took a lighter from the sideboard drawer, picked up his holdall and walked to the front door. Outside, he lit his lighter and threw it into the hallway. Just like the Tobin homestead, the lighter caught the petrol. Flames began to illuminate the room.

Tommy slammed the door and walked quickly down the street.

CHAPTER THIRTY-SIX

Malcolm opened his eyes. They still stung. But he could open them. And the headache. Man, he hadn't had one like that since nights out with the rugby boys in his youth. He smiled through the oxygen mask at Harriet, who was sitting by the side of his hospital bed. She held his hand and smiled back. Her eyes were red. The journey to the hospital had been a blur of paramedics checking everything that there was to be checked. But he was safe. He was alive.

William and Alfie hovered at the foot of the bed. Malcolm raised his hand to wave a greeting, but hospital monitoring devices attached to him limited his range.

Harriet smiled. "This pair saved you."

Both of them? Malcolm could well believe William would have rescued him, but Alfie?

Harriet's smile broadened. "Yes, Alfie too."

Alfie shifted from foot to foot.

William put his hand on the journalist's shoulder. "If it hadn't been for Alfie, I wouldn't have found yeh."

Malcolm reached to pull the mask from his face. He had so many questions.

Harriet put her hand on the mask. "Don't you dare! William, just tell him what happened, or he'll never be content."

"Alfie here was contacted by Tommy Smith – the same man who had given Hannah bother a few weeks back about accessing records. He asked Alfie to help him find his birth mother. Alfie thought it would be a good feature. Yeh know. For the paper."

Christ, did that man never stop looking for an angle? He frowned at Alfie and shook his head slowly.

"It's my job!" said Alfie in a pleading tone.

"Malcolm," tutted Harriet. "I know what you're thinking. But the man does have a job to do."

Malcolm tried to shrug.

"Anyway," continued William. "Alfie was concerned about Tommy Smith's behaviour. Is that right?" He turned to Alfie.

Alfie nodded. "He was all right at the start. Friendly enough. But he got a bit out of hand at the Tobin place, and then when we went to Elizabeth's house—"

This time Malcolm got his hand to the oxygen mask and pulled it to one side. He managed to say, "You stupid..." before the coughing took over again.

Harriet gently knocked his hand away and repositioned the mask. "Malcolm, for once in your life would yeh just do as you're told. They're trying to tell yeh what happened." Tears welled up in her eyes.

Malcolm let his hand fall to the bedclothes. Harriet had suffered enough with his stupidity. She was right, it was time to grow up. He took deep breaths and the coughing slowly subsided.

Alfie frowned. "Harriet, should I go on? I mean I don't want to..."

"Don't worry. He needs to know. Otherwise he'll never settle."

"Well, OK, if you're sure. I took him first to the Tobin place. That's where he started acting weird. Then to Paul McGonigle's. He wasn't in. When we got to Elizabeth's house..." Alfie winced when he saw Malcolm's scowl reappear. "I know, I know, I was going to bail then, but he pulled a gun on me. We weren't at Elizabeth's long, but she got really upset. It was strange. I mean, she had never met the guy before, but she seemed like she recognised him. Not in a good way. But that couldn't be possible."

So Elizabeth saw the likeness of Paul McGonigle in Tommy as well. Malcolm started to raise his hand towards his mask, but caught Harriet's stern look and lowered it again. Time enough later to fill them in on that part.

"He left me back at the office after the visit to Elizabeth. I didn't know what to do for the best. I rang William. I thought he would know if the man had done anything illegal. He would know what I should do – you know, report it officially or whatever. And I knew Hannah looked after Elizabeth."

William took up the story. "I was off duty, so I thought I'd check it out with my DI the following day. But then Harriet rang. She couldn't get in touch with you. She explained what had been going on in Portrush and what you'd found out about the Mulholland case. Knowing you're like a dog with a bone, Alfie's phone call, and then you going missing..."

"As I'd been with Smith the day before," continued Alfie, "William picked me up so we could retrace his steps. William guessed he had unfinished business. We went first to McGonigle's house. That nosey neighbour of his was really helpful. Told us two people had visited McGonigle, one after the other, but she hadn't heard any noise through the adjoining wall since one car left. She thought you'd all left together. Suggested that, given McGonigle's drinking habits, we'd be best looking for you in a local pub. We found your car and your dog."

Malcolm looked at Harriet.

"Billy's fine," she reassured him.

William stepped to the side of the bed and perched on the edge. "As this all seems to be about the Tobins, I thought that's where Tommy Smith would have taken yeh. We could see the smoke as we were on the road to the old Tobin yard." He rubbed his eyes. "Jesus, Malcolm, when we got there… I thought there was no hope if you were in there."

Alfie grinned. "But it was your wee dog. As we got out of the car, he ran towards the front door of the house and barked like crazy. The heat was wile, but William here put his shoulder to it and could see you. You were on the floor, an arm's length from the front door. He was able to pull yeh clear just in time." He shook his head in disbelief. "And the wee dog was trying his best, too. He had your coat in his mouth and was pulling away. Fantastic angle for the paper."

Malcolm was tired, suddenly. The adrenalin that must have given him a momentary boost now left him just as quickly. His eyes were heavy. He tried to fight it, but knew he was failing. Harriet squeezed his hand.

"Look, lads, I think he needs to sleep now," Harriet said.

"No bother," replied William. "I'm just grateful that he's going to be all right. Com'on, Alfie. I could do with a stiff drink."

Malcolm was a hair's breadth away from disappearing into sleep. Then he remembered. Elizabeth! He pushed himself up in the bed, as much as his strength allowed.

"Malcolm, please," Harriet pleaded. "This is getting ridiculous. You need to rest!"

"Eliz..." The coughing started again.

William moved back to the bed and put his arm around Harriet. "I think he wants to know about Elizabeth."

Malcolm nodded and rested back on the pillows.

"She's in hospital too. Hannah went to her at the same time I was looking for you. Seems like Smith really upset her. She'd taken an overdose of paracetamol. God knows where she got the tablets from. All the local shops and pharmacy know her, so they are really careful with her. But Hannah got to her in time."

No, no – it was Tommy Smith who tried to kill her. But it was no use. Malcolm's eyes were as heavy as lead, and sleep finally overcame him.

CHAPTER THIRTY-SEVEN

The ferry was on time. They weren't many foot passengers keeping Tommy company. He sat on the rear outside deck of the boat as it made its way slowly out of Belfast Lough and towards Scotland. The first step in his new life. He had nearly messed up when checking in. A momentary pause when they said his name. His new name. But the check-in desk had been deserted and the woman behind it was distracted by her boredom. No suspicions were raised.

The ferry passed Harland and Wolff with its two iconic cranes. The slow speed of the boat gave Tommy all the time he needed to say goodbye to all that he had known. Because he was sure he would not be returning. But that was good. He could now decide who he wanted to be. No being pulled this way and that by his past. He had made sure.

He patted his pocket containing the document that would ensure he had money. George Tobin would never want to lose all that he had built up, so the confession he had written would mean a steady flow of cash when Tommy needed it. And there were ways in which money trails could be hidden.

The volunteer who would be his contact for the next leg of his journey would sort that out. The old boys' system had worked in the past, in the time of the Troubles, for the volunteers who had to leave the province quickly. And the system, although dormant, was still in place. After all, what if the peace process failed? The volunteers, their guns and their escape plans, would need to be ready. Maybe the escape route wasn't specifically designed for Tommy, but using his father's name, he had called in favours.

One last thing to do. He reached into his holdall and felt the cold metal of his gun. He looked around him. No one else wanted to brave the cold wind. He walked to the side, where no windows overlooked the deck. He threw the gun into the deep, dark waters of the lough.

CHAPTER THIRTY-EIGHT

The sun warmed Malcolm as he sat in his easy chair in the conservatory. What a simple pleasure it was to be here. His chest was still wheezy, and his singed eyebrows looked a bit of a mess. But he was home. And with a lovely cup of tea and slice of lemon drizzle cake just there on the side table.

He heard the doorbell and Harriet going to answer it.

"Hello, how are you all? He's in the conservatory."

Malcolm stood to greet whoever it was. The effort made him cough. William and Hannah stood in the doorway of the room.

"William, Hannah, great to see you! Sit yourselves down."

Malcolm was puzzled by the sight of Harriet behind them, carrying his coat and with Billy on a lead. Surely she couldn't expect him to start walking the dog again just yet?

"And great to see you!" William said, smiling. "We thought you would like a bit of an outing. We have a table booked at the Northern Counties Hotel. To celebrate you getting home."

Harriet held his coat open. "Huh, I think the nurses were glad to see the back of him. He grew awful cranky as he was getting better."

Malcolm slipped his arms into the coat. "Well, I hate hospitals. And they could do with a bit of organising there. There was one man in the ward who..."

"Just listen to him!" She held out a brown envelope to Malcolm. "This was on the doormat. Looks like something official from the PSNI." Turned back to William. "Right... I know you said you would drive, but are you sure it's OK for Billy to come in your car? There might be a few hairs left behind."

William grinned. "It's my pleasure to have the four-legged hero of the day in my car. I would be honoured."

Malcolm looked at the envelope, then turned it over. Probably something about his pension or an invite to some dreary post-retirement do. He set it down on the side table. Time enough to look at it later.

The article Alfie had written about Billy's part in the rescue had been a bit overblown, in Malcolm's view. Alfie had managed to get a good bit of attention from some of the national papers, so he was happy enough. But when UTV wanted to interview Malcolm with Billy, he had put his foot down. Explained that, as an ex-police officer, it would affect his security. The excuse worked. Anyway, Malcolm had another theory about this supposed wonder dog. He had seen his coat back at the hospital when he was discharged. It was only fit for the bin after the smoke damage. But before he had put it in a black bag, he'd checked the pockets and had pulled out the torn, sodden glove that was so precious to Billy. That was what he had been after.

"Just give me two minutes." Harriet gestured for William and Hannah to sit down. "I need to touch up my makeup and put a comb through my hair."

Malcolm rolled his eyes. "It's going to be more than two minutes. Sit yourselves down. Yeh may get a cup of tea."

I know where everything is," Hannah said. "I'll get the tea."

With Hannah in the kitchen, Malcolm took the opportunity to catch up with of William without being told off by either of their women for talking shop.

"Tell me, William, what about the cold case? Any progress?"

William shook his head. "George Tobin has been interviewed; I think three times now. But no progress. He's adamant he had nothing to do with the Mulholland murder. Robinson is playing the dementia card. Says he can't remember a thing and gets confused. Dead ends there. Sorry, Malcolm, the Crown Prosecution service is taking the view that it's your word against Tobin. With McGonigle dead, there's no corroborating evidence."

"I suppose when the man has kept his secret all these years, he'll manage more. What about those payments he was making to McGonigle? Surely that would say something?"

Hannah brought in two mugs of tea. Looked down at the table. "Is that Harriet's lemon drizzle cake?" She reached over for a slice. Then she looked between William and Malcolm. "You're talking shop. For God's sake, Malcolm, after all you've been through! Isn't it time to put your feet up?"

"Ach, I know. I just need to hear the rest of the story. You were saying, William?"

William sat down and took a sip of his tea. "George Tobin was adamant it was a payment to an old and loyal employee. Said that he promised his parents he'd look after McGonigle."

"What about that Tommy Smith? Any word of him yet? If they could catch up with him then there's your corroborating evidence."

Hannah shuddered. "Horrid man."

"He's disappeared," continued William. "They've tried everything. Even got divers in the Lagan to see if maybe he killed himself. But nothing."

Malcolm stared into his tea. "You'd think, in this day and age, anybody could be found."

"Well yes, if they want to be." William shrugged. "The technology used to find someone can just as easily be used to hide. There's some intelligence suggesting that the paramilitaries have retained their getaway networks Tommy Smith's father was high-ranking. So the boy's away, probably. The bullets they retrieved from McGonigle's body... They were traced back to a gun used by a number of paramilitary operations back in the day."

"And Elizabeth?" Malcolm hoped some good would come out of this for that poor woman.

"Still in hospital," replied William.

"I'm not sure if Elizabeth will ever come to terms with it all," Hannah said, and smiled sadly. "But at least they're able to treat her knowing the truth. No more telling her she's delusional."

"Aye, that's something at least," agreed Malcolm.

* * *

Malcolm had to walk slowly up the steps of the hotel with Harriet alongside him. Hannah and William had offered to take Billy for a walk before bringing him into the hotel. As Malcolm pushed open the door, he heard a clatter of voices from the bar. He peered through the glass door and saw they were all there. Kevin and Emily, his unlikely new friends, and Sean and Alfie.

Harriet took his hand. "They all wanted to welcome you back."

The door to the bar was opened by Alfie. "Hard to kill a bad thing, isn't that what they say?" He thrust a glass of whiskey into Malcolm's hand and grinned.

Malcolm sipped the whiskey and was pleasantly surprised. "Bushmills. Single Malt. Jesus, that national paper must have paid yeh well for the story. Cheers." He clinked glasses with Alfie, whose glass contained transparent liquid. "What in the name of God is that you're drinking? Water?"

"Gin and tonic. It's all the rage. Yeh need to get with the young and trendy set." Alfie took a swig and winced. "Christ knows how this stuff caught on. Anyway, I'm a way on to talk to yonder young man. He has some skills and some stories to tell." Alfie clinked glasses again and walked off towards Emily and Kevin.

Christ, did that man never stop looking for a story? Still, you had to give it to him. He never gave up.

Harriet walked towards him with a glass of white wine in her hand. She pointed towards Alfie. "You pair are like bookends, do yeh know that?"

Malcolm grunted. "I don't think so!" How could she think that?

Sean Cahill was now at his side. "I'll get yeh the next one."

Malcolm beamed at him. "Feck's sake, Sean, how did they let you to come to the best bit of the island?"

"The wife. Can you believe it? She likes Portrush so much she wants to make it a regular trip. Huh, I tried to tell her, there's plenty of places to equal it, and more, our side of the border."

"If yeh say so, Sean. If yeh say so," replied Malcolm with a smile.

* * *

When he woke the following morning, Malcolm knew immediately he had drunk more whiskey than his doctors would have thought wise. Jesus, his head throbbed. He knew he couldn't mention it to Harriet. He wouldn't hear the end of it for weeks. Best just to soldier through. But sure, it had been a mighty night. He remembered vaguely being helped back to the house by William.

He rolled out of bed and padded to the kitchen. Rehydrate. That's what he needed to do. He was startled to see William filling the kettle.

"Head still on?" asked William with a smirk.

"Nothing wrong with me. Still recovering from the smoke inhalation." Malcolm grimaced. "They say the headaches will come and go."

"Is that so?" William's smile widened.

"Aye, well, if your hand's on the kettle, I could do with a tea." Malcolm shuffled his way to the conservatory.

William followed moments later, carrying a tray with tea and toast. "It was a good night. And yeh deserved it. Maybe we should make it a regular thing."

Oh Christ, no. He was too old for this pain. "Aye, that would be lovely, but maybe not for a while." Malcolm reached for the tea. Well stewed. A spoon could stand in it. He took a sip. Perfect. It was like manna from heaven.

Harriet pushed the door open.

"This is where you are. That was some night." She sat heavily on the settee. "Any chance of a brew?" She rubbed her temples. So Malcolm wasn't the only one suffering. "Malcolm, love, do yeh think your investigating is all over? Surely William can take it from here. I'm looking forward to a bit of peace and quiet."

Malcolm looked over at her. Harriet had settled onto the settee, lowering her head back onto the headrest with a sigh. Maybe it was time to let go, find some new interests. There must be something that would fill his time. He didn't want to put this woman through any more. She deserved better.

On the side table beside Harriet lay the brown envelope with the PSNI post stamp that had been delivered the day before. Malcolm picked it up. He eased his finger under the flap, gently ripped it open and read the contents of the single page. He rubbed his chin. Interesting. Very interesting. An invitation to a meeting. To discuss opportunities for him on a part time basis no less. Using his expertise and experience. Looking at cases that were either cold or not being given priority by the PSNI.

He looked at Harriet again. Her eyes were closed, fatigue etched on her face. She would understand. He could put it to her that it was consultancy work. Safe as houses. Mostly. And he could pick and choose what he would get involved with. After all, a man had to have an interest, and this would certainly use his skill set.

Maybe retirement – a Malcolm Bell style of retirement – would suit him after all.

THE END

DIAMOND CRIME

Passionate about the crime/mystery/thriller books it publishes

Follow
Facebook:
@diamondcrimepublishing

Instagram
@diamond_crime_publishing

Web
diamondbooks.co.uk

Printed in Great Britain
by Amazon